DATE DUE			

The Day of Creation

By the same author

THE DROWNED WORLD
THE VOICES OF TIME
THE TERMINAL BEACH
THE DROUGHT
THE CRYSTAL WORLD
THE DAY OF FOREVER
THE VENUS HUNTERS
THE DISASTER AREA
THE ATROCITY EXHIBITION
VERMILION SANDS
CRASH
CONCRETE ISLAND
HIGH-RISE
LOW-FLYING AIRCRAFT
THE UNLIMITED DREAM COMPANY
HELLO AMERICA
MYTHS OF THE NEAR FUTURE
EMPIRE OF THE SUN

The Day of Creation

J. G. BALLARD

Farrar · Straus · Giroux
New York

Copyright © 1987 by J. G. Ballard
First published in Great Britain by Victor Gollancz Ltd., 1987
Printed in the United States of America
First American edition, 1988
Library of Congress Cataloging-in-Publication Data
Ballard, J. G.
The day of creation / J. G. Ballard.—1st American ed.
I. Title.
PR6052.A46D38   1988   823'.914   87-37525

Contents

1.	The Desert Woman	page 7
2.	The Gunmen	10
3.	The Third Nile	14
4.	The Shooting Party	19
5.	Fame	24
6.	The Oak and the Spring	36
7.	The Impresario of Rubbish	39
8.	The Creation Garden	51
9.	The River Mallory	59
10.	The Cascade	66
11.	The House of Women	70
12.	Noon	79
13.	Piracy	90
14.	Out of the Night and into the Dream	96
15.	The Naming of New Things	104
16.	The Helicopter Attack	111
17.	Escape	116
18.	The Green World	123
19.	The Lanterns at Dusk	129
20.	The Documentary Film	134
21.	The Skirmish	144
22.	Into the Lagoons	150
23.	Journey Towards the Rain Planet	162
24.	A Dream of Fair Women	174

25. The Wildfowlers . . . 183
26. The Gardens of the Sahara . . . 192
27. The Stolen Channel . . . 198
28. Doctor Mal . . . 205
29. The Blue Beaches . . . 211
30. The Arcade Peep-Show . . . 215
31. The Death of the *Diana* . . . 223
32. The Poisoned Valley . . . 229
33. The River Search . . . 239
34. The Source . . . 247
35. Memory and Desire . . . 252

I

The Desert Woman

Dreams of rivers, like scenes from a forgotten film, drift through the night, in passage between memory and desire. An hour before dawn, while I slept in the trailer beside the drained lake, I was woken by the sounds of an immense waterway. Only a few feet from me, it seemed to flow over the darkness, drumming at the plywood panels and unsettling the bones in my head. I lay on the broken mattress, trying to steady myself against the promises and threats of this invisible channel. As on all my weekend visits to the abandoned town, I was seized by the vision of a third Nile whose warm tributaries covered the entire Sahara. Drawn by my mind, it flowed south across the borders of Chad and the Sudan, running its contraband waters through the dry river-bed beside the disused airfield.

Had a secret aircraft landed in the darkness? When I stepped from the trailer I found that the river had gone, vanishing like a darkened liner between the police barracks and the burnt-out hulk of the cigarette factory. A cool wind had risen, and a tide of sand flowed over the bed of the lake. The fine crystals beside the trailer stung my bare feet like needles of ice, as the invisible river froze itself when I approached.

In the darkness the ivory dust played against the beach in a ghostly surf. Nomads had built small fires, refugees from the Sudan who rested here on their way south to the green forest valleys of the River Kotto. Each weekend I found that they had torn more planks from the hull of Captain Kagwa's police launch, lighting the powdery timbers with strips of celluloid left behind by

7

the film company. Dozens of these pearl-like squares emerged from the sand, as if the drained lake-bed was giving up its dreams to the night.

Once again I noticed that a strange woman had been here, gathering the film strips before they could be destroyed. I have seen traces of her for the past weeks, the curious footprints on the dispensary floor, with their scarred right heels and narrow thumb-like toes, and her absentminded housework around the trailer. For some time now I have suspected that she is keeping watch on me. Any food or cigarettes that I leave behind are always removed. I have even placed a small present for her on the trailer steps, a plastic viewfinder and a set of tourist slides of the Nile at Aswan, the humour of which might appeal to her. Last weekend, when I arrived at the trailer, I found that the mattress had been repaired with wire and string, though perhaps for her comfort rather than mine.

The thought that I may be sharing a bed with one of these young desert women adds a special glamour to my dreams of the night-river. If she suffers from eczema or impetigo I will soon carry the infection on my skin, but as I lie in the bunk I prefer to think of her naked to the waist, bathing in the warm waters that flow inside my head.

However, her main interest is clearly in the film strips. When I returned to the trailer I found a plastic bucket tucked behind the wooden step. I knelt in the cold dust, and searched through the curious rubbish which this young woman had collected — empty vaccination syringes from the dispensary floor, the sailing times of the Lake Kotto car-ferry, a brass cartridge case and the lens cover of a cine-camera lay among the clouding film strips gathered from the beach.

Together these objects formed a record of my life, an inventory that summed up all the adventures that had begun in this shabby town in the northern province of a remote central African republic. I held the cartridge case to my lips, and tasted the strange scent, as potent as the memory of Noon's embrace, that clung to its dull metal. I thought of my journey up the Mallory, and of my struggle

8

with the great river which I had created and tried to kill. I remembered my obsession with Noon, my duel with Captain Kagwa's helicopter, and all the other events which began a year ago when General Harare and his guerillas first came to this crumbling town.

2

The Gunmen

"Dr Mallory, are you going to be executed?"

I searched for the woman shouting to me, but a rifle barrel struck me across the shoulders. I fell to the ground at the gunmen's feet, and cut my hand on a discarded canister of newsreel film which the Japanese photographer was feeding into her camera. In a few seconds, I realised, the expensive celluloid would see its first daylight while recording my own death.

Fifteen minutes later, when General Harare had withdrawn his guerillas into the forest, leaving the lakeside town he had occupied for a few frightening hours, I was still trying not to answer this all too loaded question. Thrown at me like a query at a chaotic press conference, it summed up the dangers of that last absurd afternoon at Port-la-Nouvelle.

Was I going to be shot? As the guerillas bundled me on to the beach below the police barracks, I called to the young Japanese in her silver flying overalls.

"No! Tell Harare I've ordered a new dental amalgam for his men. This time the fillings will stay in. . . ."

"The fillings . . .?"

Hidden behind her hand-held camera, Miss Matsuoka was swept along by the group of excited soldiers running down to the lake, part beach-party and part lynch mob. There was a confusion of yodelling whoops, weapons playfully aimed at the sun, and knees twisting to the music that pumped from the looted radios and cassette players strung around the gunmen's necks among their grenades and ammunition pouches.

There was a bellow from General Harare's sergeant, a former taxi driver who must once have glimpsed a documentary on Sandhurst or St. Cyr in a window of the capital's department store. With good-humoured smiles, the soldiers fractionally lowered the volume of their radios. Harare raised his long arms at his sides, separating himself from his followers. The presence of this Japanese photographer, endlessly scurrying at his heels, flattered his vanity. He stepped from the beach on to the chalky surface of the drained lake bed, stirring the milled fish bones into white clouds, a Messiah come to claim his kingdom of dust. Dimmed by heavy sunglasses, his sensitive, malarial face was as pointed as an arrowhead. He gazed piercingly at the horizons before him but I knew that he was thinking only of his abscessed teeth.

Behind me a panting twelve-year-old girl in an overlarge camouflage jacket forced me to kneel among the debris of beer bottles, cigarette packs and French pornographic magazines that formed the tide-line of the beach. Prodding me with her antique Lee-Enfield rifle, this child auxiliary had driven me all the way from my cell in the police barracks like a drover steering a large and ill-trained pig. I had treated her infected foot when she wandered into the field clinic that morning with a party of women soldiers, but I knew that at the smallest signal from Harare she would kill me without a thought.

Filmed by the Japanese photographer, the General was walking in his thoughtful tread toward the wooden towers of the artesian wells whose construction I had supervised for the past three months, and which symbolised the one element he most detested. I sucked at the wound on my hand, but I was too frightened to wet my lips. Praying that the wells were as dry as my mouth, I looked back at the deserted town, at the looted stores visible above the teak pillars of the jetty where the car ferry had once moored ten feet above my head. Behind the party of guerillas, some lying back on the beach beside me, others dancing to the music of cassette players, I could see a column of smoke lifting from the warehouse of the cigarette factory, like a parody of a television commercial for the relaxing weed. A pleasant scent bathed the beach, the aroma of

11

the rosemary-flavoured tobacco leaf which the economists at the Institut Agronomique had decided would transform the economy of these neglected people, and provide a stable population from which the local police chief, Captain Kagwa, could recruit his militia.

Turned by the light wind, the smoke drifted towards the dusty jungle that surrounded the town, merging into the haze fed by an untended backyard incinerator. Beyond the scattered tamarinds and shaggy palms the whitening canopy of forest oaks stood at the mouth of a drained stream whose waters had filled Lake Kotto only two years earlier. Their dying leaves blanched by the sun, the huge trees slumped among the stony sand bars, tilting memorials in a valley of bones.

I inhaled the scented air. If I was to be executed, it seemed only just that I, renegade physician in charge of the drilling mission whose water would irrigate the tobacco projects of Port-la-Nouvelle and supply the cities of the former French East Africa with this agreeable carcinogen, should be given an entire warehouse of last cigarettes.

Still trailed by the Japanese photographer, Harare strode towards the beach. Had one of the dry wells miraculously yielded water for this threadbare redeemer? His thin arms, touching only at the wrists, were pointing to me, making an assegai of his body. I sat up and tried to straighten my bloodstained shirt. The guerillas had turned their backs on me, in a way that I had witnessed on their previous visits. When they no longer bothered to guard their prisoners it was a certain sign that they were about to dispense with them. Only the twelve-year-old sat behind me on the beach, her fierce eyes warning me not even to look at the bandage I had wrapped around her foot. I remembered Harare's pained expression when he gazed into my cell at the police barracks, and his murmured reproach, as if once again I had wilfully betrayed myself.

"You were to leave Port-la-Nouvelle, doctor. We made an agreement." He seemed unable to grasp my real reasons for clinging to this abandoned town beside the fossil lake. "Why do you need to play with your own life, doctor?"

"There's the dispensary — it must stay open as long as there are patients. I treated many of your men this morning, General. In a real sense I'm helping your war effort."

"And when the government forces come you will help their war effort. You are a strategic asset, Dr Mallory. Captain Kagwa will kill you if he thinks you are useful to us."

"I intend to leave. It seems time to go."

"Good. This obsession with underground water — your career has suffered so much. You always have to find the extreme position."

"I shall be thinking about my career, General."

"Your real career, not the one inside your head. It may be too late. . . ."

The radios were playing more loudly. A young guerilla, his nostrils plugged with pus from an infected nasal septum, danced towards me, eyes fixed knowingly on mine, his knees tapping within a few inches of my face. I remembered the Japanese woman's question, and its curious assumption that I had contrived this exercise in summary justice, among the beer cans and pornographic magazines on this deserted beach at the forgotten centre of Africa, and that I had already decided on my own fate.

3

The Third Nile

The guerilla unit had emerged from the forest at nine that morning, soon after the government spotter plane completed its daily circuit of Lake Kotto. During the night, as I lay awake in the trailer parked behind the health clinic, I listened to the rebel soldiers moving through the darkness on the outskirts of Port-la-Nouvelle. The beams of their signal torches touched the window shutters beside my bunk, like the antennae of huge nocturnal moths. Once I heard footsteps on the gravel, and felt a pair of hands caress the steel framework of the trailer. For a few seconds someone gently rocked the vehicle, not to disturb my sleep, but to remind me that the next day I would be shaken a little more roughly.

By dawn, as I drove my jeep to the drilling site, the town was silent again. However, as I opened my bottle of breakfast beer on the engine platform of the rig I saw the first of the guerillas guarding the steps of the police barracks, and others moving through the empty streets. Beyond the silent quays, in the forecourt of the looted Toyota showrooms, Harare stood with his bodyguard among the slashed petrol pumps, his feet shifting suspiciously through the shards of plate glass.

For all his ambitious dreams of a secessionist northern province, Harare was chronically insecure. A sometime student of dentistry at a French university, he had named himself after the capital of a recently liberated African nation, like the other four Generals in the revolutionary front, none of whom commanded more than a hundred disease-ridden soldiers. But his socialist ideals travelled lightly with a secondary career of banditry and arms smuggling

14

across the Chad border. With the drying out of the lake and the virtual death of the Kotto River — its headwaters were now little more than a string of shallow creeks and meanders — he had decided to extend his domain to Port-la-Nouvelle, and impose his Marxist order on its vandalised garages and ransacked radio stores.

Above all, Harare detested the drilling project, and anyone like myself involved in the dangerous attempt to tap the sinking water table and irrigate the cooperative farms on which the bureaucrats at the Institut Agronomique had squandered their funds. The southward advance of the desert was Harare's greatest ally, and water in any form his sworn enemy. The changing climate and the imminent arrival of the Sahara had led to the abandonment of Lake Kotto by the government forces. Most of the population of Port-la-Nouvelle had left even before my own arrival six months earlier as physician in charge of the WHO clinic. Within a week Harare's guerillas had sabotaged the viaduct of galvanised iron which carried water from the drilling pumps to the town reservoir. The Belgian engineer directing the work had been wounded during the raid. Hoping to salvage the project, I had tried to take his place, but the African crew had soon given up in boredom. The few tobacco workers who remained had packed their cardboard suitcases with uncured leaf and taken the last bus to the south.

None of this, for reasons I should already have suspected, discouraged me in any way. With few patients to care for, I turned myself into an amateur engineer and hydrologist. Before his evacuation in the police ambulance the Belgian manager had despairingly shown me his survey reports. Ultrasonic mapping by the Institut geologist suggested that the enfolding of limestone strata two hundred feet below Lake Kotto had created a huge underground aquifer flowing from Lake Chad. This subterranean channel would not only refill Lake Kotto but irrigate the surrounding countryside and make navigable the headwaters of the Kotto River.

The dream of a green Sahara, perhaps named after myself, that would feed the poor of Chad and the Sudan, kept me company in the ramshackle trailer where I spent my evenings after the long drives across the lake, hunting the underground contour lines on the survey charts that sometimes seemed to map the profiles of a nightmare slumbering inside my head.

However, these hopes soon ran out into the dust. None of the six shafts had yielded more than a few hundred gallons of gas-contaminated brine. The line of dead bores stretched across the lake, already filling with milled fish bone. For a few weeks the wells became the temporary home of the nomads wandering westwards from the famine grounds of the Southern Sudan. Peering into the bores during my inspection drives, I would find entire families camped on the lower drilling platforms, squatting around the bore-holes like disheartened water-diviners.

Yet even then the failure of the irrigation project, and the coming of the Sahara, had merely spurred me on, lighting some distant beacon whose exact signals had still to reach me. Chance alone, I guessed, had not brought me to this war-locked nation, that lay between the borders of Chad, the Sudan and the Central African Republic in the dead heart of the African continent, a land as close to nowhere as the planet could provide.

Each morning, as I stepped from my trailer, I almost welcomed the sharper whiteness of the dust which the night air had washed against the flattened tyres. From the tower of the drilling rig I could see the thinning canopy of the forest. At Port-la-Nouvelle the undergrowth beneath the trees was still green, but five miles to the north, where the forest turned to savanna, the network of streams which had once filled Lake Kotto was now a skeleton of silver wadis. Day by day, the desert drew nearer. There was no great rush of dunes, but a barely visible advance, seen at dusk in the higher reflectivity of the savanna, and in the faded brilliance of the forest along the river channels, like the lustre of a dead emerald from which the light has been stolen.

As I knew, the approach of the desert had become an almost personal challenge. Using a variety of excuses, I manoeuvred the manager of WHO's Lagos office into extending my three-month secondment to Port-la-Nouvelle, even though I was now the town's only possible patient. Nonetheless my attempts to find water had failed hopelessly, and the dust ran its dark tides into my bones.

Then, a month before Harare's latest incursion, all my frustration had lifted when a party of military engineers arrived at Port-la-Nouvelle. They commandeered the drilling project bulldozer, pressganged the last members of the rigging crew, and began to extend the town's weed-grown airstrip. A new earth ramp, reinforced with wire mesh, ran for a further three hundred yards through the forest. From the small control tower, a galvanised iron hut little bigger than a telephone booth, I gazed up at the eviscerated jungle. I imagined a four-engined Hercules or Antonov landing here loaded with the latest American or Russian drilling equipment, hydrographic sounders, and enough diesel oil to fuel the irrigation project for another year.

But rescue was not at hand. A light aircraft piloted by a Japanese photographer landed soon after the airstrip extension was complete. This mysterious young woman, who camped in a minute tent under the wing of her parked aircraft, strode around Port-la-Nouvelle in her flying suit, photographing every sign of poverty she could find — the crumbling huts, the sewage rats quarrelling over their kingdom, the emaciated goats eating the last of the tobacco plants. She ignored my modest but well-equipped clinic. When I invited her to visit the maternity unit she smiled conspiratorially and then photographed the dead basset hound of the Belgian manager, run down by the military convoys.

Soon after, the engineers left, without returning the bulldozer, and all that emerged from the wound in the forest was General Harare and his guerilla force, to whom Miss Matsuoka attached herself as court photographer. I assumed that she was one of Harare's liberal sympathisers, or the field representative of a Japanese philanthropic foundation. Meanwhile the irrigation project ground literally to a halt when the last of the diamond bits screwed itself immovably into the sandstone underlay. I resigned myself to heeding the heavy-handed advice of the local police chief. I would close the clinic, abandon my dreams of a green Sahara, and return to Lagos to await repatriation to England. The great aquifer beneath Lake Kotto, perhaps an invisible tributary of a third Nile, with the power to inundate the Sudan, would continue on its way without me, a sleeping leviathan secure within its limestone deeps.

4

The Shooting Party

Fires burned fiercely across the surface of the lake, the convection currents sending up plumes of jewelled dust that ignited like the incandescent tails of immense white peacocks. Watched by Harare and the Japanese photographer, two of the guerillas approached the last of the drilling towers. They drained the diesel oil from the reserve tank of the engine, and poured the fuel over the wooden steps and platform. Harare lit the cover of a film magazine lying at his feet, and tossed it on to the steps. A dull pulse lit the oily timbers. The flames wavered in the vivid light, uncertain how to find their way back to the sun. Tentatively they wreathed themselves around the cluster of steel pipes slung inside the gantry. The dark smoke raced up this bundle of flues, and rapidly dispersed to form a black thunderhead.

Harare stared at this expanding mushroom, clearly impressed by the display of primitive magic. Sections of the burning viaduct collapsed on to the lake-bed, sending a cascade of burning embers towards him. He scuttled backwards as the glowing charcoal dusted his heels, like a demented dentist cavorting in a graveyard of inflamed molars, and drew a ribald cheer from the soldiers resting on the beach. Lulled by the smoke from the cigarette factory, they lay back in the sweet-scented haze that flowed along the shore, turning up the volume of their cassette players.

I watched them through the din and smoke, wondering how I could escape from this band of illiterate foot-soldiers, many of whom I had treated. Several were suffering from malnutrition and skin infections, one was almost blind from untreated cataracts, and another showed the clear symptoms of brain damage after childhood meningitis. Only the twelve-year-old squatting behind me among the beer bottles and aerosol cans seemed to remain alert. She ignored the music, her small hands clasped around the breech and trigger guard of the antique rifle between her knees, watching me with unbroken disapproval.

Hoping to appease her in some way, I reached out and pushed away the rifle, a bolt-action Lee-Enfield of the type I had fired in the cadet training corps of my school in Hong Kong. But the girl flinched from my hand, expertly cocked the bolt and glared at me with a baleful eye.

"Poor child . . . all right. I wanted to fasten your dressing."

I had hoped to loosen the bandage, so that she might trip if I made a run for it. But there were shouts from the quay above our heads — a second raiding party had appeared and now swept down on to the beach, two of the guerillas carrying large suitcases in both hands. Between them they pushed and jostled two men and a woman whom they had rounded up, the last Europeans in Port-la-Nouvelle. Santos, the Portuguese accountant at the cigarette factory, wore a cotton jacket and tie, as if expecting to be taken on an official tour. As he stepped on to the beach he touched the hazy air with an officious hand, still trying to calculate the thousands of cigarettes that had produced this free communal smoke. With the other arm he supported the assistant manager of the Toyota garage, a young Frenchman whose height and heavy build had provoked the soldiers into giving him a good beating. A bloody scarf was wrapped around his face and jaw, through which I could see the imprint of his displaced teeth.

Behind them came a small dishevelled woman, naked except for a faded dressing-gown. This was Nora Warrender, the young widow of a Rhodesian veterinary who had run the animal breeding station near the airstrip. A few months before my arrival he had been shot by a gang of deserting government soldiers, and died three days later in my predecessor's bed at the clinic, where his blood was still visible on the mattress. His widow remained at the station, apparently determined to continue his work, but on impulse one day had opened the cages and released the entire stock of animals. These rare mammals bred for European and North American zoos had soon been trapped, speared or clubbed by the townspeople of Port-la-Nouvelle, but for a few weeks we had the pleasure of seeing the roofs of the tobacco warehouses and garages, and the balconies of the police barracks, overrun by macaques and mandrills, baboons and slow lorises.

When a frightened marmoset took refuge inside the trailer, I tricked the nervous creature into my typewriter case and drove it back to the breeding station. The large dusty house sat in the bush half a mile from the airstrip and seemed almost derelict. The cage doors were open to the air, and rotting animal feed lay in open pails, pilfered by ferocious rats. Mrs Warrender roamed from window to window of the looted house. A slim, handsome woman with a defensive manner, she received me formally in the gloomy sitting-room, where a local carpenter was attaching steel bars to the window frames.

Mrs Warrender had discharged the male servants, and the house and its small farm were now staffed by half a dozen African women. She called one of the women to her, a former cashier at the dance hall who had been named Fanny by the French mining engineers. Mrs Warrender held her hand, as if I were the ambassador of some alien tribe capable of the most bizarre and unpredictable behaviour. Seeing my typewriter case, she assumed that I was embarking on a secondary career as a journalist, and informed me that she did not wish to recount her ordeal for the South African newspapers. I then produced the marmoset, which sprang into her arms and gave me what I took to be a useful reputation for the unexpected.

A week later, when she visited the dispensary in Port-la-Nouvelle, I assumed that she wanted to make more of our acquaintance — before her husband's death, Santos told me, she had been a good-looking woman. In fact she had merely wanted to try out a new variety of sleeping pill, but without intending to I had managed to take advantage of her. Our brief affair of a few days ended when I realised that she had not the slightest interest in me and had offered her body like a pacifier given to a difficult child.

Watching her stumble among the beer bottles on the beach, face emptied of all emotion, I assumed that she had seen Harare's men approach the breeding station and in a reflex of panic had gulped down the entire prescription of tranquillisers. She blundered between the gunmen, trying to support herself on the shoulders of the two guerillas in front of her, who carried their heavy suitcases like porters steering a drunken guest to a landing jetty. They shouted to her and pushed her away, but a third soldier put his arm around her waist and briefly fondled her buttocks.

"Mrs Warrender . . .!" I stood up, determined to help this distraught woman. Behind me, the twelve-year-old sprang to her feet and began to jabber in an agitated way, producing a stream of choked guttural noise in a primitive dialect. I seized the rifle barrel and tried to cuff her head, but she pulled the weapon from my hands and levelled it at my chest. Her fingers tightened within the trigger guard, and I heard the familiar hard snap of the firing pin.

Sobered by the sound, and for once grateful for a defective cartridge case, I stared into the wavering barrel. The girl retreated up the beach, dragging her bandage over the sand, challenging me to strike her.

Ignoring her, I stepped over the legs of the guerillas lounging by their radios. Santos and the injured Frenchman were being backed along the beach to the tobacco wharf, whose heavy teak pillars rose from the debris of cigarette packs like waiting execution posts.

"Mrs. Warrender . . .?" I held her shoulders, but she shivered and shook me away like a sleeper refusing to be aroused. "Have they taken your women? I'll talk to Harare — he'll let them go. . . ."

The air was silent. The guerillas had switched off their radios. Plumes of tarry smoke drifted from the gutted shells of the drilling towers, and threw shadows like uncertain pathways across the white surface of the lake. By some trick of the light, Harare seemed further away, as if he had decided to distance himself from whatever happened to his prisoners. The soldiers were pushing us towards the tobacco wharf. They jostled around us, cocking their rifles and hiding their eyes below the peaks of their forage caps.

They seemed shifty and frightened, as if our deaths threatened their own sense of survival.

The Japanese photographer ran towards us through the billows of smoke. Seeing her concerned eyes, I realised for the first time that these diseased and nervous men were about to shoot us.

5

Fame

Signal flares were falling from the air, like discarded pieces of the sun. The nearest burned through its metal casing thirty yards from the beach where I stood with Mrs Warrender, its mushy pink light setting fire to an old newspaper. The spitting crackle was drowned by the noise of a twin-engined aircraft which had appeared above the forest canopy. It flew north-east across the lake, then banked and made a laboured circuit of Port-la-Nouvelle. The drone of its elderly engines shivered against the galvanised roofs of the warehouses, a vague murmur of pain. Looking up, I could see on the Dakota's fuselage the faded livery of Air Centrafrique.

Harare and his guerillas had gone, vanishing into the forest on the northern side of Lake Kotto. The radios and cassette players lay on the beach, thrown aside in their flight. One of the radios still played a dance tune broadcast from the government station in the capital. Beside it rested an open suitcase, Nora Warrender's looted clothes spilling across the lid.

She pushed my arm away and knelt on the sand. She began to smooth and straighten the garments, her neat hands folding a silk ball gown. Draping this handsome robe over her arm like a flag, she walked past me and began to climb the beach towards the jetty.

"Nora . . . Mrs Warrender — I'll drive you home. First let me give you something in the dispensary."

"I can walk back, Dr Mallory. Though I think you should take something. Poor man, everything you've worked for has gone to waste."

Her manner surprised me; a false calm that concealed a complete

24

rejection of reality. She seemed unaware that we both had very nearly been shot by Harare's men. I was still shaking with what I tried to believe was excitement, but was almost certainly pure terror.

"Don't pull my arm, doctor." Mrs Warrender eased me away with a weary smile. "Are you all right? Perhaps someone can help you back to the clinic. I suppose we're safe for the next hour or so."

She pointed to the dirt road along the southern shore of Lake Kotto. A small convoy of government vehicles, a staff car and two trucks filled with soldiers, drove towards Port-la-Nouvelle. Clouds of dust rose from their wheels, but the vehicles moved at a leisurely pace that would give Harare and his men ample time to disperse. At the entrance to the town, by the open-air cinema, the convoy stopped and the officer in the staff car stood behind the windshield and fired another flare over the lake.

Shielding her eyes, Mrs Warrender watched the transport plane drone overhead. The pilot had identified the landing strip and was aligning himself on to the grass runway. Mrs Warrender stared at the charred hulks of the drilling towers, which stood on the lake like gutted windmills.

"A shame, doctor — you tried so hard. I imagine you'll be leaving us soon?"

"I think so — the only patients I have here spend their time trying to kill me. But you aren't staying, Nora — ?"

"Don't give up." She spoke sternly, as if summoning some wavering dream. "Even when you've left, think of Lake Kotto filled with water."

Without looking at me again, she crossed the road and set off towards the breeding station, the ball gown over her arm. The convoy of soldiers approached the police barracks, guns trained on the broken windows. Santos and the Frenchman ignored the vehicles and the shouting soldiers, and walked back to their offices, refusing my offers of help. I knew that they considered my medical practices to be slapdash and unhygienic. Shrugging off the pain in his swollen jaw, the Frenchman began to sweep away the glass in front of the Toyota showroom.

The Dakota circled overhead, its flaps lowered for landing. I strode towards the clinic, deciding to seal the doors and shutters of the dispensary before an off-duty platoon of the government soldiers began to search for drugs. The two trucks rolled past, their wheels driving a storm of dust against the windows of the beer parlour. As they passed Mrs Warrender, the soldiers hooted at the silk gown draped over her arm, assuming that this was some elaborate nightdress that she was about to wear for her lover.

I watched her moving with her small, determined steps along the verge, dismissing the young soldiers with a tired wave. I imagined lying beside Nora Warrender in her silk robe, watched perhaps by a stern-faced bridal jury of her servant women. Fanny and Louise and Poupée would be watching for the first drop of my blood, not my bride's. Then a battered staff car, its plates held together by chicken wire, stopped in the entrance to the clinic. A large hand seized my elbow and a handsome African in a parade-ground uniform, Captain Kagwa of the national gendarmerie, shouted through the aircraft noise.

"She's not for you, doctor! For pleasure you'll have to sit with me!"

"Captain Kagwa . . . For once you're on time. . . ."

"On time? My dear doctor, we were delayed. Where's Harare? How many men did he have?"

"More than three platoons. Don't worry, you gave them enough warning to escape." I pointed to the trucks heading towards the airstrip. "Why all this military action? I thought you'd already stolen everything in Port-la-Nouvelle?"

"Doctor, I don't want anything from you, not even your water. I've brought you something precious. What you Europeans really understand."

"Drilling bits, Captain?"

"Drilling — ?" Kagwa pulled me into the rear seat of the jeep, where I sat among the field radios and ammunition boxes. "I'm talking about something real, doctor, something you can hold in your hand, that's not going to run through your fingers like water. I'm talking about fame."

★

26

Fame? Had I been shot, along with Santos and Mrs Warrender, the news would scarcely have made the morning bulletin on the government radio station. I assumed that this was some complex game of the Captain's — perhaps Harare was about to be betrayed by his own men and I would be called upon to identify the body as it lay in state at the Toyota showroom. Since my failed courtship of Mrs Warrender, I had grown to know this amiable but unpredictable police chief more closely than anyone else at Port-la-Nouvelle. A huge and often clumsy man, well over six feet tall, Kagwa was capable of surprising delicacy of mind. He was a modest amateur pianist, and had tried patiently to teach me the rudiments of the keyboard on Santos's upright.

A fanatic for self-improvement, Kagwa spent his spare time listening to a library of educational cassettes on politics, law and economics. One evening in Port-la-Nouvelle, when the French mining engineers had run riot through the beer parlours, I tried to compliment him by remarking piously that he and I were the only sober and responsible people in the town. He had clasped my shoulders in his immense hands and said, with great earnestness: "Doctor, you are not sober. You are not even responsible. No responsible man would search for water at Lake Kotto — I could arrest you tomorrow. You are Noah, doctor, waiting for rain, Noah without an ark."

A brief cloudburst would have been welcome as we reached the airstrip. The Dakota had already landed, and was taxiing through its own dust, engines setting up a storm of white soil. The two trucks filled with soldiers drew up alongside the control tower. One squad set off to patrol the airstrip perimeter, weapons raised to the forest canopy as if the soldiers expected Harare and his guerillas to be climbing into the sky. A second platoon formed an honour guard, heels stamping as they dressed off in two files. While they presented arms I saw that the entire scene was being filmed by the Japanese photographer. From the cockpit of her light aircraft Miss Matsuoka had removed a chromium suitcase packed with lenses and filters. Mounting a small cine-camera on a tripod, she filmed the Dakota as it lumbered up and down the earth strip, casting clouds of dust and dirt over the tractor parked beside the trees at the eastern end of the runway.

At last, having convinced himself that he had landed, the African pilot shut down the engine. The noise faded, and the co-pilot's window opened to the air. A blond-haired man in a safari jacket, with a deep suntan that was more electric than solar, leaned from the window and gave a series of encouraging waves, apparently returning the cheers of a huge welcoming party. He repeated the performance as Miss Matsuoka, face pressed to the eye-piece of the hand-held camera, ducked under the starboard wing. She crept along the fuselage, her lens taking in every capped tooth in the man's confident and wolf-like smile.

Already the cargo doors had opened, and two crew men lowered a metal step to the ground. Their overall pockets carried a distinctive emblem that seemed to be both a religious symbol and the logo of a television station.

"Who are these people?" I asked Captain Kagwa as we stepped from the jeep and shook the dust from our clothes. "Are they evangelists? Or some sort of missionary group?"

"Our saviour, certainly." Kagwa saluted the aircraft with an ironic flourish. "Professor Sanger brings hope to our doorstep, salvation for the poor and hungry of Lake Kotto, comfort for the bush doctor. . . ."

The blond-haired man stood in the doorway of the cargo hold. He was in his mid-forties, and had the reassuring but devious manner of a casino operator turned revivalist preacher. He bent down and greeted Captain Kagwa with a generous handshake, while giving his real attention to the Japanese photographer, who was reloading her camera beneath the starboard wingtip. When she was ready he ruffled his hair and then brought his hands together in a snapping gesture which I first assumed was a stylised religious greeting, but in fact was a clapperboard signal. As the camera turned, he posed beside two large sacks which the flight crew had manhandled into the hatchway. He composed his features into a tired but pensive gaze, and allowed a quirky smile, at once vulnerable but determined, to cross his sharp mouth. This well-rehearsed grimace, a tic I had seen before somewhere, cleverly erased all traces of his quick intelligence from his face. Only his eyes remained evasive, looking out at the indifferent forest wall with a curious blankness, like those of an unrecognised celebrity forced to return the stares of a foreign crowd. When Miss Matsuoka called to him, he quickly slipped on a large pair of sunglasses.

"Right, Professor Sanger — I will wait for the poor people to receive your gifts. . . ."

The Japanese woman had completed her shot, and was thanking Captain Kagwa, who had clearly relished the attentions of her lens. I left the jeep and walked to the wingtip of the Dakota, running my hand against the weather-worn trailing edge of this elderly aircraft. I now remembered Professor Sanger, a sometime biologist turned television populariser. He had enjoyed a brief celebrity ten years earlier with a series of programmes that sought to demonstrate the existence of psychic phenomena in the animal world. The migration of birds, the social behaviour of ants and bees, the salmon's immense journey to its spawning grounds, were all attributed to the presence of extra-sensory powers distributed throughout the biological kingdom, but repressed in Homo sapiens. As a newly qualified houseman doing my year on the wards in a London hospital, I would see him on the television set in the junior doctors' common room. Of mixed Australian and German ancestry, Sanger had perfected the rootless international style of an airline advertisement, which his audiences took for objectivity. After a day spent in the emergency unit, treating road accident casualties and the victims of strokes and heart attacks, I would sit exhausted in the debris of the common room and watch this scientific smiler holding forth from a rockpool in the Great Barrier Reef or an anthill in the Kalahari.

Fortunately, his success was short-lived. He soon exposed himself to ridicule when he claimed that plants, too, could communicate with one another and appeared in a televised experiment in which the gardeners of Britain rose at dawn and urged their hollyhocks and lupins to deny the sun. After this fiasco

Sanger began a second career in Australian television, but he soon became involved with dubious video and publishing ventures, pop-up books and filmed histories of the Yeti and Bigfoot.

"Dr Mallory. . . ." Captain Kagwa signalled to me. I was being summoned to meet the great man, who was already in conference with his production staff—a small team of European engineers, and a scholarly young Indian frowning over his pocket calculator, whom I took to be Sanger's scientific researcher. Behind them were two African journalists from the government information office, gazing sceptically at the weed-grown airstrip and the silent forest.

"Doctor. . . ." Sanger clasped my injured hand in a strong grip, greeting me with deep respect as if I were Livingstone himself or even, conceivably, that ultimate marvel, a member of the ordinary public. "Doctor, Captain Kagwa tells me that I have saved your life."

I was unable to think of an adequate reply to this — it occurred to me that if I knelt at Sanger's feet he would have been unaware of any irony. All the more annoying was the fact that the statement was literally true.

To add to my irritation, Captain Kagwa interjected: "The guerilla attack, doctor — it was fortunate for you that the television plane arrived on time."

Sanger modestly dismissed this. "We have so many lives to save. There are mouths to feed, Africa is still starving, the world is starting to forget. The selfless work of people like yourself, Dr Mallory, needs to be brought into every living-room." Sanger pointed to the cargo hold of the aircraft, where I could see the sections of a small satellite dish among the grain sacks. Electronic equipment, lights and reels of wire were stowed between the seats. "We have complete studio facilities here. Africa Green, the television charity to which I have donated my time, has satellite links with the major Japanese networks. In fact, doctor, we thought of using you in our film."

"You would bring me into every Japanese living-room?"

"Your work here, doctor, and your escape from death." Sanger paused, looking me up and down in a shrewd but not unfriendly assessment. I was certain that he saw me as little more than a scruffy bush doctor, in my dusty cotton shorts, lumpy army boots and bloodstained shirt, the backwoods physician stuck in my ways and unable to accept the opportunities of the media landscape. Yet he may have grasped that he needed me. "But the important task is to feed the mouth of Africa. We have five tons of rice here, bought with funds donated by West German television viewers. It's only a small start . . . Will you help us, doctor?"

"I'd like to — it's very generous, and the charities have done enormous good. But one problem is that the people here don't eat rice. Their diet is sorghum and manioc. The second is that there aren't any people — they fled months ago, as Captain Kagwa should have told you."

"Well, they may be brought back." Kagwa gestured to the empty forest, uncomfortable with my churlish response. "It would be good for the Lake Kotto project, doctor."

"Fair enough. We'll bring them back. I'm sure they would like to go on Japanese television — perhaps you should starve them a little first?"

"Professor — !" The Indian assistant shouted in anger. Bookish and trembling, he stepped protectively between us, his eyes searching wildly for the Dakota's pilot and an instant take-off to a more welcoming site. "Such a remark betrays Dr Mallory's profession. In the context — "

"It's all right, Mr Pal. The doctor is naturally bitter. He was brutally mistreated. . . ."

I liked this earnest young Indian, and tried to pacify him. "That wasn't sacrilege — not everyone in Africa is starving. The people of Lake Kotto have always been well-nourished. The problem here is the shortage of water. And the Sahara. I'm afraid you've lengthened the wrong runway."

Captain Kagwa was about to intercede — I assumed he had been thinking of his future political career when he invited this small mercy mission to Port-la-Nouvelle — but Sanger suddenly took my arm. In a gesture of surprising intimacy, he steered me along the wing, unconcerned that the blood from my hand was marking his jacket. He was well-groomed, but I noticed that his teeth were riddled with caries, a surprising defect in a television performer. At close quarters his blond hair and deep suntan failed to mask an underlying seediness, and the look of immanent failure that his recent face-lift would never disguise. The subcutaneous fat had been cut away beneath the lines of his cheekbones, and his gaunt jaw was carried in a set of muscular slings. Whenever he switched off his spectral smile his handsome face seemed to die a little.

"You must help me, doctor, as long as you are here. Captain Kagwa tells me you are leaving. Stay a few more days. You and I can deal with the Sahara later. Just now I need to show the people in Europe that I am trying."

"I understand. Why not go to Chad or the Sudan? You could do real good there."

"It's not so easy — these regimes are choosy. Oxfam, UNICEF, the other big agencies are there. This was all I could find. I know — even my disaster area is a disaster."

He wiped his forehead on his jacket sleeve, transferring a smear of my blood to his right temple. The first sections of a miniature television studio were being unloaded from the plane — lights, monitor screens like pickled egg yolks, sections of the satellite dish, consoles of switches, and a trio of cameras of various sizes. Only the sight of this electronic equipment seemed to calm Sanger.

"Look, doctor, perhaps they don't eat rice here — thousands of people in Düsseldorf and Hamburg paid for these sacks with small donations. This plane charter, I have to rent microwave links, millions of yen per kilometre, a lot of expense from my own pocket. But it's a big chance for me . . . Perhaps my last chance. I have only Mr Pal and Miss Matsuoka to help me — they're my ears and my eyes. All I need is a few pictures for the evening television news. . . ."

This display of frankness and concern was so bogus that I almost believed it. Sanger had spent so long in the worlds of publicity and self-promotion that only the calculated gesture was sincere. A spontaneous insincerity was as close as one could come to the truth. Mere honesty would have seemed contrived and dubious to him, a surrender to brute feelings. The bad teeth, the antique aircraft, the fifty sacks of rice, suggested that the chief recipient of any aid was Sanger himself. It was his television career he hoped to rescue with this threadbare mercy mission. His choice of Port-la-Nouvelle marked only his own despair. The prime sites — Ethiopia, Chad, the Sudan — had been allocated to the most powerful television interests, the huge American networks and the British record companies. At the same time, I felt a certain concern for him. In many ways he was more in need of help than the vanished inhabitants of Port-la-Nouvelle. In practical terms, I had already made a small contribution to Sanger's effort. It was my tractor which had helped to clear the forest and extend the runway.

"Professor Sanger, take care!" Mr Pal, the Indian adviser, pushed me aside and placed an arm around Sanger's head, as if to shield his eyes from an unpleasant spectacle. Soldiers were running across the airstrip, some taking shelter behind the control tower, others shouting to each other as they crouched beneath the engines of the aircraft.

A single rifle shot sounded from the eastern end of the runway, its harsh report magnified by the forest wall. Hundreds of cuckoo-shrikes rose from the canopy, colliding with each other in their panic as they circled the lake.

Had Harare and his men returned? I knelt behind the sacks of rice, as the pilot and Mr Pal hauled Sanger into the cargo hold. The soldiers guarding the perimeter of the airstrip waved across the runway, pointing to the undergrowth that surrounded the tractor. They aimed their rifles at the deep grass, as if about to flush out a forest boar, or one of the released residents of Mrs Warrender's breeding station, unable to cope with the rigours of life in the wild and pining for the peace and freedom of captivity.

I followed Captain Kagwa as he strode down the runway. The soldiers had found their prey in the undergrowth. Rifles raised like spears, they jabbed and prodded a small, bloodied mammal that scuffled at their feet in the long grass.

"Doctor, they've caught a guerilla!" Camera at the ready, Miss Matsuoka ran past me, almost twisting her ankle in the dusty ruts left by the Dakota.

The soldiers stepped back as Kagwa reached them, lowered their rifles and gesticulated at the figure beside their feet. Kneeling in the long grass, whose blades were wet with the blood from her nose and mouth, was the twelve-year-old girl who had guarded me on the beach. Unable to keep up with Harare and his escaping force, she had been abandoned in the tract of forest that separated the airstrip from the shores of Lake Kotto. She had thrown away both the Lee-Enfield rifle and her camouflage jacket, and wore only her ragged shorts and a green singlet. She sat on the ground as the rifle barrels bruised her cheeks and forehead. Wiping the blood from her nose, she tied and untied the bandage around her infected foot. When she saw me approach she looked up with the same hostile eyes that had steered me on to the beach two hours earlier. Small and hungry, fidgeting nervously with her filthy bandage, she made it clear that the reversal of our fates in no way altered her judgement of me, even though a rifle stock would crush her skull in a matter of seconds.

"Dr Mallory — come with me." Captain Kagwa pushed through his men. He bent down and slapped the girl, stunning her with a blow. He held her cropped head in a huge hand and tilted it back. "You recognise her? She was with Harare?"

Miss Matsuoka brushed past me. "Yes, Captain — she tried to kill the doctor."

"Well, doctor?"

The bandage flicked to and fro as a pair of small eyes watched me from between Kagwa's fingers.

"I haven't seen her before." I tapped Kagwa's elbow, hoping that he would order the soldiers away before they began their sport. "This is a different girl."

"But, Captain — !" Miss Matsuoka began to protest, and then noticed the satellite dish being erected beside the Dakota. Her attention veering away, she beckoned to us both. "Back to the plane — Professor Sanger is setting up the interviews, Captain."

The girl shook her head free from Kagwa's grip. He reached down and threw her backwards into the grass, where one of the soldiers kicked her with his rubber boot. She scuffled away through the undergrowth, dragging her unravelling bandage like a snakeskin.

I watched her vanish into the trees and said: "I'll take my tractor, Captain. Perhaps your sergeant would drive it for me."

"Of course." He seemed glad that at last I had something to distance me from my hostility to Professor Sanger. "May you find just one gallon of water before you leave, doctor. Enough to wash away all memories of Port-la-Nouvelle."

6

The Oak and the Spring

As smoke pumped from its exhaust funnel, the tractor laboured through the soft soil beside the runway extension. I stood a dozen yards in front of the unsteady vehicle, trying to attract the driver's attention. Confused by the steering levers and by the slow but powerful response of the engine, the sergeant had barely mastered the heavy clutch. The tractor slewed in the soft mud, the metal scoop swinging from side to side. Its scarred blade cut fillets of damp soil from the sloping ground. They curled back beneath the treads and were stamped into the ground by the metal links.

I walked along these rectilinear grids, a trace of the passing imprint of western technology on the African land, as the tractor reversed down the slope. On either side of the runway the army engineers had cleared the forest for a hundred yards, and the uneven ground was a forgotten terrain of mud-filled gulleys, hillocks of pulverised earth, and clumps of flourishing underbrush.

The tractor blundered across this no-man's land, the driver straining his arms to hold the machine on its course towards the forest road that ran from the eastern end of the airstrip to the shores of Lake Kotto. He climbed the last of the hillocks, and then faced a ramp of compacted earth which the engineers had erected for their supply vehicles. The sergeant throttled up his engine, lowered the scoop and thundered forward in a roar of smoke and oil. The metal blade sank into the ramp, and cut away a huge block of compressed gravel mounted on a section of underlying soil that contained the root-tree of a forest oak.

This immense black core lay partly exposed, like the petrified

36

heart of an extinct bull, or the crown of an underworld deity ripped
from the ceiling of a subterranean palace whose arches supported
the airstrip, a submerged cathedral of mud. The soil wept through
its roots and fell into the dark maw of the cavern below, an open
mouth wide enough to swallow a small car.

The sergeant reversed his gears, and briefly cut back his engine.
He looked up at me, as I watched from the edge of the runway,
clearly expecting me to order him to ignore this obstacle and make
a sensible detour around it. But I waved him forward, curious to
see how large this root-system might be — clearly the felled tree
had been one of the tallest oaks in the forest, sitting for hundreds of
years at the water-table of Lake Kotto, until cut down to make way
for Sanger's runway extension and his preposterous mission. I felt
the ground under my feet, hoping to hear a rumble of subsidence
— with luck, the removal of this ancient root would undermine the
runway and the Dakota would crash on take-off. . . .

The sergeant worked up his engine, smoke pumping from the
exhaust stack behind his head. He engaged the gears and drove
forward, gradually forcing the root-crown from the cavity where
it rested. To my disappointment, it failed to put up any great fight,
but lay passively against the tractor's scoop, a gnarled mass of dead
roots some six feet in diameter. Forced on to its back, it rolled
soundlessly into a hollow between two nearby hillocks and expired
there in a cloud of sandy dust, a long-dead god of the earth.

I waited as the tractor rumbled forward, its treads easily
straddling the cavity below. As the sergeant headed towards the
forest path I walked down the earth ramp and peered into the open
mouth. Scores of torn roots emerged from the ground-soil, the
crop of a strange subterranean plantation. To my surprise,
however, a small pool of water had appeared at the base of the
cavity. As if leaking from the amputated roots, the dark liquid
slowly covered the sandy floor, the last sap of the dead oak
irrigating its own grave.

All too aware of the irony that I had at last struck water, I
gathered the loose soil between my feet and swept it into the cavity.
But the water was already several inches deep, fed from some

37

underground stream, part of an artificial reservoir, I assumed, created by the construction of the airstrip. I gazed down, seeing my own face reflected in the black mirror from which the dead roots of the oak rose to greet me. I kicked a last shower of earth into my reflection and strode down the remains of the ramp, following one of the parallel pathways left by the tractor.

Fifty yards into the forest, I stopped to wait for the tractor's smoke to dissipate through the trees. Looking back, I could see the pattern of metal tracks stamped into the long bracelets of soil that led to the airstrip.

A thin stream of water, little more than the width of my arm, flowed along the track, carried by the slight gradient that ran down to the lake. While I waited, it crept towards my heels and touched them, moving in a zigzag of lateral and forward movements that seemed to notch up a series of coded messages, computerising itself around my feet.

An hour later, as I stood on the jetty beside the police barracks, above the beach where the twelve-year-old had tried to kill me, I saw the stream emerge from the forest and make its way down to the drained bed of the lake. It formed a small pool beneath the debris along the beach, nudging at the cigarette packs and beer cans which were already floating on its surface, as if trying to stir this dusty rubbish into a second life.

7

The Impresario of Rubbish

Behind my back, a mirror was forming. All morning, as I worked among the packing cases in the looted clinic, I was aware of the vivid reflection from the lake, as if someone had switched on the underwater lights of a swimming-pool. For reasons of its own the sun had come closer to Port-la-Nouvelle, perhaps intrigued by the appearance of this dark water that had spent so many aeons within the earth.

Resigned at long last to closing the clinic and returning to England, I tried to ignore the lake and the line of drilling rigs. Harare's guerillas had ransacked the dispensary, stealing at random from the drug cabinet in my office, scattering powdered milk over my desk and crushing scores of glass vials under their feet. I swept the debris into the yard, and packed the last of the medical supplies into a suitcase with the few clothes that Harare's soldiers had left me.

At dusk the previous evening, when I opened the door to the trailer, I first thought that the guerillas had detonated a hand grenade as a farewell present. Exhausted after the hours in Harare's custody, and the tomfoolery of Sanger's mercy mission, I cleared a space in the heap of clothes, books and crockery, pulled the mattress from below the upended refrigerator, and fell asleep as Captain Kagwa's men patrolled the deserted town, playing their radios through the darkness of the surrounding forest. Twice I was woken by the sounds of gunfire, and heard the explosions of mortar shells in the tobacco farms, as the rival forces shifted the furniture of the night.

All in all, it was time to go. My short career as hydrologist — an absurd venture from the start — had been part of the same curious obsession that had brought me to central Africa in the first place. After a childhood in Hong Kong, where my father had been a professor of genetics at Kowloon University, I was sent to school in England, and then graduated from Trinity College, Dublin. Although a qualified physician, in the ten years that followed I had gone to any lengths to avoid actually practising medicine in either Europe or North America, whose populations, it eventually became clear, had failed to be sufficiently ill to meet certain bizarre needs of my own — in Europe, I argued dubiously to myself, most of the sick were physically in better health than many of the healthy in Asia. I became editor of a specialist medical journal, and then the so-called research director of a small pharmaceutical company, in reality its publicity manager and Fleet Street lobbyist. One day, while lecturing to a paediatric conference on the merits of a new infant cough linctus, I recognised a fellow Trinity student in the audience, now a child neurologist at a state hospital. In his eyes I saw myself as he saw me, a drug company salesman beginning to believe my own patter.

Three months later I joined the World Health Organization, and by a roundabout route — Toronto, Puerto Rico, Lagos — I found myself in central Africa. After six months in northern Nigeria, trying to isolate a suspected outbreak of smallpox — a disease which WHO had eliminated from the world — I began to forget my uneasy life in London, although it seemed ironic that I should find fulfilment in an unnecessary struggle against an imaginary disease. But I was then transferred to the Central African Republic, still devastated after the rule of Bokassa, and finally sent across the border to the former French East Africa. Yet even in Port-la-Nouvelle I was never happier than when I embarked on the futile drilling project. Lying in my derelict trailer, I knew that it was time to return to England before I could discover why.

When Captain Kagwa called to see me soon after daybreak, I told him that I was closing the clinic and would leave Port-la-Nouvelle whenever he could provide me with transport.

"My regrets, doctor." He gazed at the shambles in the dispensary, and at the bloodstains on my hand and legs. With only a few bottles of drinking water, there had been no means of cleaning myself. Clearly he was relieved to see me go. "Six months at Port-la-Nouvelle, and so little achieved. You cannot even play your national anthem. However, I can arrange your flight with Air Centrafrique. The Dakota returns today."

"So soon? Hope comes and goes. That doesn't say much for Professor Sanger's concern for the starving."

"The journalists are restless — perhaps they feel disappointed here."

"I can understand. Now about the plane. Thank you, Captain, but no — I don't trust that Dakota. The thought of being incinerated at the end of a runway my tractor helped to build is bad enough, but being strapped into the seat next to Sanger when it happens. . . ."

"Charity, doctor — or, if you prefer, self-interest — besides, Professor Sanger is not leaving with you. He is to stay here and make me famous. This very morning he will interview me on our local television station."

"Our local what . . .?" I started with wonder at Kagwa, aware now of the source of his good humour. Cool and confident, he was resplendent in a freshly pressed uniform, as if about to be promoted to General of Police by the President himself. "This is obviously an important interview. To whom will it be transmitted?"

"To Port-la-Nouvelle and the Lake Kotto area, doctor. Professor Sanger has all the latest equipment — he isn't drilling for water in a desert. A large part of Lake Kotto is within range of his station. His local antenna has a ten-mile radius."

"A new career for you, Captain." I could see that the absence of an audience mattered nothing to Captain Kagwa. No doubt he had his own reasons for keeping Sanger in Port-la-Nouvelle, probably to publicise his bush war against the guerillas. "This means that Sanger will be staying on at Lake Kotto?"

"Of course — he has his mission to perform."

"His fifty sacks of rice? Do you think that's his real reason for being here?"

"You've become too suspicious living with us. What else?"

"He could be working for French Intelligence — or even Harare. . . ."

"That's dangerous talk, doctor. It's small-minded of you. I think it's time for you to go."

"All right. I'll take that mercy flight after all."

"Be at the airstrip by twelve noon. It's a shame, doctor. Professor Sanger tells me that the world is hungry for a new Schweitzer . . . All those keyboard exercises will have gone to waste." Kagwa gazed at the strange light over the lake, and shook the powdered milk from his boots. "What will you do when you return to England, doctor? You won't be happy there."

"I dare say I'll find some dry wells to drill . . . See you at the plane, Captain."

An opal light lay over the lake, and transformed the surface of white sand and fish bone into a faint mother-of-pearl. As I stood outside the clinic with my two suitcases I saw a fleeting mirage, a second forest that hung below the first. The undergrowth and the canopies of the shabby oaks were more vibrant, perhaps bathed in the televised aura of Captain Kagwa being transmitted at that very moment from the airstrip antenna, preparing the local flora and fauna for the electronic world order to come. Perhaps Sanger had stumbled upon a method of reviving the flagging agriculture, a new fertility rite for the television age. Along the borders of Chad and the Sudan, the images of provincial leaders and local police chiefs would be broadcast to the arid sand. Already I could see the colossal spectre of Captain Kagwa beamed out like the electronic statue of a new Ozymandias. . . .

A cloud of grit swept against my legs as one of the police trucks stopped outside the barracks before returning to the airstrip. A suitcase in each hand, I walked between the bullet-riddled fuel pumps on the Toyota forecourt. Swinging my cases on to the tailgate of the truck, I told the teenage driver that I would walk to the airfield.

Beyond the garage was a looted appliance store. Captain

Kagwa's sergeant emerged from its office with two soldiers. Between them they carried a large video-recorder, which they handled with the respect due to an ancient tabernacle, and bore swiftly into the barracks.

When they had gone the town returned to its silence. The cooperative factory which had once produced cotton textiles, soap and beer, and the small assembly plant for cheap motor cycles and radios stood dustily in the heat. The streets were empty, as if the entire population were indoors watching television, and reminded me of those English suburbs which I had fled, where on a summer's afternoon everyone would sit behind drawn blinds watching a tennis final or a royal wedding. Captain Kagwa had made the ultimate leap forward, dispensing even with the need for an audience.

But I was searching for a different kind of magic. I stepped on to the beach below the wharf of the tobacco warehouse. Again I saw the mirage along the shore, the same illusory forest that hung among the clouds of mother-of-pearl. Then, as I touched the lake-bed, I realised its source.

The lake was damp. My cleated boots left firm imprints as sharp as those scored into the forest trail by the tractor. The fire at the cigarette factory had been put out by Kagwa's soldiers, and now that the smoke had faded the vivid light over the lake was undimmed. The surface gleamed like a salt flat still moist after a few minutes of rain.

As for the mirage, I could see the inverted forest even more clearly, the high canopies of the jungle oaks reflected in a shallow pool of water, two hundred feet in length and some thirty wide, that lay along the beach. Even now this narrow crescent had attracted a few birds. Parties of jacanas and plovers stood in the water, pecking at their reflections.

Had my wells at last reached the water-bearing strata below the lake, tapping the giant aquifer that would carry a third Nile into the Sahara? I ran through the damp sand towards the nearest of the drilling rigs.

The footsteps behind me were already filling with a clear fluid. I

43

reached the rig and rested against the wooden frame. Looking down into the bore, I felt a curious relief that the well was still dry. I pressed my head against the fire-scarred platform, staring at the charred timbers that had fallen from the derrick. The water which had moistened a small corner of Lake Kotto had come from the spring beside the airstrip, whose mouth the tractor had opened the previous afternoon.

Why did I feel so strong a sense of relief? In part, it would have been galling to leave Port-la-Nouvelle and then find that Captain Kagwa or, even worse, Professor Sanger, was taking credit for the successful drilling operation. When I reached the crescent pool I stopped within a few feet of the water's edge. It seemed an alien element, with its clear geometry conforming so agreeably to the contours of the shore-line, containing nothing in its shallows but concealing everything, like the eyes of the adolescent Chinese girls I had pursued so keenly in Hong Kong.

A jacana waded past me on its overlarge claws, leaving ripples like the spoor of submarine flight in the forest canopy that loomed from the reflection. Fifty feet away, the mouth of the stream emerged from the forest. Little more than a small drain, it leaked a trickle of clear water into a shallow gutter that crossed the road and flowed down to the lake.

I stepped into the pool and washed the dust from my boots, then knelt down and bathed my face and hair, aware that this might be the last useful task to be performed by the small reservoir before it evaporated. Days had passed since I had taken my last shower, and the white dust shed itself from my arms and chest, revealing a second, darker skin. Looking down at the surface, I was surprised to see that it teemed with life — water-spiders flickered to and fro, fishing for the swarms of hydra and infusoria. Microscopic creatures glimmered in the turbid water, as if generated from the sweat and dust of my skin. I seemed to have sloughed away the older, desert version of the up-country physician I had become for a younger, riverine self. Seeing my slim face and shoulders — the product of a poor diet and intermittent dysentery — I remembered the boy of eighteen who had taken a last eccentric sail trip to the mouth of the Canton River, before reluctantly agreeing to my father's wish that I study medicine, and had spent three days marooned on a rocky headland with several hundred screaming gulls for company.

Refreshed by this cool bath, I climbed the beach and stood on the forest road. Then, almost without thinking, I began to kick the sand into the mouth of the stream. The water backed up behind the dam, forming a small pond which soon disappeared into the dust.

Pleased with myself, in an absurd way, I strode forward through the trees. It was childish of me to have blocked the stream but I had created the spring the previous afternoon. Before I left I would warn Kagwa to replace the root-bole of the old oak, or the seeping water would undermine the airstrip.

My feet slipped in the damp undergrowth between the trees. Confused by the darker air below the canopy, I had strayed from the forest road. I blundered among the ferns and palmettos and fell to my knees in a pool of black water. I assumed that this was a stagnant channel, but even as I crouched there, shaking the mud from my hands, I could feel the pressure of a current against my legs.

I was standing in a jungle stream more than ten feet wide. It flowed through the trees, hidden by the dead lianas and debris of the forest floor. For some fifty yards it followed the road, and then swerved into the brush, seeking out the darker gradients that ran down to the lake.

As my eyes sharpened, I saw that the original stream had divided into several channels, only one of which had so far reached the lake. The others pooled in the hollows, seeping between the fallen trunks and turning the forest into a sombre bayou.

I returned to the forest road and set off towards the airstrip. I felt elated but vaguely guilty, and remembered a childhood visit to Kowloon with my parents, when I had broken the earth dyke that held the water within a small paddy field in the hills of the New Territories. By the time I returned to my mother and father, setting our picnic beside the parked car, the escaping water had run down the hillside and was washing the car's wheels. Puzzled by the shouts of the farmers from the rice terraces above, my parents set off through the valley for another picnic site. It had taken hours for the moisture on the tyres to dry, hours of nervous excitement and small-boy guilt. . . .

However, I already realised that this stream running through the forest would be a boon to Port-la-Nouvelle. Calming myself, I stepped from the trees at the eastern end of the airstrip. One of Kagwa's sentries stood by the runway, rifle slung over his shoulder, throwing pebbles into the shallow brook that ran among the tree stumps and hillocks of the waste ground. He stared at my drenched clothes and muddy arms, as if I were a plumber who had just released some infernal stop-cock in the earth's cistern.

I climbed the shoulder of the runway, following the stream's course. The huge root of the forest oak lay beside the cavity from which the tractor had dislodged it. The black bull's head, like the crown of a minotaur with its snake-like roots, the primal deity of the river, was now covered by a swirl of brown water, beer cans and aerosol cylinders. A steady current moved among the mounds of earth, flowing from a secondary source in the overgrown terrain to the north of the airstrip. Two hundred yards away, a small arm of the stream moved through the scrub, its green back already attracting two kingfishers that leapt from branch to branch of a baobab tree. By dislodging the dead oak from its bed, I had released a flow of water from an underground reservoir beneath my feet, and the hydraulic vacuum had cracked the natural containment wall. I assumed that the weight of the airstrip itself was expressing this trapped fluid, perhaps from a relic of the original water-table of Lake Kotto.

Angry voices crossed the airstrip, an altercation that moved like a skidding stylus from French to German to Sudanese. Between the parked Dakota and the control tower Sanger had set up his aid station and television studio. A plastic tent with a transparent window flap served as the control booth. A portable generator behind the tower throbbed quietly in the sun and fed its current to the monitors within the tent. On the two screens mounted on a card table I could see a distant image of the journalists remonstrating with Sanger. Their exasperated gestures were carried from the unmanned camera fixed on its tripod in front of them, along a land-line to the twenty-foot-high local antenna secured to the roof of the control tower.

His safari suit crumpled after an unsettled night, Sanger was trying to pacify the journalists, while the Dakota's pilot watched from the rice-sacks that lay slackly in the sun like the carcasses of a dream. The bookish young Indian, Mr Pal, stood at Sanger's elbow, doing his best to interpret for him, while Miss Matsuoka strode about moodily in her flying suit. The remaining members of the team leaned against sections of the satellite dish, watching this quarrel with dour expressions, extras in a dubious film production cut short by lack of funds. Only Captain Kagwa seemed in good spirits. He gave a light-hearted salute to the driver of the truck bearing my two suitcases, and then beamed serenely at the forest around the airstrip, as if expecting to see his magnified image projected upon the green canopy.

I assumed that his interview had taken place, transmitted on the local antenna's weak signal to an audience consisting, literally, of the birds in the trees — and, no doubt, the sergeant in the police barracks recording the occasion on the looted video. Relayed later from the government station in the capital, it would guarantee Kagwa's promotion to Major, if not Colonel. . . .

Happy to leave him to his new fame, I stepped from the edge of the runway and climbed down to the stream. More than fifteen feet wide, it slid through the undergrowth, barely visible in the long grass. Fed by the main channel, pools of waters had formed in the waste ground, and now carried a regatta of used condoms, jettisoned by the French oil-company workers who had built their camp beside the airstrip. Looking down at this floating parade, I felt as if I had conjured up, not just this miniature river that would irrigate the southern edge of the Sahara, but the entire consumer goods economy which would one day smother the landscape in high rises, hypermarkets and massage parlours. As the scummy debris drifted past, I could almost believe that I had invented Professor Sanger himself, somehow conjured this third-rate television producer to serve as its presenter, the impresario of rubbish. . . .

I walked along the bank, even more curious now to find the source of the stream. One of Kagwa's soldiers stood naked in the long grass, washing his uniform in the water. He draped his camouflage jacket and trousers over a bale of telegraph wire that lay coiled in the shallows. Whistling through a stem of dried grass, he seemed almost to be talking to the stream, guiding it towards him, just as his primitive forebears in the forest had found the magic to summon rain and turn winds.

One engine of the Dakota began to whine, then coughed into a throaty roar. The plane would leave in fifteen minutes, but I placed the sound at the back of my mind. Leaving the naked soldier and his flute, I followed the stream as it flowed towards me from the heavier undergrowth. Narrower here, the stream had concealed itself among the overhanging branches that thrust themselves against my chest. I pushed them aside, and waded through the knee-deep water.

The walls of a steep culvert enclosed the stream. Holding to the lianas which hung from the boughs above me, I climbed over the trunks of dead palms lying together like the timbers of a rotting raft. Then the culvert opened into a green basin, a forest drawing-room shaded by curtains of moss and dead creeper. In the centre sat the hulk of a rusting motor car, thrown into this makeshift tip by the construction workers of the oil company. The shallow water flowed through the radiator grille of the car, emerging between the glassy eyes of the headlamps as if from a fountain's mouth. Behind the rear wheels the grass was sodden, the water leaking from that same underground reservoir which I had fractured.

I kicked the damp grass, and scattered a spray of water into the rusty interior of the car. The Dakota's engines sounded from the airstrip. The slipstream raked through the trees, and a whirlwind of dusty air seethed around the basin. Behind me, the sunlight briefly touched a metal rod pointing through the leaves, the barrel of a rifle trained upon my chest. Too startled to run, I saw a small figure crouching among the tamarinds, head hidden by the fronds that thrashed its shoulders.

The Dakota completed its take-off check at the western end of the runway, and the trees in the basin settled themselves. The armed figure had vanished, presumably one of Harare's guerillas sent here to keep watch on Captain Kagwa and the cargo brought in by the Dakota.

As I left the basin and followed the stream into the culvert I could hear the impatient engines of the aircraft. I guessed that the plane was waiting for me, and that the pilot would soon tire of standing on his brake pedals. But I was thinking only of the stream. Already I was convinced that by finding its source between the wheels of the rusting car I had somehow broken its magic, and that my wells in Lake Kotto would no longer be under threat.

However, even before I reached the waste ground beside the airstrip the stream was flowing more strongly. The current tugged at my calves, overtaking me in its rush towards the waiting lake. The pools of standing water among the hillocks had been drawn into the main channel. The foliage of the trees was more vivid, readying itself for the brighter world to come. The naked soldier was moving his clothes further up the bank. When I splashed past him, he raised his rifle as if I was some latter-day savage emerging from this floating jungle of condoms and cigarette packets.

The Dakota had aligned itself on the runway and edged forward through the swirling dust. Sanger stood by his makeshift television station, almost alone among his cameras and antennae. Ignoring him, I set off along the forest road towards the lake. A hundred yards away I saw an adolescent girl standing above the beach, the twelve-year-old with the infected ankle whose life I had saved. Her right foot still dragged the unravelling bandage. She stared at the lake, her hands dancing excitedly at her sides, and then scuttled away when she saw me approach.

I climbed the bank and stared at the sheet of silver water, rippled by the hot wind, that stretched towards the jetties of Port-la-Nouvelle a quarter of a mile away. Already the edges of the pool had touched the bows of the stranded car ferry and the white rudder of the restaurant barge beached on the shore beyond the cigarette factory. Little more than an inch deep, the water extended towards the line of drilling rigs, and had almost reached the nearest tower. The stream sluiced down the bank with the comforting splash of an ornamental fountain. My earth dam had been swept aside in a flurry of small heels. In the scattered sand were the prints of a child's foot with slender but prominent toes.

For reasons of her own the girl was defending the stream, accepting some self-imposed challenge. She scurried through the trees, fierce eyes watching me from her pallid face, like a child-terrorist who had planted a bomb and was waiting half-fearfully for it to explode. Behind her she towed the filthy bandage, as if trying to confuse me by trailing this thread of her own blood.

I shouted to her, but my voice was drowned in the blare of the Dakota. It swept above the lake, barely clearing the forest canopy. I stepped into its trembling reflection and walked through the warm water towards the nearest drilling tower.

A silver arm of the lake had reached the well before me. I leaned between the trestle posts and peered into the bore, where a pool of dusty fluid rose through the discarded newspapers. A horn sounded from the police barracks. Captain Kagwa was waving to me from his jeep. He lowered my suitcases on to the wharf, shook his head in disapproval and drove away. No doubt he had assumed all along that I would stay at Port-la-Nouvelle and had thoroughly enjoyed the irony of my wells filling with water from the forest stream that I had accidentally created.

Kagwa or no, I would stay at Port-la-Nouvelle and reopen the dispensary. And I would defend my dry wells.

8

The Creation Garden

"We're threatened, Mallory! Forget your dam!"

"Go away, Sanger. Make a film about someone else."

"No! Doctor, it's time to build an ark. . . ."

A familiar shabby figure in a sweat-stained safari suit hailed me across the water. Sanger lounged back in the stern of his skiff, in relaxed good humour, as always when he saw me working on one of my various futile schemes. He watched me shovel the soil on to the crumbling wall that I hoped would be one shoulder of an earth dam. As hard as I worked, the current carried away the damp clods.

Mr Pal, his scientific adviser and general factotum, stood in the bows, punt pole sunk into the bed of the stream. He held the craft against the current, staring at my modest efforts with an expression of deep gloom, and then confided his verdict to Sanger.

"Median depth is now three feet, Professor, rising approximately at one inch per hour." He spoke in a light educated voice, his diction giving a lilt of good news to his depressing litany. "Current estimated three miles per hour, capacity six hundred cubic feet per minute. Flood table imminent."

"Mallory, did you hear Mr Pal? Flood table imminent."

I drove the spade into the bank and rested my reddened palms on the handle. Somewhere below my knees a pair of mud-caked boots had vanished into the brown water. My shorts and chest were spattered with the red mud.

"What are you doing here, Sanger? Do you want to interview me?"

Sanger gestured in an artless way, as if this was a prospect beyond all his dreams. "You don't want to be interviewed, doctor. For you, television is vanity, the death-warrant of the human race written in 625 lines. Yes, you told me so, very bluntly." He spread a hand across the water, like a card-sharp about to tamper with a pack. "We might be looking for gold."

"Good, you'll be able to pay the journalists to come back to Port-la-Nouvelle. And return my fifty dollars."

"Fifty? As little as that? I feel better about my debt to you. Every dollar you lend me is a deposit in the bank of friendship. Still, it might be worth panning here — there is equipment in the tobacco factory we could modify."

"Sanger, you're wasting your time. As Mr Pal will tell you, the geology is against you. Anyway, this stream will soon cease to exist, once I've managed to divert it."

"Stream?" Sanger beckoned Mr Pal to the bank. Holding the Indian's arm, he stepped from the skiff and stood beside me. He touched my shoulder in his frank and engaging way. Behind his dark glasses I could see his weak but curiously trusting eyes. "Stream, doctor? You still call it a stream? This is a river. You have created a *river*."

His voice carried through the trees, catching the ear of the young Japanese woman who was photographing the channel. Still wearing her flying overalls, she followed Sanger everywhere, flitting about him like the Ariel of this threadbare Prospero. His eyes and his ears, Sanger called these two assistants, the shy young Indian with the mind of a breast-pocket encyclopaedia, and the busy-as-a-bee photo-journalist who ran here and there, endlessly performing the intricate mating dances that united nature and her camera lens. They were forever feeding him scientific facts and possible film locations. At times it seemed that nothing had any real significance for Sanger until Mr Pal and Miss Matsuoka had pre-digested it for him in the terms of an imaginary film documentary. Sanger existed in a fictionalised world, remade by the clichés of his own "wild-life" nature films. These were not soap operas but soap documentaries. The makers of TV documentaries were the conmen and carpetbaggers of the late twentieth century, the snake-oil and fast-change salesmen purveying the notion that a raw nature packaged and homogenised by science was palatable and reassuring.

"A river?" I repeated. "Not yet. Strictly speaking it's no more than a freak rise in the local water-table." We were standing below the shoulder of the runway extension, a few yards from the site of the original spring. All trace of the access ramp had been swept away by the rushing waters of the past eight days. The north-east corner of the runway had vanished, and a cliff of once compacted earth was now collapsing into the stream.

Whether stream or river, brook or burn, the channel was fifty feet wide. Draining from the unmapped forest swamps two miles to the north-east of Port-la-Nouvelle, it flowed past the airstrip to empty into Lake Kotto. Each morning when I woke in the trailer the light reflected from the surface rippled ever more brightly across the ceiling of the cabin. Already the western end of Lake Kotto was covered to a depth of twelve inches by a vast brown pool of silt-filled water that stretched six hundred yards from the quays beyond the tobacco factory.

All my drilling wells had been flooded. The line of towers stood like harbour buoys, linked to the shore by the charred sections of the viaduct. I had tried to defend the wells by building an earth rampart around them, a wall of dust which the advancing lake had soon penetrated. By the third day, when the last of the wells began to fill with water, I abandoned the effort and ordered the sergeant to return the tractor to the clinic.

Even then, a substantial delta had formed. This miniature river carried tons of fine soil and humus from the forest floor and deposited them at its mouth, where they lay in banks of silt as smooth as pillows of wet satin.

When I followed the stream's course through the forest, past the airstrip and Nora Warrender's breeding station, I soon found that the secret basin to which I had traced it no longer existed. The basin and the service road of the French oil-company workers had been obliterated by the strong channel that flowed among the trees, and which each day seemed to place its source ever deeper into the forest. Two miles to the north of the airstrip the stream was still ten feet wide, flowing through the scrub and undergrowth, but I was then turned back by a patrol of Kagwa's soldiers. At night I heard the sounds of rifle fire and mortar shelling, and guessed that Harare's guerillas had been drawn back to this unexpected supply of fresh water.

Kagwa seemed to concur. At first the Captain was eager to rid himself of this nuisance that threatened the airstrip, distracted his men, and altered the strategic balance of the arid region under his rule. After my meeting with the armed patrol he clearly suspected that I was acting in some way as an emissary between Harare and dissident elements to the south. But Kagwa merely warned me of the dangers of trying to penetrate too deeply into the forest, and then assigned three men to help me dam or divert the stream.

Even with their aid it was soon obvious the current was too strong for us. The earth dam we built at the mouth of the stream — a rampart of sand and soil driven over the delta by the tractor — was overrun within hours. A second, which we constructed using a section of the runway extension, was washed aside before we could bridge the two banks. Meanwhile the stream continued to grow, deepening and widening its channel, sweeping with it a freight of uprooted saplings, rafts of brushwood, and a legion of beer bottles and aerosol cans. Watching this tide of man-made rubbish, I could almost believe that this small stream was trying single-handedly to cleanse the continent of the garbage which the century had deposited there.

Within a week of my creation of the river, the first brown water reached the pier of the police barracks, and Captain Kagwa reassigned the three men, leaving me on my own. His mechanics were working on the engines of the police launch and the car ferry stranded on the beach beyond the cigarette factory. Already the bows of the restaurant barge — a floating bordello once patronised by the oil-company workers — were washed by the lake. The plaster goddess with yellow hair who hung below the bowsprit, crudely painted to resemble a future Queen of England, dipped up and down on the shallow waves, as if the venerable craft were preparing itself for the trade to come.

Meanwhile this mysterious stream continued to transform the forest. The foliage was brighter, and a green lustre filled the once blanched canopy, as if the stream had bathed everything with a subterranean light. As I walked through the trees, trying to devise some means of building an effective dam, I sensed around me the atmosphere of a new world. I breathed the fresh, Edenic air, almost believing that I had planted and watered a forgotten corner of the original Creation garden. I felt light-headed on the sweet scents of blossom and rotting bark, and yet curiously at rest, as if I were waking into a dream that had slept within me since my childhood. I remembered the derelict kitchen garden of the house my father had bought in Kowloon, a miniature wilderness where I had played as a boy among tomato and cucumber frames overgrown with wild sugarcane. Rats and small snakes infested the deep grass, but I had made my child's world there until, when I was seven, my father had brought in a local contractor, cleared the ground and built an asphalt tennis court. However, even as an adolescent playing with my friends, I could still sense the lost jungle of the rubbish tip around me.

I waded in the silvery water, washing the dust from my arms and face. In my fancy I imagined that this stream was a forgotten tributary of the primordial river in the desert gorges of central Africa, where man's primitive ancestors had broken their pact with the tree, the giant river which had descended beneath the Sahara and lain dormant for thousands of years.

Perhaps aware of the refreshing light in this waking forest, others were also drawn to the stream. By night Harare's guerillas haunted the upper reaches of the channel, now and then firing a mortar shell into the deserted streets of Port-la-Nouvelle. By day Kagwa's soldiers walked naked in the cool water, washing their clothes and hunting for gold.

Even Sanger had crossed the runway to inspect the stream, and twice a day would fill a flask of water for the boiled rice on which he and his two aides subsisted. Abandoned in disgust by the journalists and the freelance film crew, who had soon realised that this risible mercy mission was merely a publicity stunt, he now lived on at the airstrip, waiting for the Dakota to return and collect his broadcasting studio.

Stranded in Port-la-Nouvelle until Air Centrafrique received payment from his sponsors in Tokyo, Sanger camped with Mr Pal beside the control shack, surrounded by his bags of rice, the cameras and recording equipment, and the dismantled sections of his satellite dish, an electronic dream already overgrown by the runway grass. He was now his own famine victim, benefactor and documentary historian, a self-contained one-man television disaster area. Once he came down to the dispensary and borrowed money from me, ostensibly to purchase supplies from Captain Kagwa's quartermaster, but I saw him hand the cash over to the Japanese photographer, who had already threatened to leave. She lived alone in her pup tent, below the wing of her aircraft, refusing to share her supplies. It was clear that Sanger's documentary needed a radical change of script, some new theme that would revive the project and satisfy the Tokyo networks.

While I worked with my spade, I noticed that Sanger was listening intently to Mr Pal. The slim-shouldered Indian stood beside the beached skiff and kept up his endless commentary, now and then glancing at me in a knowing way, as if I had already suggested to him the germ of a new wild-life programme, perhaps on the subject of amateur dam-building. Even Miss Matsuoka had begun to point her camera at me when she had no other subject in view. I was all too aware that this intense young Japanese saw me as one of the odder denizens of the forest.

Irritated by this air of small conspiracy, I threw the clods of earth at their feet.

"Sanger — tell Miss Matsuoka to aim her camera at someone else."

"You're careless of life, doctor." Sanger instantly came forward when he saw that I was waiting for him to go. "Like all your profession, you dismiss everything that doesn't fit into some punitive scheme of things. That's why the public venerates you."

"Why don't you leave Port-la-Nouvelle? There's nothing here for you."

"There's nothing for me anywhere else." Sanger shrugged, with one of the displays of frank despair to which he often treated me, as if testing me in some way. "I'm waiting for funds to be telexed. I need to lease a big plane for the rice. People don't realise what all this charity weighs."

"Then leave the rice here. Go to Gambia, make a tourist documentary about crocodiles."

"It's been done too many times. The natural realm is exhausted, everyone got there first in the sixties. Nobody wants to know how the world is, they want emotion and imagination rolled across it like a soft carpet. Believe me, Dr Mallory, you need new ideas these days. Just as we need new vices."

"What you really need is a new set of lies." I said this without malice — in an unexpected way, I found myself drawn to this amiable impostor. I thrust at the oozing mud between my feet. "Still, that shouldn't be too hard to find."

"Very hard." Sanger held my shoulder, oblivious of the flecks of mud on his suit. "You are wrong again, doctor. Television doesn't tell lies, it makes up a new truth. In fact, the only truth we have left. These sentimental wild-life films you despise simply continue that domestication of nature which began when we cut down the first tree. They help people to remake nature into a form that reflects their real needs."

"And that justifies any invention?"

"No. It must chime with their secret hopes, their deep-held belief that the universe is a kindly place. Besides, everything is invented and then pondered upon. God rested on the seventh day in order to look at the rushes. These trees, these leaves, flowers and roots, are fictions invented to trap the sun, catch an insect, suck the water. Look at your river — that's a complete invention."

"A television company might even have thought it up?"

"Perhaps it did. And what difference? Sooner or later, everything turns into television. Consider, Dr Mallory, you may already be the subject of a new documentary about a man who invents a river. . . ."

A cascade of gravel fell on to the bank beside me, splashing into the water at my feet like the pellets of a shotgun. The sharp stones stung my arms and neck, and I dropped my spade into the mud. I turned to see the Japanese photographer standing above me on the crumbling face of the runway, the stone chips falling from her flight boots. She had listened to Sanger and now fixed me in the viewfinder of her camera, already accepting that I was her new project.

Sanger was kneeling at the water's edge, filling his flask as Mr Pal pushed the skiff into the stream. The clear liquid poured into the chromium flask, its silvery reflection dancing happily in its private vault. Sanger wet his hands, and then raised his sunglasses and bathed his tired eyes, as if they had already seen enough of my real motives.

"Sanger. . . ." I picked up the spade and struck the earth wall at my feet, sending a shower of wet mud through the air. "Leave that water. And get out!"

"Of course, doctor." Spattered with the mud, Sanger stood up, searching for Mr Pal's shoulder. "I should have asked for your permission. It is your river." With a formal bow, Sanger decanted the water into the stream. He wiped the neck of the flask on his sleeve and then allowed Mr Pal to help him into the skiff.

With an effort, I controlled myself, listening to the rapid clicks of Miss Matsuoka's motor-drive. What had annoyed me, I realised as Sanger sailed upstream, was not the thought of being filmed, even by some imaginary programme inside his head; rather, I had been angered by his taking of my water. Much as I was trying to stifle the stream, or point it in some other direction, preferably north, I now regarded every drop it contained as my own.

9

The River Mallory

Spade in hand, I set off along the bank. I was certain that Sanger was deliberately stealing the water, not merely to boil his rice, but in some way to subvert my own image of the stream, and to trivialise my awakening sense of that richer world I had glimpsed in the forest. As if reassuring me, the bright waves rushed towards my feet, tumbling over a cascade of truck tyres that lay on the sandy bed.

As I waded through the shallows, following the trail of bubbles left by Mr Pal's punt pole, I saw the skiff pulled up on to a beach of red sand. Sanger knelt with his flagon, helping himself to the current.

Twenty yards upstream, a second watering-party had arrived. Mrs Warrender and two of her servant-women stood knee-deep in the water, skirts fastened around their bare thighs. They had brought with them a wooden cart, to which a fifty-gallon drum was lashed with copper wire. Scanning the stream for the clearer currents free of leaves and dead insects, they filled their ladles with water and emptied them into the drum. While they worked in this leisurely but efficient way they were watched by Mr Pal, who framed his fingers to form a camera viewfinder, recording this pastoral glimpse of the sisterhood under the sign of Aquarius.

I, in turn, was watching Nora Warrender. She held the handle of the cart in her firm grip, and gazed across the river at two of Kagwa's soldiers who were bathing by the opposite bank. Between them, moored in midstream to the branch of a collapsing beech, was the twelve-year-old with the injured foot. She had built a small coracle by stretching green plastic sheeting over a frame of bamboo. One foot over the side, she played with her bandage as it unravelled in the flowing stream.

Mrs Warrender ignored her, and watched the naked men sedately soaping themselves behind the veil of beech leaves. Her strong face was set in an expression of stony hostility. I assumed either that this was the racist response of a former white Rhodesian, or that she had recognised a former guerilla who had killed her husband.

"N'doc. . . ." There was a soft grunt of alarm. Noticing me, the girl sat up and reeled in her bandage. Using a home-made paddle, she moved swiftly across the stream and stationed herself a few yards from the women. Eyes fixed on me, she whistled to the water, as if urging the river to be alert, spurring it on with encouraging strokes of the paddle.

"Mrs Warrender . . . I meant to warn you." I strode past Sanger, aware of my mud-caked hands and legs, and the wild smears on my face. "I take it you aren't drinking this water?"

She turned to face me, looking me up and down with the same expression that I had seen as she gazed at the soldiers. "Why not? It seems pure enough. Doctor . . .?"

I caught my breath, aware of the half-naked bodies and heavy perspiration of the women, and unable for a moment to think of an answer. "All this water — it's part of the Lake Kotto irrigation project."

"Fair enough. I'm glad to see it irrigate Lake Kotto. There's plenty left over for the rest of us."

"No. . . ." I gestured to the African women to stop ladling, but after the barest glance they ignored me. "It may well be infected. Nora, it's best to leave it alone."

Nora Warrender stared at me in a sympathetic way, shaking her head. "It's infected you — I can see that straight away. God only knows with what strange virus. . . ."

She bent down to fill her ladle, the loose lapels of her dressing-gown exposing her breasts. She dressed in this offhand manner, though not out of coquetry. By casually revealing her body, she was telling me in the most matter-of-fact way that I did not exist.

Irritated by all this, I seized the ladle. Her arm pressed against mine, and I felt the tension of a fierce body inside the shabby bath-robe.

"Nora . . . This water may not be safe — there are bodies buried here."

"Don't be a fool. You don't own this river. . . ."

We struggled together around the cart, bumping into the African women, who turned and began to shout at me. The water leapt from their ladles, drenching my shirt. I lost my footing in the wet sand, slipped and fell on to my back in the stream. Instantly the girl in the coracle paddled forward. With a flick of her oar she pivoted the small craft and churned the water over my legs, as if trying to bury me.

Ladles in their heavy hands, Fanny and Louise stared down at me. They hooted derisively, and then dragged the cart on to the beach. Nora Warrender stood on the bank, watching in a concerned way as Sanger and Mr Pal helped me to my feet.

I was still reflecting on Nora Warrender's last words when I went to see Captain Kagwa in the police barracks three hours later. My absurd wrestling match with this increasingly odd young widow had at least cleared my mind. With Sanger and Mr Pal at my heels, I set off along the bank towards Port-la-Nouvelle. Through the trees I could see the girl in the coracle, coasting on the current behind the screen of trees. Her eyes were forever on me, this self-appointed guardian of the stream, as if she were now responsible for this river which I had conceived.

For all the humiliation of being thrown into the water, I knew now that Mrs Warrender had spoken only the truth — I had made the river but I did not own it.

"You want to buy the river, doctor?" Captain Kagwa walked around his desk and gazed through the broken windows at the brown surface of Lake Kotto. "Simply to buy it?"

"Exactly. Land here is for sale — thousands of acres are bought and sold, including hundreds of lakes and streams. WHO has leased miles of malarial creeks. Even Lake Kotto was once offered to a Franco-Belgian consortium."

"Of course. A pity they didn't take it, I would be a rich man. A General of Police." Kagwa glanced at the television screen in the corner, where a video of his interview with Sanger was playing on an endless loop. Now that Captain Kagwa was a celebrity, the upright piano had been moved into the orderly room. The soft tones of Sanger's obsequious questions and Kagwa's resonant replies, as he stood by the Dakota like Hannibal beside an elephant, sounded through the noise of the soldiers working on the police launch and the car ferry. But Kagwa was vaguely intrigued by my strange proposal, and curious enough to question me further.

"But this river, doctor. A week ago you were leaving us in despair. Now you have these dreams of property. Is there gold here?"

"Not that I know of. But don't worry, I will assign to you all mineral rights."

"Perpetually?"

"Of course. And fishing rights, navigation rights, everything. Anyway, I only want to own the river for a short time."

"For what purpose, doctor?"

"I want to divert it, or conceivably drain it. All this water has ruined my irrigation project. Besides, Captain, it's best to stop thinking of it as a river. It may look like a river, but in fact it's merely an accidental surface flow. At any moment it will dry up, leaving a huge swamp that may take years to drain."

"A malarial swamp? That's true. Perfect cover for Harare's forces." Kagwa sat at his desk, pondering the prospect of millions of mosquitoes descending on this empty town over which he presided. He stared at his image on the television screen, comparing his resplendent uniform with my ragged shirt and mud-stained shorts. "You work so hard, doctor, it would be a pity to see so much effort go to waste. A bad advertisement."

"Good. I appreciate your support, Captain. As soon as I drain this stream I can return to the drilling project. That's much more important to you and to Port-la-Nouvelle than this little creek."

I opened my leather map-case to reveal the damp-proof bag that contained my WHO accreditation, the Health Ministry's passe-partout, my return ticket to Lagos and a wallet of bearer cheques in lieu of my salary.

"Now, I have control of a small WHO contingency fund to deal with suspected outbreaks of malaria or smallpox — but before spending this money I must have some kind of title to the channel. I'm sure I could spend seven hundred dollars."

"Very good, doctor." Kagwa was well aware that no such fund existed, and that I would be buying the river with my own money. "I'm sure something can be arranged. Perhaps for a thousand dollars . . .?"

I stood on the wharf below the police barracks, looking out over the widening expanse of Lake Kotto. The brown surface was now more than two feet deep, extending far beyond the line of drilling rigs, those water-mills against which I had tilted. A skiff was moored to the nearest rig, and one of Kagwa's soldiers was fishing for frogs with a length of net that he had stretched between the tower and the collapsed viaduct. The water continued to flow from the river, its currents drifting in clockwise eddies around the lake, giving off the stench of the broken land.

Two hundred yards from me, the girl sat in her plastic coracle at the mouth of the river, surrounded by the tilting oaks whose roots had been loosened by the ceaseless passage of water. She paddled against the current with strong, impatient movements, obviously suspicious of my meeting with Captain Kagwa.

For all her scowls, little was she aware of the powers I now had over her. For a thousand dollars I had bought a year's lease of the river. As agreed, I had ceded all mineral, fishing and navigation rights, but in return I had sole management of the waterway and whatever role it might play in the Lake Kotto irrigation project. I had the right to dam, divert or drain the river, to vary its flow and gradient, to adjust its banks and course. In short, for a year I was master of this impossible channel.

A year, I calculated, would be more than enough time to be rid of it. With the tractor, and the four men whom Kagwa had promised to assign to me (all seconded to WHO for wages which I would pay and the Captain disburse) I calculated that I would block the channel with enough infill to reverse the flow. Perhaps I would breach the bank, enticing the river into the low-lying ground beside the airstrip, and let it expire in a hopeless duel with the dust and the sun. Meanwhile I would drop a huge earth barrage, fortified with the trees uprooted by the river, across the full width of the channel. Then I would cap the original spring with the root-crown of the great oak. . . .

These plans were still half-formed, but I felt almost light-headed at the prospect of scotching the river. Unexpected feelings of revenge ran through me; I was surprised by my eagerness to set about mutilating this harmless mass of water. I checked myself, thinking of my first sight as a young medical student of the cadavers in the dissection room, laid out on the glass tables like the forgotten patrons of a Turkish bath who had waited too long for their massage. Most of the bodies donated were those of physicians, and in a sense we were dismembering our future selves. Under the scalpels and scissors, a nervous humour had flowed; we had needed to avenge ourselves on these yellowing cadavers for the fears they prompted.

"Not that again. . . ." As I calmed myself I saw one of Kagwa's mechanics frowning at me from the diesel engine of the *Salammbo*, the car ferry moored to the police wharf.

I bowed my head, pretending to bless this elderly craft, and walked along the jetty. I noticed that Kagwa had not withdrawn his men from either the ferry or the former French landing-craft beached beyond the restaurant barge. If the river failed, as I intended, Lake Kotto would be dry again. But no doubt the Captain viewed my plans with some scepticism.

At the same time, I was intrigued with the notion of leaving the river to flow. Sooner or later the hydraulic levels within the subterranean aquifer would even themselves, and this mysterious creek would dry out of its own accord. Perhaps it would become a small brook, a few feet across, a pleasant scenic reminder of my work on the drilling project.

"All set, Mallory . . .!" Followed by Mr Pal, Sanger strode

along the wharf, waving three copies of the provisional agreement. "The lease is signed, the river is yours for a year — you can swim in it, vomit, urinate, make love to Mrs Warrender under water — it's at your beck and call."

"Right, Professor, I may well do so, in that order." I took the ill-typed documents from his unsteady hand. Sanger leaned against Mr Pal, his face as pallid as the bone-like surface of the lost lake-bed. I realised that both men were hungry and under-nourished, and were looking at my thin but well-muscled body with envious eyes. "Sanger, I'll give you some flour and one or two cans of fish. You can help me with the drainage project."

"Of course, doctor. Mr Pal is a hard worker."

I knew that I was already starring in Sanger's next documentary. My creation of the river, my purchase of it from the local police chief, and my obsession with destroying it had all touched his fancy.

"By the way, doctor," Sanger added. "I borrowed the Captain's radio-phone and sent a message to the German legation in Nairobi. At my request they will register the river with the National Geographic Society in Washington. For the sake of convenience I had to give it a name."

"Thorough of you — and what did you call it?"

"The Mallory — what else?"

I turned away and stared at the mouth of the river where the girl watched me from her coracle. The River Mallory. I felt a curious pride. Yet knowing that it bore my name made me all the more determined to destroy it.

IO

The Cascade

Unaware of its coming end, the Mallory continued to flow below me. I stood on the earth rampart which Captain Kagwa's men had constructed beside the airstrip, and looked down at the channel of brown water that emerged from the forest and swept towards the lake. Now seventy yards wide, the river had settled into a sedate middle-age, its course littered with the half-submerged trunks of the palms and forest birches whose roots it had undermined. Their foliage still thriving, the trees lay at all angles in the warm stream, a roosting place for hundreds of painted snipe and oystercatchers.

Behind the tractor, the soldiers sweated in the sun, moving the last of the oak piles into position behind the rampart. Now that the river was about to be extinguished, I felt pleasantly drunk — the combined effects of the sun, the whisky I had been drinking since breakfast, and the disapproving eyes of the coracle girl who had restlessly watched the preparations from midstream.

From the roof of the police barracks Captain Kagwa kept an eye on our progress through his binoculars. A hundred yards upstream from the rampart, Mrs Warrender and her women stood on the bank, watching with their expressionless faces, like a party of Norns. I was only sad that my underwater tryst with Nora Warrender would not now take place.

On the opposite bank Mr Pal and Sanger waited behind their cine-camera, while Miss Matsuoka darted around the tractor, tape recorder slung over the shoulder of her flying suit, pushing her microphone into the faces of the bad-tempered soldiers.

For once I was happy to let Sanger record these final hours of the

Mallory. I had worked for three weeks with Kagwa's men, planning a final assault on this ever-growing river, recruiting three elements of nature against the fourth. Earth, air and fire would be brought to bear together — the mass of soil and gravel which we had excavated from the shoulder of the airstrip would be driven forward by the tractor and dropped across the river at its narrowest point, forming a huge rampart fortified by the oak piles. Through breaches in the banks the dammed water would pour into the waste ground beside the runway, and soon evaporate in the hot air. Lastly, I had transported a hundred gallons of diesel fuel from the drilling project, to be tipped into the stream and ignited, scorching the last moisture from the bed of the channel. The river would die here, where I had first loosed it upon the unsuspecting light.

"Dr Mallory — the river is ready for you. . . ." Miss Matsuoka called to me from her vantage point beside the oak piles. She danced among the heavy logs, ready to skip out of their way when they began to roll. She beckoned me on, but then held up her hand, as usual finding it impossible to satisfy herself.

The tractor waited below me. The sergeant had backed the last of the earth into the rampart. Covered with dust and sweat, he hung from his controls, watching for my signal. Downstream, two of his men waited to release the water through their sluice-gates. On either side of the rampart the logs lay in place, about to tumble forward.

The smoke from the tractor billowed into my face, forcing me to choke. Already queasy from the effects of the whisky, I waved the fumes away, tripped over a plastic carton half-buried in the rubble and sat down heavily. Cock of my dunghill, I gazed at the river for the last time, and raised Captain Kagwa's flare pistol above my head.

Through the smoke I saw a small fir tree drift below the rampart. Partly hidden within the foliage was the girl in the coracle. Paddling fiercely, she was trying to undo the soldiers' work, freeing the river of all obstacles so that it might flow with its greatest strength. She swerved to and fro, sweeping the water on its way, and steered herself to the foot of the earth wall. Small fists clenched around her paddle, she looked up at me, willing me to do my worst.

Above the rumble of the tractor I heard the higher note of an aircraft engine. Fifty feet above the forest canopy a helicopter of the provincial gendarmerie was approaching the airstrip. Once owned by a French oil consortium, its shabby paintwork still carried the company's livery on the dented plates of its hull, over which were superimposed the gendarmerie insignia. At the controls a fair-haired European pilot peered through his windshield, surprised to see the bizarre tableau below him.

As a million dead leaves swirled into the air I tried to wave the helicopter away. My feet slipped in the soft earth, sending a shower of pebbles into the water around the girl. She winced and pinched herself, then paddled more furiously, hunting down each dilatory eddy and speeding it on its way.

Deafened by the helicopter's engine, and happy to misinterpret my signal, the tractor driver released his clutch and propelled the vehicle into the rampart, sinking the huge blade into the earth shoulder. I slid down the shifting slope, as the soil and beer cans spilled around my waist, shouting to the girl in the coracle and urging her to move out of danger. Confused by the noise and the cascade of gravel, the three soldiers holding back the oak piles began to loosen the halyards of their derrick and tip the giant logs into the water.

"Hold on — not yet . . .!" I waved to them with the flare pistol, but their faces were confused by the whirling dust and the noise of the helicopter. Trying to include the circling craft in her composition, Miss Matsuoka stood with her back to the straining logs, eyes fixed to the viewfinder of her camera.

The earth slipped below my feet, a soft, swift avalanche into the peppered surface of the water. I found myself sitting in the muddy shallows at the foot of the rampart, as a cascade of earth, gravel and garbage poured around me. Huge logs were tumbling into the current only a dozen feet away, and I caught a last glimpse of Miss Matsuoka stumbling among them, face stunned and hair dishevelled, the flying suit torn from one shoulder. Twisting between them was the plastic coracle. The child flailed with her paddle through the clouds of earth and spray. The helicopter had overflown the airstrip, the pilot unnerved by the sight of part of the runway shoulder disappearing beneath his landing rails. Miss Matsuoka had vanished and an empty silver sleeve floated on the brown foam.

The ledge on which I sat sank beneath me. An intact section of the rampart fell forward into the river, and the wave of displaced water swept me off my feet. Carried into the yellow depths, I saw one of the oak logs rolling above my head like the wheel of a truck. I felt myself drawn down, and my feet touched the wall of a funnel within the gravel-bed, that cavern from which the stream had first emerged and which my body would fill, setting the Mallory free at last to run its course.

II

The House of Women

Around me I could hear the voices of women, muffled as they made their beds in rooms always somewhere beyond my sight. Softened by the thick drapes that hung from the doors of the veranda, the low sing-song murmur moved between them as they worked. In my mind the liquid clicks of their dialect merged with the sounds of the river tapping at the terrace below the veranda, so that the brown waves seemed to draw the endless chatter from the hidden rooms of the breeding station and were in turn teased on their way by the voices of these invisible women playing among their beds.

For three weeks I had rested on the veranda, sitting in the high steel cot which the nuns at Port-la-Nouvelle had purchased for their ageing priest, and on whose hard Victorian springs the poor man had died. For days I listened to the women, but never caught what they were saying. The large house had been converted into a maze of bedrooms in which the women murmured all day like the contented inmates of a seraglio, falling silent only when they entered the veranda.

Every day they bathed naked in the river below the terrace, but it was clear that they did not regard me as a wounded pasha being lovingly restored to health. Three pairs of strong hands changed my sheets and dressings with the same briskness they used when pounding cassava in the kitchen yard. But for Mrs Warrender, I was sure that Fanny and Louise and Poupée would have wheeled the cot on to the terrace and tipped their unwelcome guest into the nearest whirlpool. However, I was content to watch these handsome women bathing in the river, and put up with their ill-humour, only puzzled why Nora Warrender had accepted me at the breeding station.

I had been rescued from the tumbling logs by two of Kagwa's soldiers, and pulled half-drowned on to the river bank. The following day the body of Miss Matsuoka was washed ashore on the beach below the tobacco warehouse, although it was a week later that I learned of her death. With a fractured vertebra in my neck, a bruised liver and spleen, I had been left in my trailer at the clinic, but rapidly slipped into shock before being moved to a disused cell at the police barracks. For three days Kagwa had gazed at me with expressions that ranged from boredom to concern, as the reflection of Sanger's video played on the ceiling above his head. At last he decided to send me by truck to the provincial capital, a journey over sabotaged bridges and cratered roads that would have ruptured my spleen and killed me within hours.

Then, as I was being lifted over the tail-gate of one of the trucks, I was rescued by Nora Warrender. She and her three women trundled me back to the breeding station on the same wooden cart which I had forbidden them to use as a water-carrier. From then on, a diet of cassava, the sight of soft arms and hard hands, and the sounds and smell of the river set me on the mend.

Above all, it was the river, which had once tried to take my life, that now revived me. In the weeks that I spent on the veranda I watched it flow past the grounds of the breeding station. It was now an immense brown current two hundred yards wide, filling the entire valley beside the airstrip, which the waters had swept away since the fiasco of my attempt to smother them. Ten feet deep at its centre, the river emerged from a wide rent in the forest two miles to the north of Port-la-Nouvelle. Through the canyon of red earth which the current had cut between the trees, I could see its upper reaches winding across the open savanna as it emerged from the Chad and Sudan borderlands. At night I watched its silver back through the darkness, crossing the horizon like the traffic stream of a continental highway.

The speed of the river's growth had overwhelmed Lake Kotto, which was now an expanse of deep brown water thirty miles in length, teeming with the fish and small snakes that had emerged from the meanders of the Kotto River at its southern end, and furnished with its own micro-climate. Already the first clouds had formed above the lake, and there were hints of rain. An entire landscape was being remade. During my first week the women had walked the full length of the estate in order to fill their water pails from the slippery bank, but the river had soon shortened their journey. The strong brown tide, seething through the debris of toppled trees lying in midstream, quickly overran the brick wall beside the gates, then swept up the drive and demolished the fence of the kitchen garden. Within the second week, the water had crossed the weed-grown lawn to the steps of the terrace, as if to seek me out and remind me how much it had grown since my attempt to destroy it.

The stone veranda was now a jetty across which waves would often break, depositing dead rats, empty after-shave bottles and drenched copies of *Paris-Match*. The tide swirled around the house and in twenty-four hours swept away the brick cages of the breeding station. Led by Mrs Warrender, the women had moved the few remaining macaques and marmosets into the smaller cages in the surgery. They filled flour-bags with earth from the kitchen garden, and laid them in a makeshift wall across the drive.

As I could have told them, their oozing defence wall had soon been demolished. They laboured knee-deep in the mud, wallowing like the members of a female wrestling team, and I remembered their strong hands and felt almost proud of this great channel. I had left part of my blood in the river, and although we were enemies a special bond had formed between myself and this strange waterway.

The cot trembled against my back, the castors turning on the stone floor as the house shifted under the pressure of water. Within a few weeks, unless the river abated, it would be swept away, and already Nora Warrender had conceded to Captain Kagwa that she would have to evacuate the breeding station. Hidden tides rolled below the smooth surface of the river, taking their beat from a different pendulum whose swing was as wide as the horizon. A faint shudder moved through the walls, and I saw a broad swell sidle across the river. On its brown back it carried a police patrol launch which it swept sideways on to a narrow sand-bank in midstream. After a change of helmsman the crew pushed themselves free with a flurry of oars and boathooks. On its starboard bow a second patrol boat was trying to cross the channel in a cloud of diesel smoke, drifting towards a clump of drowned oaks fifty yards from the bank, where a party of soldiers were constructing a small jetty.

As if aware of all this military activity, the river had smoothed its surface and withdrawn into itself, into those secret deeps where part of me had drowned. I could feel the water still flowing through my veins and was aware of those changes, in the realms of time and the senses, that the Mallory had imposed. I knew that my obsession with the river had led to the death of the Japanese photographer, and that her body lay in the cemetery behind the deserted Catholic mission, beside the oil-company workers and the former manager of the Toyota garage. Yet in my mind she and I still swam through that bright, gravel-filled stream. I wanted to immerse myself in the great rivers of the world, to be drawn down into their deeps. Already I guessed that it was not the Mallory that I had wanted to kill, but myself, and that this river which I had created was in fact trying to save me. . . .

"You're dreaming too much, doctor. See what you've been doing with all this water. . . ."

Poupée, the youngest of the African women, who had once been a hostess on the *Diana*, strode across the veranda on flat heels, her handsome hip striking a corner of the cot and jarring my neck. Ignoring me, she stepped on to the terrace, the water streaming around her bare feet. She picked up a willow branch washed on to the flagstones and ambled along in a jaunty way, as if to throw it into the channel, but then lashed viciously at the water below the veranda.

A child's head emerged into view, hands raised against this

fusillade of blows. Poupée flailed at her shoulders, knocking away the paddle. She bent down and seized the side of the coracle and tried to overturn the craft, working herself into a fury at the girl.

All this anger unsettled me, and I tried to climb from the cot. I saw the girl every afternoon, paddling across the river to inspect a new sand-bank raised by a shift in the current, hanging on to the branch of a half-submerged tree as she kept an eye on my convalescence. She spent the morning near the military camp at the airstrip, watching Professor Sanger's television monitors and scrounging for scraps from the company of bored field engineers brought in by Kagwa to build a pontoon bridge. The attempt had proved another fiasco — the river had doubled in width during the week which the engineers had taken to assemble the bridge. A single surge in the current swept away the metal pontoons and scattered them far across Lake Kotto.

Clearly pleased by this, the girl paddled swiftly to the breeding station. I had never spoken to her, but every day, while the women dozed after our afternoon meal, I would leave some of my food for the child on the veranda steps. However, she had not sped across the river to eat, but to make sure that I was aware of the engineers' failure.

Caught in the face by the flailing willow branch, the girl cried out. She abandoned her oar and paddled backwards with her hands, wiping the tears from her nose and eyes.

"Poupée, leave her alone! She only wants food!" When I reached the veranda the current had carried the child out into the channel. I took the oar from Poupée's hands, but in her anger she tried to wrestle it away from me. Something about the girl, perhaps her tribe, or simply her delight in the river, touched a reflex of extreme hostility.

"Come in, doctor. We can't have you trying to drown yourself again."

I felt Nora Warrender's hands on my shoulder. She steered me away from the water, as if I were a senile patient at a private clinic, one of those so-called nursing homes that line the banks of the Thames and Long Island Sound and are in effect private prisons.

She still wore the old dressing-gown, a badge of whatever outrage she had suffered — before leaving Port-la-Nouvelle, Santos had suggested that Mrs Warrender and her women had been beaten and probably raped by Harare's guerillas.

However, my accident, or our imminent departure from Lake Kotto, had catalysed a remarkable change in Nora Warrender. She was as stretched and vulnerable as ever, but she had woken from the muffled sleep of bereavement, her walking numbness, and now moved purposefully about the breeding station as she supervised the packing. And, though I found it hard to believe, she even seemed to show some interest in recruiting me into whatever half-formed scheme circled around her mind. Often in the early evening she would come on to the veranda with two tumblers of whisky, sit on the bed and talk to me in an eerily level way. I even had some vague idea of restarting our affair. At that time she had been unable to cope with my problems, my endless talk of remythologising myself and making a new life somewhere else, as if somewhere else existed. Now, however, she took an intense pleasure in the river and its growth, and was clearly undismayed by the prospect of the breeding station, and all trace of her marriage, being washed away by its waves.

"Do they need to be so hard on the child?" I tossed the oar over the water towards the coracle. The girl's eyes locked on to mine, her only concession to thanks. She retrieved the blade with a grimace, and then spun the coracle in an eddy and slipped away like a dodgem driver into the current.

Without thinking, I waved to her, a small show of sympathy. "Strange creature. Why do your women hate her so much?"

"She's always stealing food. Don't feel too sorry for her. She tried to kill you."

"Hardly, Nora. She's little more than a child."

"Is death less final when the trigger-finger belongs to a twelve-year-old?"

"I like to think so."

Mrs Warrender settled me against the pillow. "It's a good thing you're leaving, doctor. I'll have a word with them — they connect

75

her with the river, and feel she might even be some sort of partner of yours."

"Partner? She tried to shoot me."

"Perhaps she thinks you have special powers — I'm sure she can see that you're half-way to the dream-time."

"She fired her rifle at my chest."

"Well, now she knows you have stamina. She comes from some mountain tribe to the north — probably she's decided to marry you. At twelve or thirteen she's practically an old maid."

"Not for much longer, the way your women go on — they're trying to blind her."

"I'll keep them away from her. They know she was with Harare."

"And they haven't told Captain Kagwa?"

"They would — but I've explained to them that she's important to you."

"Is she?"

"Of course — you don't realise it, but she's your little messenger. You have her flitting around everywhere. She keeps you informed."

"About what, for God's sake?"

"The river . . . *Your* river."

I followed a large swell that crossed the brown stream, moving like the submerged carapace of an immense leisurely turtle. Already parts of the terrace were awash. "*My* river? As a matter of fact, it is my river. I still have the deeds."

"I hope Captain Kagwa recognises them. At least it bears your name."

"The River Mallory — I paid a thousand dollars, more than Kagwa bargained for."

"He's impressed — you're a figure of potency. One day he'll erect a shrine to you, like the De Lesseps statue at Port Said."

"Maybe . . . I'm sorry about the Japanese girl. It all got a little out of hand, like most things I touch. All the same, it's the only real achievement I've managed to pull off here."

"Then why try to destroy the river?"

"Destroy it? I was trying to divert the channel and save the drilling project."

"With that dam and all those drums of gasoline? I call that deliberate murder."

I watched the water sluicing across the terrace, strangely soothed by the sight of the calm brown channel. "It provoked me — the stream springing from the ground, why there rather than a hundred feet away? All that water gushing about, it was too much. And then it wouldn't stop growing. When Sanger named it after me . . . I had to scotch it."

"And now?"

"Everything's changed. This is a third Nile. Strangling it will take more than a few drums of gasoline."

"Why try? Strictly speaking, you didn't create the river. According to Mr Pal, an earthquake in the Massif du Tondou has shifted the watersheds. It's simply coincidence."

"No. That's the one thing it isn't." In the doorway one of the women stood in the shadows, her sullen eyes watching me. I gazed at the far bank two hundred yards away, where a patrol of soldiers was pulling a tree trunk from the water. Ignoring the women, I spoke softly. "I created this river, Nora. It's named after me. I own it."

She stepped back and fastened the dressing-gown tightly around her waist, regarding me with a sympathetic but distant eye, as if I were an exotic primate which she and her husband might breed for some eccentric keeper of mammals at a fashionable zoo. "So you will try again? All this water to waste. I can think of better uses."

"Irrigating the Sahara?" The gendarmerie helicopter passed overhead, the down-draught from its blades denting the surface. "Think of it, Nora — thanks to the River Mallory this area is about to become a war zone. Already Harare calls it the Red Nile. Kagwa thinks he's going to be the proconsul of a new Saharan province with secessionist ambitions. Any moment now a Pan-African commission will arrive and the bickering will start. The mineral concessions will be carved up, the multi-nationals will start recruiting mercenaries. . . ."

"Men must play their dangerous games." Mrs Warrender spoke with offhand but bitter tones as the water splashed across the veranda. She stared at a drop that glistened on her finger like a diamond, and for a moment resembled a child wondering how to preserve it. "I'd let the river run free. Then it might sweep them away. All of them, Harare and Kagwa and the mercenaries, and you, too, doctor. I could open the station again. I'd like to breed leopards and impala, not these toy macaques for petting zoos in California. That's something to dream of . . . A new game reserve in the Sahara, populated by every living species — except one."

She sat on the cot, like a widow in an almoner's office, forced to accept the sympathy of others, but only sustaining herself by a desperate dream of better times to come. I held her shoulders, hoping to comfort this still numbed woman. "Nora, you can build another station. And you'll breed leopards there — but first you have to leave. Where will you all go?"

"Captain Kagwa says we can move into the *Diana*. His engineers claim the hull is sound."

"The oil–company brothel . . .?" When she frowned and pushed my hands away, I asked: "Tell me — why did you decide to look after me? You could have left me in the truck."

"I thought you might help us. You're so totally possessed."

"But how? To do what?"

She stood up, lips pursed as she stared at the brown channel. "I don't know . . . yet. To enlarge the river, doctor. Think hard, I want you to draw all the water from the mountains, make it wider and deeper, so wide that it overruns its banks. . . ."

She spoke softly, but her small fists drummed on the chromium rail at my feet.

12

Noon

The helicopter soared low across the river, the young French pilot intrigued by the breeding station and its women. I stepped from the terrace on to the narrow silt beach that ran between the river and the abandoned kitchen garden, fastening Alan Warrender's faded silk bath-robe around my waist. Did his widow imagine that I had conjured this vast channel from inside my head? I felt the warm water run at my heels. The small waves lassoed my ankles, trying to draw me into the deeper stream. The river fished for the fisherman. As the spray flicked at my calves I again remembered that liquid, gravel-filled crypt in which I had almost died. Already, part of my mind believed that the river would never harm me, any more than my own bloodstream would try to drown me.

Raising my eyes from the hot, sunlit surface, I deliberately forced back my head, feeling the bruised disc and the pinched cervical nerves that pricked my shoulders. For a few seconds the pain held back the river. I strode along the shore, kicking the waves out of my way.

A group of shaggy palms leaned from the bank, their roots exposed by the water. I stepped between the trunks and found myself in a narrow inlet of calmer water, where the forest wall leaned over a beach of yellow sand.

Squatting beside her plastic coracle was the girl whom I had last seen being whipped by Poupée's willow branch. The dark skin of her shoulders and arms was scored with blue blisters. She rocked to and fro on her knees, crooning to herself as she arranged a set of glass and metal objects on the beach.

Beside her, at the edge of the forest, was a miniature hutch built from driftwood and bamboo, the palm leaves on its roof held down by a rusty bicycle wheel. Through the doorway of this little kennel I could see an old blanket on which I assumed she slept each night, but the den was otherwise filled with small pieces of glass and scraps of electrical equipment she had found in the looted stores of Port-la-Nouvelle.

A selection of these she was arranging on the sand — a broken light-bulb, a plastic washing-machine dial, a piece of printed circuitry from a transistor radio, and several lengths of copper wire. She knelt over these, whistling and grunting as she moved them about like chess pieces on a board, trying to urge them into some kind of life.

I watched from the trees, a few steps behind her, guessing that she hoped with her guttural hoots to reproduce the sound and colour of Sanger's monitor screens. When they lay inertly on the beach she gave a cry of disgust and flicked the damp sand across them.

"Don't give up yet. . . ."

Still on her knees, she sprang round, staring up at me as she protected the weals on her shoulders. My gifts of food had not yet won her approval, but at least she had not bolted into the forest.

"Yes, me — N'doc . . . It's all right. You're as nervous as a bird."

When I knelt beside her she moved back but watched me in a level way. She treated me to a close scrutiny, running her eyes over my bruised arms, thinner thighs and calves, as if assessing my prospects as a work-horse.

I brushed the wet sand from the light-bulb. "Let's see what we can do with this. What do they call you?" Close to her, and without a rifle barrel to separate us, I could see that the girl was a primitive from some northern mountain tribe, her black skin lit by a faint blue sheen. Her solemn and elegant features were marked with old scars around her brows and lips, and I guessed that she had been abused as a child, driven away after her mother's death and left to fend for herself. Somehow she had enrolled herself into Harare's guerilla unit. She was either mute or autistic, or had suffered slight brain damage after a beating. However, she seemed alert enough as she pursed her lips in a sceptical way, confident that I could not reconstitute these pieces of glass and wire into one of Professor Sanger's monitor screens.

I picked up the broken light-bulb and pulled away the brass socket. "I'll try to get Mrs Warrender to take you on. Now, what about this?"

I broke off the brittle fragments of the bulb's stem, and then slid a bottle-top into the bulb, pressing it against the underside so that the red letters of the medallion glowed through the frosted glass.

"Good?"

Refusing to be impressed, the girl gave a vigorous snort through her small nostrils. However, she kept a discreet eye on the bulb, intrigued by this simple ruse. For all her primitive background, there was a stylishness about her neat movements, the small flourishes with which she opened her hands and knees, as if she were endlessly rehearsing the elements of a richer and more elegant life.

"Shall we see Mrs Warrender?" I stood up and offered to take her elbow, but she withdrew from me, and crouched in the door of her hutch. "All right. I'll put some food out for you tomorrow."

I was about to leave when she sat up on her knees. She raised a hand to her throat, preparing her damaged vocal cords for some sustained effort.

". . . N'oon." With a faint smirk, evidently pleased by this odd noise, she turned her head in a shy profile.

"Noon — ? Fair enough. I'll tell Mrs Warrender."

I walked towards the palm trees, but after two steps heard a race of feet across the sand. The girl ducked behind me, half-hidden in the trees. Her over-lit eyes set in a fierce warning, she pointed to the police launch that was heading across the river towards us, a brown spray slicing into the hot sunlight. Captain Kagwa stood beside the helmsman, a black waterproof over his police tunic.

"It's all right, Noon. The Captain won't harm you."

But she had slipped away through the underbrush, leaving me a last glimpse of her intense face, with its expression of concern like that of a teenage mother whose child is threatened.

I walked along the beach to greet Captain Kagwa. I realised that it was not I who had befriended Noon, but this simple child of the waterways who, for whatever reasons of her own, was protecting me.

The police launch approached the terrace, a constable reaching to the tiled steps with his boat-hook. I stood beside Mrs Warrender and her women, and looked up at the imposing figure of Captain Kagwa silhouetted against the sun, aware of how much the river had risen. The swells that undulated across its surface gave its back a marked camber, as if even the present channel was too confined for its immense body.

Hand on holster, Captain Kagwa grandly surveyed the river, like a mahout placed in charge of a magnificent but unpredictable elephant. With the growth of the river there had been a corresponding rise in the Captain's fortunes. He now controlled a force of a hundred men, a landing craft and helicopter, and had put on both weight and authority. It occurred to me, not for the first time, that by creating the river I had given Captain Kagwa and everyone else at Port-la-Nouvelle a new sense of purpose. The river had cured them of their malaise, and irrigated their arid lives.

"Wake yourself up, doctor. Then you can get dressed." He stepped ashore, almost catapulting his constable into the stream. "Mrs Warrender, bring your women together. My sergeant will collect you in one hour."

"But, Captain — " Mrs Warrender looked over her shoulder at the vibrating house. "You said next week. We have to pack up the laboratory."

"No sentimental packing, no last-minute farewells. This is evacuation — you leave Port-la-Nouvelle tomorrow. Look!"

He pointed to the kitchen garden behind the house. The large pools of water that lay among the vegetable beds had coalesced into a stream ten feet wide, a small arm of the river which crossed the gravel drive and then rejoined the main channel. The breeding station now stood on an island of waterlogged mud no larger than a football field. The Dutch gable at the eastern end of the house was already leaning forwards from its joists. The softening foundations had begun to split the wooden frame, and I could see daylight through the attic roof and between the loosened boards of the balcony.

"You come back now, doctor," Kagwa told me. "Two of my men are injured in a motor accident. This river — " He stared at the channel, inhaling deeply as if to synchronise his own breath with its great measures. While Mrs Warrender and her women returned to the house, he remarked with a touch of his old humour: "All your obsessions, doctor. They cause a lot of trouble. . . ."

Ten minutes later, as the launch swung out into the stream, I looked back at the tilting house on its dissolving rostrum of mud. Mrs Warrender stood on the terrace, her small figure veiled by the spray. I waved to her, hoping to raise her spirits, but she ignored me, quietly dreaming of the deluge that would spread southwards from the Sahara, after ten thousand years of drought, to drown the race of men.

Swept along by the current, we entered the faster water of the central channel. Caught beam-on, the craft drifted on the heavy, sun-filled swells. The engine stalled, and in the silence we floated backwards while the Corporal at the helm struggled with his throttle and starter. The banks slipped past, carved by the river out of the red earth. The trees leaned over the water, their roots exposed like chandeliers, the boughs dipping their leaves into the stream. A road ended abruptly at the bank, and a steel fence ran along the perimeter of a tobacco field, the line of wire vanishing into the flood. On both sides the dense forest crowded against the water's edge. The overhead canopy was richer and more luminous, islands of green light about to float away into the sky. The huge trees advanced towards the water like an army of knights, happy to be cut down while wearing their full caparison of boughs and foliage. As we approached the airstrip I watched a giant beech lose its hold on the eroding banks and topple into the water, an immense cathedral drowning itself before me.

I sat in the stern among the flares and ammunition boxes, enjoying the cool rainbows that lifted from this continent of water. But Captain Kagwa, eager to get on, stepped forward and worked the ignition.

"These village boys," he confided when we were under way. "They can polish a guard-room floor, but anything else confuses their minds . . . I need trained men now."

"Why, Captain? There's no point in trying to build dykes around the tobacco fields — I'm afraid they're lost."

"Tobacco fields? Port-la-Nouvelle is under water now, the town only exists in a technical sense. I'm thinking of larger matters, doctor. Northern Province is now a strategic zone. We can hold back the desert, and begin our advance against the Sahara."

"So you think the river will last?"

"Of course! When the hour of a dream has come who can stop it?" Kagwa seemed to have forgotten my own abortive attempts. "We caught two of Harare's deserters, they came on a raft after sailing for three days. They say that this may be only one branch of an even bigger river flowing from the Massif du Tondou."

"The Red Nile? I'm told Harare already calls it that."

"The Black Nile, doctor — carried by this river, black Africa will move north against the Arab world."

He sat back, arms outstretched to touch the river, a black conquistador sailing up his private Amazon, with one eye alert for the nearest television lens. As we approached the airstrip, however, I noticed that all trace of Sanger's film equipment had vanished from its site beside the control tower. I had expected that the newsreel footage of the dam fiasco and Miss Matsuoka's death would have placed Sanger's face on television bulletins across the globe. Yet, for all the military activity along the banks, there was no sign of that second army of bureaucrats, agronomists and World Bank advance men whom I expected to see swarming around this vast new waterway.

"A grand vision, Captain — is it shared by the provincial governor?"

Kagwa loosened his holster belt before replying. "Not yet, doctor — it's too early to inform him. Everything is in a state of flux."

"And too much information might confuse him?"

"Of course. I've explained that your drilling project has been a success and persuaded him to lend me a helicopter. Soon I will carry out a reconnaisance across the Chad and Sudan border. Hot pursuit, in search of Harare and his dangerous bandits. While there, to save expense, I will also make a geological survey, to define any matters of territoriality and ownership."

"I thought the ownership was established, Captain."

"In what way, doctor?"

"The River Mallory — it is my river."

"Doctor. . . ." Although angered, Kagwa placed his large hand on my shoulder with surprising gentleness, as if soothing a fractious patient. "My dear fellow, you must separate dream from truth."

"I have a lease, Captain. I paid you a thousand dollars. The river is even gazetteered in my name."

"But. . . ." Kagwa gestured to the broad expanse of water. "This is not the same river — its headwaters lie in the Massif du Tondou, two hundred miles away. That little stream sprang from your head."

"Perhaps — but it remains the same river. I could insist that you honour the lease, Captain."

"So that you can try to destroy it? You are not being practical."

"On the contrary, I was only concerned with the drilling project."

"And you succeeded!" Kagwa shouted, alarming the young helmsman. "You succeeded beyond all your dreams. Beyond my dreams, too. Your project is a triumph, you will be honoured throughout Africa, you will often be interviewed by *Newsweek* and *Paris-Match*."

"I thought you were keeping the news to yourself, Captain."

Kagwa sighed to himself, and directed a less than friendly smile towards me. "Doctor, the world is full of rivers. If you want to fight a duel with a river, choose one in your own country."

We were nearing the mouth of the channel, where it emptied into Lake Kotto. To our right was a ragged cliff-face of earth and gravel, marking the point at which the airstrip ended abruptly at the water's edge. The soil had stained the water a milky yellow, and formed smooth sand-bars that rose above the surface. In the shallows lay what seemed to be the head of a black bison, the submerged root of the oak from which, in my imagination at least, the river had been born. Washed by the current, it lay among the drifting logs and tree-trunks, not far from the original spring.

Even Kagwa seemed to recognise this wounded but still threatening object. He gave a grimace of distaste and spat into the water.

Between the last of the trees we swept forwards across the broad back of Lake Kotto. The white bed had vanished. From horizon to horizon the landscape was engorged with water. The great oaks that lined the banks of the lake now stood on narrow causeways of mud only a few feet above the surface. A tide of brown water had overwhelmed Port-la-Nouvelle. Waves lapped to within a few feet of the wharf below the police barracks. Arms of the lake filled the streets, and a squad of soldiers were laying duck-boards from the barracks to the forecourt of the Toyota garage, which was now the army motor pool and gasoline store. My trailer sat outside the clinic, oily water swilling around its hub caps.

We tied up at the police wharf. Moored alongside were the car ferry *Salammbo* and the French landing-craft. On the freight deck of the ferry stood an elderly Mercedes limousine, presumably purchased with the money I had given to Captain Kagwa. Beside it were six drums of diesel oil for the ferry's refurbished engines. With pride Kagwa surveyed the car, whose polished but dented bodywork reflected decades of service in provincial motorcades and funeral corteges. I easily imagined him reclining in its passenger seat as the ferry, guarded by the helicopter and landing craft, made its imperial progress towards the source of the river.

The Captain disembarked and strode into the barracks with a flourish, first making sure that I was three steps behind him. In his eyes I was a mere mission doctor, attached on sufferance to his court. During my convalescence at the breeding station all my medical supplies and surgical equipment had been moved from the clinic and were now stored in a room next to Kagwa's office, sharing the shelves with his modest library of video-cassettes.

He scanned the sunlit waters of the lake from the window of his office, waiting for the helicopter which would take him on an aerial inspection of his domain. In the orderly room next door I treated the two soldiers. Both had been injured while manhandling the Mercedes on to the ferry. Playing with the controls of the heavy limousine, the sergeant had released the handbrake and thrown the two men against the diesel drums. I dressed the abrasions on their scalps and shoulders, and tried to calm their fears at being involved in this water-borne traffic accident.

Later, as I washed my hands in the corridor sink, I looked down into the internal courtyard of the barracks. Among the military stores, bales of barbed wire, and chickens in bamboo coops was a large packing case filled with electronic equipment — the monitor screens, control panels and cameras that I had last seen beside the Dakota.

I assumed that Sanger had abandoned his farcical mercy mission, but I was surprised that he should have left Port-la-Nouvelle without his travelling studio. I turned to question Captain Kagwa, and knocked the lid from a mess-tin which an armed soldier was carrying down the corridor. He replaced the lid on a dish of sweet potato and boiled fish, and let himself through the locked door beyond the medical storeroom.

Following him, I glanced over his shoulder into a windowless cell lit only by the dusty fanlight in the ceiling. A mattress lay along the wall, beside a stained slops pail. An emaciated European was asleep on the mattress with his face to the grey brickwork, bearded chin resting on a pillow of his rolled-up jacket. On a card table below the fanlight lay a collection of half-plate photographs of Captain Kagwa in his best uniform, some of which I recognised as stills from the interview that Sanger had conducted on the day of his arrival. Others were police academy photographs of Kagwa graduating with his cadet class, and of the Captain saluting from the passenger seat of his helicopter. Before losing interest in the project, or becoming too ill to pursue it, the prisoner had been arranging the photographs on to a wooden frame, constructing a crude story board of a documentary about the illustrious career of this provincial policeman.

"Doctor. . . ." Kagwa's strong hand gripped my right elbow, his fingers deliberately bruising the ulnar nerve. He closed the cell door on the soldier, who had placed the mess-tin on the floor beside the European and was about to remove the slops bucket. "Your duties now are complete. You may return to your clinic and finish your packing."

I let him steer me along the corridor to his office. "The beard — I couldn't see the man. Was that Sanger?"

"Of course not — he has left Port-la-Nouvelle, many weeks ago."

"His film equipment is here." So, I surmised, when Kagwa embarked on his expedition a documentary would record his proconsular progress. "If that isn't Sanger, who is it?"

"A drug smuggler, awaiting trial. A most dangerous man. You will go now, doctor."

"First, I ought to see him. A month in that airless room. . . ."

"Dr Mallory!" Kagwa punched my shoulder with the palm of his hand. He stared down at me, trying to establish in what strange organ my compulsion to be a nuisance resided. "Doctor, I have considered your position — Lake Kotto is now an operational war zone, for your safety you will leave tomorrow with Mrs Warrender. Your resident's permit is now withdrawn."

I started to protest, but the clatter of an approaching aircraft sounded through the window, shaking the galvanised roof of the tobacco warehouse into a cacophony of frenzied tin. Captain Kagwa's helicopter had arrived. As it hovered above the car ferry, I noticed that a light machine-gun had been fitted in the cabin floor beside the pilot. Attached to the starboard landing rail was a cylindrical pod once armed with rocket flares, the empty orifices now stuffed with rags.

While the navigation light rotated, flicking its small beam across the floor of Kagwa's office, the young French pilot peered down at the soldiers running on to the quay. Waiting for them to get out of his way, he set off slowly along the shore, the down-draught from the helicopter's propeller sending up a storm of dust and cigarette packets.

Ignoring me, Kagwa shouted over the noise of the engine, summoning a squad of soldiers from the orderly room, where they lounged among their weapons, picking their teeth and playing with each other's transistor radios. They clattered down the stairs and ran along the quay, following the remote-control camera mounted between the landing rails of this chimeric machine, like the devotees of a new televised religion.

13

Piracy

I stood in the dusk beside the trailer, watching the last cerise bars of the sunset sink into the western rim of Lake Kotto. The forest drew closer to the abandoned town, the palm fronds dipping over the tin roofs. Within the heavy, green darkness the water seemed to rise above the containing banks, as if the huge swells that rolled across its surface were about to inundate everything around me, immersing my mind within its amniotic dream. I stared at the broad mouth of the river, which had incorporated even Lake Kotto into its channel, feeling an undimmed pride in having played my part in its creation. The task of halting this immense mass of water was clearly an impossible one. I realised that I could no longer hope to defeat the river by tackling it here at its mouth — I needed to trace its course towards the borderlands of Chad and the Sudan, and then find its source in the mountains of the Massif du Tondou. Besides, I now wanted to explore the river, which I had brought into the light from its subterranean tunnels. I had freed it from the dark and steered it towards the day. Now the sun and the air would take over from me, and I was eager to see how it would grow and change.

I held the broken door of the trailer. The wooden panel bore the imprint of a rifle butt, and the contents of the cabin had been looted repeatedly by Kagwa's off-duty soldiers. I looked down at the flattened tyres, submerged in the pool of water that ran through the open doors of the clinic and washed the floors of the ransacked office and dispensary.

Somehow I needed to find a truck strong enough to take me more than two hundred miles up-country, with enough fuel for the journey. Yet if I tried to stay on in Port-la-Nouvelle I would be imprisoned by Kagwa. If I left with Mrs Warrender and her party the next day it was likely that we would be sent, not to the provincial capital, where we could talk to the press and the UN agencies, but to some remote village, held under house arrest by one of Kagwa's cronies.

Over the water's edge, a strange creature hovered in the darkness. Its long tail swung to and fro between its claws as it hung above the lake, like some reptilian bird washed by the river from its fossil resting-place.

I left the trailer and walked through the shallow water, curious to see this macaw or parakeet released from Mrs Warrender's breeding station. As I reached the bank, I realised that I was looking at the skin of a small crocodile suspended by its nose from the tip of a bamboo pole. Below it, Noon sat in her coracle, oar in one hand, the pole in the other, moving the skin to and fro in the darkness.

Paddling along the shore, she continued to wave the skinned reptile. No doubt she had heard from the sentries outside the barracks that I was leaving the next day, and this curious gesture was an attempt to keep me at Port-la-Nouvelle, to commit myself again to the river.

A hundred yards from the barracks, when we reached the first of the wharves, she let the coracle run aground on the beach. She sat in the darkness, surveying me with the same grave eyes, as if understanding all my motives.

Careful not to unsettle her, I watched the crocodile skin swaying in the night air, its armoured plates lit by the kerosene lamp on the barracks steps. Rifle over his shoulder, the sentry argued in a desultory way with two fishermen who squatted on the wharf beside their display of dried carp. Behind them, in the darkness, the high sterns of the car ferry and the restaurant barge rocked on the evening swells. Captain Kagwa was spending the night at the airstrip beside his beloved helicopter, and only a small guard unit manned the barracks.

I knelt next to Noon in the warm sand. Taking the bamboo pole from her scarred hand, I lowered it into the coracle.

"Right. But I can't take you with me. Now, where's the rifle?" I placed the oar against my shoulder, aiming the handle at the sentry.

"The rifle? You hid it somewhere, Noon. . . ."

When she ran off into the darkness I held the bamboo pole in my hand and listened to the distant murmur of the river as its waters met the lake, the deep reverie of a drowsing giant into whose mouth I was about to slip.

Within an hour she returned from the forest, weighed down by a damp parcel of matting and plastic sheet. While she crouched below the beach road, keeping watch on the barracks, I unwound the old Lee-Enfield from the camouflage jacket in which she had wrapped the weapon. I dismantled the bolt and felt the intact firing-pin, remembering Noon's attempt to shoot me on this same beach. Satisfied with the trigger mechanism, I released the rusting magazine. The girl had been given two cartridges with which to defend herself, but had forgotten to drive one of them into the breech.

Had Noon known this at the time? She scuttled down the beach and squatted beside me, gazing with pride as I handled the rifle, the first show of emotion I had seen in her face. Did she think I could slay the river with these two bullets? Since our first meeting, her motives had been as unreadable as my own. At times she had defended the river, at others she seemed to provoke me into destroying it. . . .

The camouflage jacket over her shoulders, she paddled away into the darkness. I waded through the shallow water below the wharf, while she sat in the coracle fifty feet from the beach. As the fishermen argued with the sentry, patting the dried carp with their hands, I slipped between the sterns of the car ferry and the restaurant barge. The current pressed between my legs, drawing the hulls from the jetty.

Below the wheelhouse of the ferry there was cargo space for three vehicles. Despite the weight of the Mercedes limousine, barely a foot of freeboard separated the waterline from the metal deck. The dark lake-water flowed around my waist as I loosened the starboard mooring lines and let them sink below the surface. I climbed aboard, hidden from the police barracks by the square bulk of the wheelhouse. When the port lines fell away into the water one of the fishermen looked round, but the young soldier on sentry duty was demonstrating his looted calculator watch. The ferry swayed sideways and drifted against the white hull of the restaurant barge, but the truck tyres hanging from its sides muffled the soft impact. Urging on the current, I leaned across the gap between the two vessels and pushed at the barge's ornamental railings.

The ferry slipped from its berth, drifting forward into the darkness, where the girl sat in her coracle, small face reflecting the distant light of the kerosene lamp on the barrack steps. She looked up at me as I moved past, her wan face creased by a shy smile. She gestured with the crocodile skin, as if still hoping that I might take her as a passenger.

There was a shout from the wharf, and the soldiers and the two fishermen ran across the wooden planks. The ferry was only fifteen feet from the wharf, drifting slowly into the current. Rifle above his head, the soldier clumped down a flight of stone steps and waded into the shallow water.

The surface broke around his thighs. Within an arm's length of the propeller, he reached up to the truck tyre hanging from the stern rail. Although the steel vessel weighed some thirty tons, the soldier was strong enough to hold the craft until the men sleeping in the barracks came to his aid.

I waved helplessly at the air, trying to start the huge diesel in its pit below the helm, following the laborious sequence I had watched from Kagwa's office. I primed the carburettor of the gasoline starter-motor, switched on the magneto and began to hand-crank the small engine. When it came to life I could release the clutch and engage it with the main diesel, then in turn connect the drive-shaft of the propeller.

Seeing me inside the wheelhouse, the soldier raised his rifle and leapt forward through the water. He shouted to me when I tried to hide behind the helm, and then strode alongside, beating the rifle butt against the ancient plates of the hull.

Crouching behind the fuel drums, I levelled the Lee-Enfield at him. In the darkness twenty feet away Noon stood in her coracle, waving the crocodile skin in an attempt to distract the soldier, who was now trying to climb on to the moving deck.

Raising the sights over his head, I drove the bolt forward, ramming one of the two cartridges into the breech, and then fired a single shot at the kerosene lamp on the barrack steps. In the roar of noise the soldier fell back across the water. He stumbled through the ferry's lace-like wake, his eyes lit by the flames playing among the broken glass and the pieces of dried carp. His attempt to mount the ferry had given the vessel a parting impetus, and it drifted out into the lake, as the light flickered in the swinging tail of the skinned crocodile.

A few desperate minutes later, as the last wild shots from the barracks crossed the water, I had started the engine of the *Salammbo* and was heading at a steady three knots towards the entrance of the river. The beat of the heavy diesel jarred the metal deck beneath my feet, drumming at the wooden helm as I steered into the silver mouth of the channel. The smooth surface lay in the moonlight like the gateway to a continental highway, whose first toll-gate I had passed without payment.

"N'doc . . .!"

Looking down at the dark water beyond the starboard rail, I saw Noon in her coracle. She paddled furiously with her small oar, arms smothered by the camouflage jacket. She barely kept pace with the ferry, and the coracle was already filling with water washed from the *Salammbo's* bows.

I stepped from the wheelhouse and waved her away, although I knew that Kagwa's men would shoot her on sight if they saw her again.

"Go back! Hide with Mrs Warrender!"

"Doc Mal . . .!"

Necessity had taught her another word. The coracle collided

with the ferry for the last time. The metal hull and the rushing water crushed the bamboo frame as I reached down and took the girl's hand. Upended, the coracle vanished into the wake, chopped to matchwood by the blows of the heavy propeller as it beat the water. I swung Noon on to the deck, surprised by her lightness. A moment later, as the water spilled from my shirt and trousers, she already stood on tip-toe beside the helm in the wheelhouse, gazing at the approaching mouth of the river. She tapped the glass and pointed to an island of floating trees behind which we could hide, to the first of the sand-banks that might seize our keel, and to the great root of the old oak lying in our path, the amputated head of the beast from whose loins the waters of the Mallory had sprung.

14

Out of the Night and into the Dream

We were entering a world without time. For six days we had moved upstream, against a slow amber current that slid smoothly between the forest walls. The immense softwood trees shut out the sun, whose fierce presence floated far above us in the jungle canopy, the travelling rose window of an inflamed cathedral. The clicking of the cutwater and the steady beat of the diesel engine below the wheelhouse reminded me of clocks ticking to the same rhythm, but these were clocks without hands.

Each morning we set sail soon after dawn, casting off from an overnight mooring beside the bank. Within a few hundred yards the drumming of the engine and the unchanging green walls would erase any sense of the real passage of time, of minutes, hours or days. Noon would whistle to me from her perch in the prow of the *Salammbo*, and point to the vertical sunlight that filled the centre of the channel. Only then would I realise that it was time to boil a pan of rice and resume the hopeless task of trapping a shrike or plover. Hours had slipped by in seconds, falling like dust through the open grilles of my mind.

Since our midnight escape from Port-la-Nouvelle, we had seen nothing of Captain Kagwa, and had overtaken the two advance patrols which he had sent to explore the river by boat. The flight from Lake Kotto had been a dangerous scramble among the sandbanks and islands of waterlogged trees at the mouth of the river. I had barely learned to control the heavy diesel — changes of speed on the wheelhouse throttle, even after a week of practice, would transmit themselves only erratically to the propeller, whose huge blades continued to thump the water like the arms of a boisterous hippo long after I had disconnected the drive-shaft.

From the moment she came aboard Noon had tried to guide me, but I was too excited during our escape to listen to her. Struggling with the heavy helm, I steered the ferry into the widest of the three channels that formed the delta of the river, only to run the craft on to a submerged telegraph pole. The *Salammbo* gave a sudden sheer to port and would no longer steer. Fortunately, the pressure of the current against the hull soon freed the keel. Around us raced the silver back of the river, lit from below by the reflected searchlights of the airstrip, like the floor of an open-air nightclub. Drifting trees, trunks locked together by their roots, collided with the prow. The foliage climbed the bows and swept across the car deck, brushing a pane of glass from the wheelhouse before swerving away into the darkness. Standing beside me, Noon picked the glass fragments from her lips. Already she was trying to take over the wheel. Convinced that I would soon run us aground on the gravel cliffs below the airstrip, she left the wheelhouse and ran forward to the bows.

Signalling to me with a series of guttural whoops and whistles, like those used by Port-la-Nouvelle's pig-farmers, she steered our course past the airstrip. At first I ignored her, but when a huge sand-bar loomed towards us like the partly submerged hull of a submarine, I decided to follow her croaks and signals.

As I expected, the soldiers at the police barracks had radioed Captain Kagwa and told him of my armed theft of the ferry and the rifle shot fired over the sentry's head. I had hoped that Kagwa might think we were crossing the lake and trying to escape southwards down the Kotto River, but he knew my motives too well. Floodlights blazed around the airstrip command post and the soldiers were setting flares for the helicopter. Its blades turned in the darkness as the turbine whined, throwing spears of light across the river. The noise masked the *Salammbo*'s diesel, but a soldier stumbling along the gravel cliff had seen the foam thrown up by the propeller. A ragged volley of shots was fired into the darkness, and a bullet punctured the windshield of the Mercedes and buried itself in the rear seat.

The helicopter rose from the airstrip, but we had already left the buoyed waterway, free of the sand-bars and floating tree-islands of the delta. We passed Mrs Warrender's ruined house, its roof collapsed as the walls sank into the mud. Then we headed into the open channel, where the forest walls closed around the river, a private highway which shut out even the stars, a tunnel leading out of the night and into the dream.

Sheltered by the trees, we sailed on through the darkness, hiding beneath the boughs which extended their leaves above us, as if in thanks for this abundant watercourse at which they drank. In a sense I had saved the oaks and conifers from the advancing desert, and they now repaid me. Calm at last, I was careful not to overstrain the engine, or to alert Harare's patrols with any excessive noise. The ferry's cruising speed of five knots could barely match the flow of the current, and it was almost dawn when we finally left Captain Kagwa's helicopter behind us. I could hear the drone of its engine as it scoured the river valley, and see the probing eye of its searchlight moving across the wooded hills.

Then, as the river widened to form a long, elliptical lake, I almost ran the *Salammbo* on to the sand-bar that divided the shallow channel. Cutting the engine, I let the craft drift backwards with the stream, only to find that an unexpected current was carrying us towards the western bank. We plunged through the overhead branches, snapping the steel hawsers that supported the mast and loosening the stove-pipe funnel from its mounts. We sat there in the darkness while the current swirled past us, whispering its little warnings against the hull, as if confiding to Noon. We were trapped by the heavy boughs, the propeller embedded in the narrow beach that ran below the trees.

Noon clambered down from the prow. She squatted beside the radiator grille of the Mercedes and thoughtfully strummed one of the guy ropes that secured it to the deck, curious to see how I would set us free.

I throttled back the engine, but as I stepped from the wheelhouse a violent blare of noise and light filled the air. A siren wailed through the flashes of a rotating beacon, and a cold down-draught drove the dark surface of the water into a series of concentric waves. The helicopter settled above the river, like a visiting spacecraft descending from the sky. The huge machine hovered ten feet from the surface, its searchlight racing across the trees. The veering light and the shadows of the leaves threw a dappled camouflage across the ferry, but before I could hide behind the wheelhouse the helicopter had moved away, at the centre of its tornado of noise. It climbed over the hills, following its shadow across the forest canopy. We waited in the seething darkness as the sound of its engine faded into the night, and fell asleep in the firm embrace of the waterside oaks.

I woke into a brilliant riverine light. Reflected in the stream, the sun shone through the awning of leaves that formed a green marquee over the wheelhouse. The surface of the water gleamed like warm lacquer as it slid past the forest walls. The whoop of a strange bird sounded from the canopy above me, answered by the chittering hoot of a small arboreal mammal.

I climbed through the branches that pinned the *Salammbo* to the bank. Noon slept in the rear seat of the Mercedes, thumb in her mouth, her shoulders wrapped in a quilt of green leaves that had fallen through the open window. As she lay asleep, one eye wide open, her cheek rested against the bullet hole in the black upholstery.

Careful not to wake her, I looked up at the forest slopes of the river valley, listening for any sounds of Harare and his guerillas. But the trees were packed so tightly together that the green walls shut out everything but the birds. The river had revived the dying rain forest, and the trees crowded towards the bank like a herd of animals standing shoulder to shoulder at a water-hole.

While Noon slept I took stock of the fuel and supplies aboard the ferry. Brushing the broken glass to one side, I examined the contents of the wheelhouse. The wooden cabin had been the pilot's combined bridge, shipping office, pantry and sleeping quarters. A straw mattress lay on a shelf along the rear wall, and above it hung a collection of time-tables, bills of lading, fuel dockets and military passes, together with a display of sun-bleached pin-ups.

Among the rubbish on the floor lay a Renault road-map dating from the colonial days of the former French East Africa. I spread the mildewed pages across the desk, trying to gain some idea of the terrain that separated us from the mountains of the Massif du Tondou. From Port-la-Nouvelle the original road had cut through the rain forest to a mining settlement thirty miles to the north-west, following the course of a jungle river long since erased by the southward march of the desert. From there the road set out through the open savanna that stretched across the central basin of Northern Province. Little more than a dust track, the road linked the small farming communities with their vanished French names, crossing a single-track railway line from the south where the latter reached its terminus at Saliere, a trading post and military depot. Fifty miles to the north and west lay tracts of marsh and salt desert which the road avoided, circling eastwards to reach the now abandoned airbase at Bonneville, on the edges of the open Sahara below the foothills of the Massif.

All in all, a journey of some two hundred miles. Although covered with warnings of flash floods, treacherous viaducts, scarcity of fuel and spare parts, the map carried no contour lines, and I could only guess that my new river, assuming it flowed from the mountains of the Massif, followed a course close to the lost road.

I folded the map and placed it on the pilot's shelf beside the helm. An enamel pail stood on a metal stove by the door, and served as washing-up bowl, hand-basin and saucepan. On the floor under the mattress were two ancient canvas deckchairs, and an almost empty hessian sack stamped with a familiar cipher: "Africa Green".

I opened the sack and ran my hand through the dry rice grains —there were some five pounds in all, enough to feed us for a week, and longer if we could learn to trap the birds and small mammals.

The Lee-Enfield rifle leaned against the helm. I pulled back the bolt, ejecting the spent cartridge I had fired the previous night. I touched the one round left in the magazine, then drove it into the breech. The last bullet was to be saved for an emergency, but already I was reluctant to shoot any of the creatures in the forest.

The river swept by, enveloped in its great calm, fingers tapping against the steel hull of the *Salammbo*, reassuring me that all was well. I swayed against the rail, still light-headed after my night's sleep. I was hungry, bruised and nervous, my ears tuned to the trees and the river with an almost amphetamine sharpness. Stealing the ferry had been a stupid and dangerous act. I knew that Kagwa would try to kill me, tracking down his precious Mercedes. In every way I was now a hunted animal, but I felt more confident than at any time since arriving at Port-la-Nouvelle. I had begun to shed the hard core of misanthropy, often masked by a professional dedication to good works, that is more common among physicians than their patients realise. My sense of failure and lack of purpose had vanished in the night, replaced by a keen pride not only in the great waterway I had created, but in its abundant flora and fauna. In a giddy way I felt the first hints of certain delusions of grandeur — already I imagined the Mallory irrigating the Sahara and saw myself as the third world's greatest benefactor. . . .

At the same time, my duel with the Mallory had still to be settled. Roped together below the wheelhouse were six 50-gallon drums of diesel oil, enough to power the craft's engines for at least 300 miles, and carry us safely to the river's source in the Massif du Tondou. Reminding myself of all I had risked, I stared at the sleek, swollen surface of the river, like the fleshy body of a sleeping woman. In my mind I saw a rocky burn bubbling from a remote cavern among the peaks. I would use the last of the fuel as an explosive cap, and drive the icy spring down into the deepest veins of the mountain. Only then would I seal the mouth of the underground aquifer that I had opened, and close the door upon the great fossil river that had once irrigated the Sahara.

However, for the moment these dreams belonged to the night. When Noon woke half an hour later, roused by the green smoke from the stove, I was preparing a bowl of boiled rice. Her scalp covered with leaves, she watched me gravely through the rear window of the Mercedes, frowning as I stirred the rice with a greasy screwdriver. Once again I was puzzled by the way in which she had attached herself to me, making no attempt to hide her disapproval, like a serious-minded child watching a clumsy adult. I could almost believe that some invisible power had assigned her the task of steering me to the river's source. Or, more prosaically, was she under Harare's orders, using me and my obsession as a decoy that would lure Captain Kagwa across the border . . .?

She was still watching me as she stepped through the passenger door of the limousine. When she lowered her right foot to the metal deck I noticed that the infected wound had at last drained. The scar, like a small red snake, curled around her heel, emerging from its lair within her instep.

"Comfortable, Noon? The girl-friends of gangsters and police chiefs have slept in that car."

She squatted by the stove and gazed without expression at the sunlight on the river and the forest walls that enclosed us. Using the pilot's clasp-knife, I cut twigs from the branches overhanging the deck and fed them to the stove. The green smoke lifted through the trees, merging with a mist that rose in the morning heat.

As I fanned the hissing flames, she reached out and picked a handful of rice from the pot.

"Hold on — that isn't cooked yet."

I tried to take her wrist, but she snatched the knife from the deck and backed away from me like a nervous animal.

"It's all right — I won't hit you. Noon, you're safe with me."

She ducked through the branches and slipped behind the limousine. I waited for her to return, deciding not to pursue her through the tangled foliage that lay across the deck. One false step, and this odd child would stab me through a kidney.

A few minutes later I heard a splash from the water beside the ferry. A freshly cut spear in her right hand, Noon swam across the river. Her left hand glided through the water, releasing the grains of partly boiled rice she had taken from the pot. She peered intently into the water, as if threading a needle with her toes. Then the thin spear, little more than a sharpened reed, flicked from her fingers.

With a hoot of pleasure she stood up, lifting an impaled fish into the sunlight. The water ran from her naked shoulders, but seeing me she sank quickly into the stream. She swam to the ferry and passed the small gudgeon up to me, then drifted away with a satisfied smile towards the *Salammbo's* bows, where she had hung her clothes, the green vest and fatigue trousers cut off at the knees.

As soon as we finished the meal that Noon prepared, we set out on our journey up-river. The channel had risen a further foot during the night, and the current had lifted the ferry's propeller from the beach. Once I cut away the overhanging branches we swung slowly into the centre of the stream. I hand-cranked the starter motor, soon aware that I had torn the tendons of my right elbow in my panic to escape from the police wharf. When the diesel began to turn, I waited for its cylinders to fire and then engaged the shaft. The prow of the *Salammbo* cut through the glassy surface, through which hundreds of fish changed course to accompany us. Trapped for so long in the meanders of the Kotto River, they had swum all the miles from Port-la-Nouvelle, as excited as I was by this new channel that had flowed into their lives. I was happy to see them, and glad that they had chosen to travel in the same direction.

The decks of the ferry were speckled with leaves and branches, a useful camouflage that began to peel away in the light breeze. Through the heavy thrumming of the engine I listened for Captain Kagwa and his helicopter. But he and his fierce machine, a metal fist clenched around its own anger, belonged to another sky. We had entered a maiden world, a realm that I had invented and which the child and I would continue to invent together.

15

The Naming of New Things

Capped by crowns of mist, the green walls of the valley slid past us. During the following days the landscape had changed, and the rain forest of the equatorial hills gave way to the flatter ground of the savanna. Some twenty miles from Port-la-Nouvelle the last of the great softwoods fell away behind us, and the banks were crowded with smaller trees, flowering shrubs, desert lavender and magnolia. The river was wider here, almost two hundred yards from one bank to the other. Sometimes it divided to embrace a narrow island, and then seemed to wander in long curves, as if aware that my own imagination had flagged. Frequently we were halted by floating barriers of sudd, a water plant like small polyanthus with long trailing roots that fouled the propeller.

Looking through the broken glass of the wheelhouse, I was constantly surprised by the richness of this riverine world. Long-dormant seeds that had lain in the desert for decades were now germinating. Revived by the cool flood that crossed the parched land, horse-tails and feather-palms dipped their leaves into the stream. Groves of green bamboo formed a gentle palisade through which I could see the dusty bush beyond. A quarter of a mile from the river lay the harsh white fields of the dying savanna, where rusting water-wheels leaned above dry irrigation ditches, and forgotten fences marked the boundaries of abandoned farms.

But along the Mallory a young life teemed. We had entered a riverside garden planted for the day of our arrival. Watching this pastoral scene through the spokes of the helm, I could almost believe that my own imagination was inventing the river as we moved along its course. Trumpet vines, winter-sweet and pretty nectaries decorated the banks. Thinking of the birds I had heard hooting in the forest behind us, I saw marsh rails and finfoots by the water's edge. A yellow-throated wagtail sailed above our bow, halcyon bird guiding us to fairer weather. At one of the quiet beaches, a small gazelle drank from the stream. On the opposite bank a forest lynx, tired of roving the arid savanna, loped through the shallows, its pelt gleaming as it sparred with the fish. I reduced our speed, trying not to disturb these creatures with the wash of the *Salammbo*.

No longer needing to guide me, Noon lazed away the days in the warm sun, lounging in the driver's seat of the limousine, and trying to work the dials on the dashboard. I was unable to find the keys to the Mercedes in either the car or the wheelhouse, but I wired the ignition so that Noon could amuse herself with the radio.

Soon bored by the news and propaganda from the government radio-station, broadcast in a language unknown to her, Noon rooted about in the chauffeur's locker. There she discovered a parcel of educational cassettes which Kagwa had ordered, popular guides to political philosophy, colonial history and third-world resources. For Noon these cassettes became her guides in a basic English language course, the first tuition of any kind that she had received in her life. She moved to the front seat, befitting a pupil, and nodded gravely to the lecturer and his interlocutor while the fragments of dialogue were recited in the over-formal tones of the correspondence schools. Adept with the push-buttons, she punched the playback and fast-forward controls, as if her fingers had become her surrogate vocal cords. In the pregnant pauses, Noon first whispered and then tried to repeat aloud the catch-phrases.

". . . tourism and bourgeois hegemony . . . the natural park as neo-colonialist folk-lore . . . African wild-life and the exploitation of racist stereotypes. . . ."

Embarrassed at being unable to get her tongue around these polysyllables, Noon turned up the speaker. Sounds of jargonised dialogue with a Marxist slant boomed across the water, and two small zebra drinking by the bank looked up at us in alarm. Delighted with this, Noon began to play the cassettes to the passing birds, informing the oystercatchers of the merits of solidarity and the rails of the hazards of exploitation.

Another reminder of the world we had left behind came on the seventh day — I had almost lost count, measuring our voyage in terms of the changing flora and fauna. We had entered a stretch of the river where the channel divided into the waterways of an internal delta. Huge sand-banks rose through the surface, and we moved across an almost abstract landscape of golden bars that emerged from the water like the limbs of a bathing giant. Noon sat in the prow, too proud to signal with her arms and muttering confused fragments of dialogue remembered from the cassette lessons.

"For heaven's sake, Noon." I cut the engine and called her to the wheelhouse. I gestured with my arms. "Let's agree on this. Left equals 'solidarity'. Right equals 'exploitation'. Okay?"

Frowning fiercely, she returned to the bows. Hands deep in her trouser pockets, she planted her legs astride the anchor, now and then turning to bark at me:

". . . 'ploitation! . . . 'ploitation!" Then, in panic: "Doc Mal! — soderality!"

At last we emerged from this delta into the open channel, and Noon returned to her classroom in the Mercedes. I drove the throttle forward, increasing our speed to six knots. For a quarter of a mile we sped steadily between the submerged sand-bars. Then, when the deep water began to surge against the bows, I felt the deck rear upwards against my feet, as if the diesel had broken loose from the engine pit. A violent scraping ground the length of the keel, a ragged shudder that threatened to strip the plates from the hull. The wheel spun clockwise, knocking my hands from the spokes, and the vessel lurched to a stop, tilting to starboard. While I climbed to my feet on the sloping deck the ravenous scraping continued. Something had seized the ferry, trying to split the hull from bows to stern and devour the engine.

From the foaming wake beside the port rail a cascade of red-flecked spray leapt into the air. A huge spine, more than fifty feet long, rose from the water. Encrusted with weed and scale, it resembled the armoured back of an ancient saurian, feet planted on the river-bed, jaws gripping the ferry's rudder.

The spray and foam subsided, and the ferry groaned into an upright position. Tipped from the passenger seat of the limousine, Noon sat on the deck among the scattered cassettes. I switched off the engine and stepped from the wheelhouse, watching our assailant subside into the water.

We had run into the steel gantry of an ore-conveyor, part of a mining excavator that had worked the now submerged quarry beneath us. I opened the starboard side of the after-peak, and removed the manhole door, exposing the propeller to view. The blades were undamaged, but a steel hawser that trailed from the gantry had wrapped itself around the shaft.

As Noon watched, intrigued by the Mercedes' resources, I took the tyre levers and jack from the limousine's tool-kit. From the rail I lowered myself on to the catwalk of the conveyor. I sat astride the box frame, trying to free the steel tentacle that tied the ferry to this underwater leviathan.

Noon swam near the bows, spear raised, casting rice on the cool stream.

"Doc Mal. . . ."

She dipped a finger into the water, and pointed downwards with a knowing smile, as if the snaring of the ferry had given her an idea.

"What is it, Noon? I won't take your bait."

She feinted with the spear, and then ducked and dived beneath the water. I rested astride the gantry, watching the semaphore of Noon's pale feet. A coquettish water-nymph, she was as smooth and agile as a seal puppy, a child-siren inviting a passing mariner down to her bower. I assumed that she wanted to impress me, to tempt me down into a realm where she, without doubt, would have the upper hand. But perhaps, too, she wanted to demonstrate that the river would no longer harm me, and that I was safe now within its depths, wrapped in the mantle of its dream. And given that I had created the Mallory, I could almost believe that I would not have drowned had I tried to follow Noon. Its waters flowed from my own bloodstream. . . .

I watched her swim to the narrow beach on which she had laid out her clothes. Around my thighs the current was softer, and the pale green trees and flowering shrubs seemed to be holding their breath, as if involved in some secret complicity with Noon.

Covered with oil and flaking paint, I decided to rest before cutting away the last of the frayed cable. Standing on the conveyor, I took off my trousers and hung them from the stern rail, then dived into the water and swam the fifty feet to the beach.

A grove of wild myrtle ran down to the narrow strip of sandy clay. I rubbed the oil from my arms, breathing the thick scent of desert lavender. Fan-palms and slender saplings of bamboo formed a cool waterside garden, an arbour filled with succulents and passion-flowers. I walked through this charming glade, placing my bare feet between the aloes and armoured rosettes of century plants that sprang from the damp floor. Nourished by the river, a vivid new flora had emerged in the past months, a cool realm that extended a hundred yards into the parched savanna. Curious tubers and corms, scarlet drupes, and culinary and medicinal herbs grew in the pale light, and I saw the yellow tubes and flared mouths of fragrant datura, their alkaloids promising drowsy potions on which the river might dream. As I looked down at the hundreds of green shoots rising between the saplings I seemed to be witnessing the birth of the flowering plants, which had brought colour and scent to the sombre world of the ferns and cycads.

Through the trees I noticed Noon returning from her foraging expedition. Under her arm she carried the sticks and tinder which she had gathered from the desert's edge. She paused to pluck a wild herb to add to the dish of rice and fish that she would prepare. She strolled between the flowering shrubs, her shoulders covered with the downy catkins and the tissue leaves of hibiscus, as if she too had just been born into this arbour. Her smooth limbs and pensive eyes had also sprung from the moistened earth. Seeing her, I was almost certain that I had thrown my spit on to the ground and created the river, which in turn had given life to this child.

She walked through the dappled glade towards the beach. Hearing my breath, she saw me among the spears of bamboo, standing naked with my paint-reddened arms and chest, the black streaks of oil like the display of a solitary forest male.

"Doc Mal. . . ." She spoke distinctly, and then uttered a fetish word, as if she could place me at a safe distance by marking me with my name. But I saw that she accepted my nakedness.

Did I trust myself with Noon? Bathed in the scent of the flowers, I rested on the beach before returning to the propeller. The meagre diet — a shared bowl of rice morning and evening, with whatever fish Noon could catch — left me exhausted after the smallest effort but I was too exhilarated to eat properly, or to look after the chafed skin of my arms and face, already suffering from the effects of exposure. Spectres swam beneath the calm surface of the river, caravels freighted with a treasure that would ransom all the debts and memories of the unhappy years.

Trying to calm myself, I gazed at the placid stream. Anchored to the steel gantry of the conveyor, the *Salammbo* rocked gently on the current. Dreams of pagan powers moved across the surface of the Mallory. I tried to stand back from my obsession with the river, but already I was thinking of the irrigation of the entire Sahara, of the transformation of the desert into the Edenic paradise that I saw around me in these green glades and sensed in its sweet airs. A new race would spring from Noon and myself as we lived peaceably in these forest bowers. It was time for a naming of new things, of new hours and new days. I would christen this quiet beach, bathed in the baptismal waters of the Mallory . . . Port Noon.

Through this sun-filled reverie I saw her standing at the starboard rail, waving to me fiercely with both fists. When I failed to stir she leapt into the limousine and switched on the cassette player.

". . . neo-colonialist folk-lore. . . ."

The fragments of amplified dialogue boomed along the shore, then stopped abruptly. Noon returned to the rail, fingers to her scarred mouth as she grimaced at the southern sky. An ugly shadow had crossed the water and was now speeding towards the ferry. I heard the shriek of an approaching engine, and saw Captain Kagwa's helicopter loom out of the air above our heads. Two yellow pontoons were attached to its undercarriage like huge poison sacs. It scrambled across the cool light, a malevolent creature emerging from a more primitive sky.

16

The Helicopter Attack

I knelt beside the radiator grille of the Mercedes, trying to conceal myself from the French pilot. Noon had taken refuge in the rear seat of the limousine, terrified by the noise and violence of this threatening machine. The down-draught dented the water, and then scythed through the riverside trees, driving away a whirlwind of coloured blossom. As the petalled cloud drifted towards the desert a storm of furious air thrashed the groves of myrtle and bamboo beside the beach, erasing all memory of our riverside idyll.

Captain Kagwa sat in the cockpit beside the pilot, sunglasses propped on to his broad forehead. Clearly he had not expected to find the handsome limousine in the charge of a naked man and his twelve-year-old companion. He signalled to the young Frenchman, ordering him to circle the *Salammbo*, still unsure whether the savage figure stained with red and black stripes was the former WHO physician at Port-la-Nouvelle.

The helicopter approached the ferry, barely twenty feet above the wheelhouse. The navigation lights kept up their monotonous pulse, reimposing the rule of the electric circuit on the tranquil day. Already hundreds of birds were rising from the wooded banks of the river, and fleeing out into the desert.

Kagwa leaned against his lap-strap and loosened the buckle of his holster. The noise of the engine sank to a flatter pitch as the pilot levelled his rotor blades before coming down to land.

"Noon . . .!" I ran around the Mercedes and opened the passenger door. "Stay there. I'll find the rifle."

She lay across the rear seat, one thumb in her mouth, the other plugging the bullet hole in the leather upholstery as if this would ward off any further missiles.

"Doc . . .?"

"Don't move . . . Kagwa won't shoot his precious car. . . ."

I closed the door and darted between the fuel drums to the wheelhouse. The helicopter settled on to the water beside the ore-conveyor. The pilot throttled back the engine, the blades thudding as they cuffed the warm air. Mooring line in hand, Captain Kagwa stepped from the cockpit on to the starboard float, and secured the cable to the gantry of the conveyor. He tested the exposed trellis-work, head lowered below the flicking propeller blade, and then walked towards the ferry. Already he was sweating in the sunlight as his buffed leather boots picked their way among the upturned ore-buckets, clearly concerned with more important matters than this minor episode of river piracy.

I watched him through the broken glass of the wheelhouse. Beside me on the bunk was the Lee-Enfield. Careful not to reveal the rifle to the Captain, I cocked the firing-pin.

"Dr Mallory . . .?" Recognising me with difficulty, Kagwa shook his head. He scrutinised the Mercedes parked on the cargo deck. Grudgingly satisfied with its condition, he glanced up and down the length of the ferry, noting the stove and piles of firewood, Noon's clothes and other evidence of this odd menage. He then peered beneath the stern of the ferry, and examined the coils of cable looped around the propeller shaft. I had cut away almost all the steel threads, but Kagwa seemed to decide that the shaft was hopelessly snagged.

"You've come a long way, doctor. But again you've been thinking too much. You are very tired. We'll take you back to Port-la-Nouvelle."

"I'll stay here, Captain. My journey isn't over."

"Your journey is finished." Kagwa stood on the metal catwalk twenty feet from me, hands on hips, still shaking his head in sympathy at my tragic mental plight. From the brutal inter-rogations I had witnessed, I knew that it was during these moments of understanding when Captain Kagwa was at his most dangerous. "Piracy, doctor. You assaulted my men and carried out an armed seizure of this vessel and cargo. A most valuable cargo. WHO will have to pay much compensation."

"They aren't keen on ransom, Captain. I'll return the ferry to you when my mission is over."

"You have no mission. What is this mission? The same foolishness about destroying the river?"

"*My* river, Captain. I created it, I gave my name to it, and I'll do what I want with it."

"My dear Dr Mallory . . . this river is now a strategic waterway. You are in a military operational zone. Also — " he pointed to the Mercedes " — you are giving shelter to one of Harare's guerillas. . . ."

"She's not with Harare, Captain. The girl is working for me."

"The *girl*? Is she still a girl, doctor? Your medical dictionary might say something else. I won't harm her, doctor, Mrs Warrender can care for the child. Everyone is concerned for you — I had to stop Mrs Warrender hiring a boat to follow you. . . ."

"Tell her to care for Professor Sanger — the last time I saw him the poor man needed it."

"That was for your sake, doctor. To save you being a laughing stock on Japanese television. He was making a secret programme about you. . . ."

Kagwa stepped on to one of the ore-buckets, shouting in Sudanese at the Mercedes. Noon's face appeared in the rear passenger window. She stared back at the Captain, and squeezed her trembling nostrils, wiping the phlegm on to the driver's headrest. The door opened, and her scarred heel touched the deck.

Captain Kagwa braced his feet against the gantry. I saw his hand move to the heavy police holster on his left hip. His broad fingers lifted the leather flap.

"Get down, Noon . . .!"

I shouted to the child above the soft thudding of the helicopter's propeller, and stepped from the wheelhouse on to the deck, waving Noon behind the car. Fifteen feet from me, Kagwa's service revolver was already in his hand. As I stood naked beside the funnel, waving my paint-streaked arms at Noon, the young French pilot watched me without expression through the aircraft's bubble canopy, like a tourist observing some curious native rite.

Without hesitating, Kagwa levelled the revolver and fired a single shot at my head. The discharge burst into my eyes, and I heard the bullet strike the funnel. It shattered against the cast-iron casing, and a small fragment hit the side of my head. The metal spur cut my right ear and then tore through my scalp. Stunned by the noise, and by the calculated way in which Kagwa had lured me from the wheelhouse, I felt the blood run on to my shoulder. On the deck behind me lay a bloody pelt of hair and scalp. Although Kagwa was aiming his revolver at my head for a second shot, I stared at this leaking fragment of myself, unable to move.

". . . wild-life and the exploitation of racist. . . ."

The lecturer's voice boomed from the limousine's loudspeaker. Noon sat forward over the cassette player, working the volume control. When Kagwa hesitated, I ducked back into the wheelhouse and switched on the magneto of the starter motor. As the blood dripped on to the deck at my feet I primed the carburettor. Working the crank with both hands, I swung the small motor into life, and then released the clutch and engaged the main engine. Above the noise of the helicopter I heard the diesel turn and begin to fire, its cylinders one by one shaking into motion.

Already the steel gantry of the ore-conveyor was dipping in and out of the water. Kagwa swayed on his feet, revolver lowered, riding the switchback as smoke pumped from the ferry's funnel. I advanced the throttle, winding up the diesel's heavy pistons. The ferry lumbered forward, and there was a brief scream of metal from beneath the stern when the propeller chopped through the last threads of cable around the shaft.

In a roar of foam and rusty water the *Salammbo* moved away, tilting to starboard as I spun the helm to keep us in the deeper stream. The ore-conveyor began to sink below the surface. The waves swilled across the trellis-work, the wash running over Kagwa's boots as he sank knee-deep in the *Salammbo's* wake.

Drenched to the waist, he pulled himself over the last few struts to the helicopter's mooring line. He freed the anchor and tried to reach the nearer pontoon, but the aircraft was already drifting on the current.

I steered the ferry into the centre of the channel, heading for a right-hand bend two hundred yards away. Through the mist of my blood sprayed across the window of the wheelhouse I saw Kagwa holding to the mooring line, while the young Frenchman tried to pull him towards the passenger door. Head ducking among the waves, he was carried along below the cloud of blossom that sailed high into the air above the floral shore.

17

Escape

As I well knew, the Captain would soon be back. Still shaking with panic, I tried to steady myself against the helm, steering the ferry away from the submerged sand-banks that might have stranded us. The great brown back of the Mallory flowed towards us, its beaches already striped by the shadows of the trees in the late afternoon sun. For all their welcome, these pleasant groves of feather-palms and spring bamboo offered far less protection than the overhangs of the rain-forest we had left behind.

Noon sat in the front seat of the limousine, one hand over her mouth, the other resting on the buttons of the cassette player, as if she could again save me from Kagwa and the helicopter with a few paragraphs of correspondence-college sociology. I was still naked, but she had not seen the blood caked on my right shoulder in a dark red epaulette. The wounds to my ear and scalp had dried, but I could already feel the effects of a mild concussion, and the first stray mental confusion. Inside my head the pain seemed to merge with the roar of the *Salammbo's* engine, the clicking rush of water against the hull plates, and my own anger at the river below my bloodstained feet. I looked down at the rifle beside me, unsure whether I should have fired the last bullet into Captain Kagwa or the treacherous current that had lured me into his sights. Had the river possessed a heart, I would have stepped from the wheelhouse and fired at the warm stream that had lulled us with the day-long idyll at "Port Noon". I could almost believe that an unconscious conspiracy existed between Kagwa and the river, that the Mallory had enlisted the policeman in its own defence. Naively I had taken for granted that the river would allow me to sail unmolested to its source and cut off its headwaters. Instead, it had beguiled me with sweet winds and floral groves, and dressed Noon in its gayest blossoms. . . .

There was a surge of dialogue from the cassette speaker. Noon pushed the driver's door to and fro, trying to fan the sound towards me. Through the blood on the stern window I could see the helicopter's navigation lights reflected in the darker water of the late afternoon. Fifty feet above the river, it came up behind us and cruised alongside, slightly aft of the *Salammbo's* funnel. Kagwa crouched in the open passenger seat, a police carbine across his knees. His face was without expression, all trace erased of our sometime friendship. The down-draught from the propeller had already dried his uniform, and the creased and shrunken cotton made his thickset figure all the more menacing, as if in his rage he were about to burst through the rumpled fabric.

Noon climbed into the rear seat of the car and closed the door. She sat back, head against the bullet hole in the seat, clasping a cassette between her hands and crooning to herself. I made a last effort to calm my arms and hands, searching the banks for any foliage that might give us cover. The saplings and shrubs formed a thin palisade that would shelter us if I beached the *Salammbo*. However, once we abandoned the ferry to Kagwa we would have to make our journey on foot, and be relentlessly hunted from the air.

Fifty yards beyond the port bow a steel post rose from the water, bearing a display of broken glass lamps set into a rusty metal bracket. Here the river had overrun the abandoned French army base which guarded the mining concessions at Saliere. We passed more posts that had once formed a line of landing lights in the approach to the military airstrip. The metal humps of a hangar and several workshops stood in the channel like a family of elephants around their bull, asleep with their heads in the water.

The helicopter drew alongside, its pontoons almost as long as the *Salammbo*. Above the clatter of its propeller I heard the harsh report of a gunshot, its sound swept behind us in the wake of foam and diesel exhaust that lifted into the air. Kagwa leaned sideways in the cockpit, and fired again at the wheelhouse. The first bullet passed through the wooden roof and knocked the glass from a window, but the second struck the helm between my hands, and tore out a foot-long dagger of stained teak. Exhausted by the heavy rudder, I forced the wheel to port and drove the ferry below the helicopter, trying to clip the pontoons with the iron funnel.

The young pilot pulled his craft away, his level eyes watching me without comment, and set out on a wide circuit of the river. As I steered past the upper storey of the airstrip control tower, still marked with the name of the French commanding officer, the bows sent a gust of spray against the galvanised iron panels. Then the helicopter lowered its nose and came in towards the ferry.

Through the approaching clatter of its engine I heard the machine-gun fire a short burst. A bullet rang against the steel hull and another kicked the last of the bloodstained glass from the stern window of the wheelhouse. The helicopter soared past and banked above the partly submerged hangar, ready to attack again. I rolled the wheel to starboard, in an attempt to tack to and fro. The deck tilted and the Mercedes lurched forward and jumped its wooden chocks. Still held by the guy ropes, it slid several feet across the deck, radiator grille overhanging the water.

I tried to change course, throttled back the engine and reversed the rudder. Too late, I saw the long white crescent of a sand-bank emerge from the brown water. The *Salammbo* ran gently aground, the hull hissing along the sand, and then began to right itself, lifting the nose of the limousine in whose rear seat I could see Noon looking out with the wide-eyed gaze of a child after her first ride on a roller-coaster.

I switched off the fuel pumps to the diesel and cut the engine. In the brief silence I listened to the water lapping at the hull. The river ran past, making its way through the open doors of a drowned workshop. The helicopter flew towards the western bank, its tail pointing towards us, and for a moment I hoped that Kagwa had decided to give up his pursuit, not realising that the *Salammbo* was grounded. But then it changed course, banked and approached cautiously across the water. Kagwa had put away his carbine, and sat in the cockpit, looking down at the tilting bonnet of his Mercedes.

He signalled to the pilot, who began a slow descent. Wary of the suction that the wet surface of the sand-bar might exert upon his floats, he landed in the shallow water nearby.

Kagwa jumped down into the knee-deep stream. He stepped on to the white beach of the sand-bar and stood in the fading sunlight, looking up at the grounded hull of the ferry. He walked forward, unbuckling the flap of his holster. As he passed the Mercedes he touched the chromium fender and wiped away the brown silt caked over the headlamps and radiator grille. His face remained closed, and I knew that in his eyes I was already dead, and that my present survival was no more than a brief administrative oversight.

When he drew abreast of the wheelhouse and glanced up at me, he was obviously surprised to see the Lee-Enfield levelled at his chest. I snapped down the bolt, steadying the barrel against the doorpost of the wheelhouse. Kagwa looked back at his footprints in the soft sand, puzzled that they should have led him into this modest ambush. He made no attempt to draw his revolver, and retreated awkwardly along the sand-bar. He raised his right hand in a signal to the young Frenchman, who was watching me from the cockpit of the helicopter, carbine at the ready.

I trained the rifle's sights at the triangle of sweat above Kagwa's heart, and listened to the soft thudding of the engine and the silver ripple of the current. I knew that I could not shoot the Captain — if I did the pilot would take off and rake the ferry from stem to stern with his machine-gun, igniting the drums of diesel oil and killing Noon and myself. Even if we abandoned the ferry he would soon track us down. Although Kagwa was determined to kill me, I needed him in order to stay alive. In his attacks upon us he had been careful not to damage the Mercedes, and the car played a potent role in his dream of establishing himself in his secessionist capital.

The pilot had disconnected his head-set. He tidied his seat and dashboard in a matter-of-fact way, and then climbed from the cockpit, carbine in hand, as the idling propeller cuffed the air over his head. Kagwa stepped backwards into his water-filled foot-steps, almost within the shelter of the ferry's bows. The pilot stood on the port pontoon, his weight tilting the helicopter to one side and exposing the underbelly of the starboard float. The water dripped from the rusting metal, revealing its patchwork of cheap welding.

I turned the sights away from Kagwa, and took aim at the underside of the starboard float. Before the pilot could jump into the water I fired the last bullet, then ejected the cartridge and drove the bolt forward, as if loading another round.

Already the pilot had climbed into his cockpit. The rifle bullet had passed through the lower hull of the pontoon, and I assumed that he would already feel the water rushing through the punctures. He replaced his headset and shouted to Kagwa, beckoning him back to the aircraft. While the Captain hesitated, the Frenchman throttled up his engine, dragging the pontoons through the wet sand. In a rush of noise and spray the helicopter rose six feet into the air, and a trickle of water emerged from the lower of the bullet holes. I raised the rifle, as if to fire another shot into the float, but already Kagwa was running to the aircraft.

Five minutes later they were gone, heading south along the river, the noise of the machine vanishing into the dusk.

"Right, Noon, out of the car. They won't be back until tomorrow."

She had crawled between the front seats and now crouched against the driver's door, the cassette pressed to her lips. She had been terrified by the aerial attack and by Kagwa's presence, and the scar tissue around her mouth and eyebrows was flushed with blood. The harsh red lines formed vivid pain-marks in her blue skin, a notched score of her abused childhood.

Trying to reassure her, I held her arm, fearing that the violence of the helicopter assault had driven her back into her mutism. But she pulled her elbow away from me. She tapped the cassette rapidly against her teeth, as if trying to talk to me by proxy through this garrulous device. Despite her terror, she was looking me up and down, examining the wound on my head and the blood caked across my arms and shoulders, making certain that I still possessed the will to go on.

"Fair enough, Noon — I understand you. First we'll get free of this sand-bar. Then we'll set off. . . ."

As Noon squatted between the drums of diesel oil, I slackened the guy ropes and then kicked away the chocks from the wheels of the Mercedes. Held by its handbrake, the heavy limousine overhung the starboard rail. I sat in the driver's seat and gradually released the brake. As the car edged across the deck, held by its cradle of guy ropes, I could feel the ferry tilting into the water. The river was still rising, and the *Salammbo* was almost free of the sand-bar.

"Noon, we're on our way. Later, I'll teach you to talk. More lessons soon."

I replaced the chocks beneath the wheels of the car, unlashed the diesel drums and began to roll them across the deck. Filled with oil, the huge cylinders were almost too heavy for me. The wound in my head began to bleed again, and Noon watched solemnly as the drops fell on to the deck, staining the paintwork of the Mercedes. But with a third drum the ferry was already free. With a faint sigh the water rushed beneath the keel. The vessel slipped off the sand-bar and fell astern on the evening tide. I sat exhausted on the deck, holding a bloody hand to my head, tempted to let the *Salammbo* drift all the way back to Port-la-Nouvelle. It coasted for a quarter of a mile, and ran down one of the landing light masts before I could recover my strength and start the engine. Then I steadied the helm and moved the ferry up-channel, tilting to starboard as the stern of the Mercedes hung over the rail, its rear bumper washed by the bow wave.

The darkness settled over the river, and thousands of birds, driven away by the helicopter and the gunfire, began to return to their perches along the wooded banks. Noon squatted in the bows, warning me away from the sand-banks. We had seen off Kagwa for another day, time for us to make a few more miles up the channel of the Mallory, which had grown even broader as we moved towards its source. Wary of running the ferry aground in the dark, I steered through the open doors of the partly submerged hangar. There we moored to the rusting superstructure below the galvanised iron roof. Too tired to clear the glass from the wheelhouse, I fell asleep on the mattress among the oil drums, while Noon sat in the front seat of the limousine, crooning to herself as she softly rehearsed the phrases from the instructional tapes, the language of a private liberation that would one day set her free.

18

The Green World

A reverie of great rivers had overwhelmed me, moments marked by the measures of dream and myth. I sat under the canvas awning in the bows of the ferry, as the hours and days slid towards us through the copper haze that lay over the distant channel of the Mallory. Even the progress of the *Salammbo* failed to disturb the river. Behind the slow beat of the propeller the wake of bubbles soon dissolved and the water smoothed out any memory of our passage. Around us the river flowed between its ever wider banks, the surface as cool as green chrome. The reflected trees hanging below the beaches seemed more real than the feather-palms and desert lavender that had sprung from the dusty savanna along the margins of the channel. I watched the fish jump as they caught the hovering dragonflies. Bitterns and black herons dived through the surface, moving freely through a realm where air and water had merged into each other. A broader sun lay over us, its warm hand pressing upon the air, which had become thicker and heavier, muffling the sounds of the engine and the distant cries of the birds.

I had lost all sense of how many days had passed, or of how far we had travelled since the helicopter attack. We had rested through the night under the roof of the hangar, where the wounds to my head and ear had dried again. But the torn muscles of my scalp set it askew on my skull, and in turn seemed to tilt my mind, so that it perceived the world at an odd angle, like a misaligned camera.

Noon had kept away from the circle of oil drums where I lay on the mattress, not wishing to be present if I were to die in the night. But at dawn, when I returned to the wheelhouse, I found that she

had swept away the glass and pulled the wooden splinters from the
bullet hole in the helm, laid the rifle on the bunk and tidied
everything like the servant of a wounded warrior.

However, within minutes of casting off I was already too
exhausted to hold the helm. The pressure of the current against the
ferry's rudder almost forced me on to my knees as I steered the
Salammbo between the submerged telegraph poles that marked the
northern limits of the military base. Noon stood beside me, and
when I faltered she pressed her strong hands over my own. She
tugged at the helm with the same grunts with which she had first
driven me on to the beach at Port-la-Nouvelle. Clicking to herself,
she caught sight of an approaching sand-bank. She pushed my
hands aside and spun the helm to starboard, then released the clutch
and disconnected the propeller shaft.

Dead in the water, the ferry stopped fifty feet short of the sand-
bank, around which a school of excited fish darted to and fro as if
waiting for us to run aground. Once we had drifted out into the
deep channel, Noon re-engaged the propeller, and we set off again,
scarcely disturbing the green lacquer of the surface. As she snapped
the spring-loaded clutch lever, Noon mimicked my own gestures
and fumbles. She spat on her hands, pretending that the throttle
was red hot, and reproved herself in a bass voice that partly
imitated my own and partly the cassettes from whose instruction I
would clearly benefit.

"Are you in charge, Noon?" I patted her head, aware how much
she had grown in the three months that I had known her. She was
still a child, but her legs were longer and less bony, and her hips had
begun to swell. In a gesture of annoyance she butted my hand with
the back of her head. Glad to leave her to it, I stepped from the
wheelhouse and made my way to the bows. There I sat in one of the
ferry pilot's canvas chairs. Bathed in the cool air funnelled through
the anchor housing, I listened to the clicking of the cutwater, and
watched the passing parade of the green world that I had created.

I had intended to sit in the bows for only an hour until my head
had cleared, but in fact I was to spend several days in that canvas
chair. Noon had already recognised the combined effects upon me

of exposure, fatigue and the infected wound in my head. I found that I could no longer smile at her, for fear of tearing at my scalp. In the wheelhouse locker she found a cotton flag bearing the Toyota emblem. She tied lengths of cord to its corners, fastened them to the bow-mast and to the door pillars of the limousine, and set up a small awning to protect me from the heat.

There I sat like a totem, propped in the bows of this strange ship piloted by a child on its journey towards the sun. As my mind drifted into a shallow fever, I was already convinced that Noon's presence at the ferry's helm would in some way shelter us from any further act of treachery by the river. After our escape from Captain Kagwa I had become aware that a duel was taking place between myself and the Mallory.

Since its birth from beneath the root of the oak tree, springing to life between the tracks of the bulldozer, the river had done everything to survive. It had tried to trick, evade and kill me, it had set traps for me, and given me delusions of grandeur by showing me ever more lavish parades of flora and fauna that were no more than cunning decoys.

Yet my wariness of the river soon dissolved in its dividing glass. At nightfall, as a mauve light lay over the water, we moored beside a grove of fan-palms whose foliage would shelter us from Kagwa's helicopter. When I woke in the canvas chair the next day, my fever had passed and with it all my fears of the Mallory. As Noon slept in the Mercedes, I gazed out at the green channel that I had created, now almost three hundred yards in width. Once again I was struck by the richness of the vegetation that sprang from the desert's edge, and by the abundant birds and flowering plants, as if an army of aviarists and florists had moved downstream in the night, casting their blossom over the shrubs and saplings, perching the colourful birds among the fragrant nectaries.

Even Noon was impressed by the transformation brought about by this immense flow of water. Child-woman, but still a child, Noon slept late in the rear seat of the limousine. She woke, rubbing her eyes as she sat up, and gazed at the vivid orchids that had fallen across the windshield of the car, like a young actress surprised by the bouquets left outside her bedroom door by an invisible admirer.

The rifle slung over my shoulder, I stood on the roof of the wheelhouse, and scanned the long reaches of the river behind us. During the night, moving in and out of my fever, I had seen lights flickering a mile or so behind us, perhaps Harare's men signalling from one bank to the other. But the morning channel was as smooth as an unremembered past, and the sky rose in a cobalt wall towards the sun, unmarked by the exhaust fumes of Kagwa's helicopter.

I watched the water coursing along the bank, overrunning the narrow beach and swilling round the roots of the tilting palm trees. The Mallory was still growing, fed by that primal Saharan river that I had woken from its subterranean sleep. Already I resented others sharing the river with me, and wanted to keep it to myself and Noon. However, destroying or at least diverting the Mallory was now closely bound up with our survival. Kagwa and his soldiers would have their hands full for the next few days — I guessed that the military camp at the estuary had been inundated — but sooner or later the Captain's imperial expedition would resume. Once Kagwa had established a forward base and fuel depot for the helicopter, the machine would attack us again.

Noon had begun to housekeep, washing the decks with water to keep them cool, gathering kindling for the stove. She carefully measured our ration of morning rice from the sack that she kept in the trunk of the Mercedes. From the small fraction removed each day she seemed to estimate that our journey would end in five or six weeks — either that, or we would have moved to a realm beyond hunger. Tapping her strong teeth, she cast an expert eye over my paint-smeared body, pleased to see that I had recovered. Then she turned to inspect the fish drawn to the cinders which she scattered overboard.

Still modest with me, she stripped behind the limousine, then dived into the green current. I knew that she preferred not to let me see her naked, so I sat on the edge of the steel deck and lowered myself into the chest-deep water. Carrying the rifle over my head

—despite its lack of ammunition, the weapon would chase away any roaming deserters — I reached the narrow beach, which was little more than a rim of polished silt below the palms. Along its slope was scattered an exhibition of washed stones and smooth limestone fragments, a palaeontology waiting for its future, laid out like the elements of a kit from which a creator might select the fossil bed of a new world.

Noon dived and plunged beside the forward anchor of the ferry, trailing the precious rice grains through the water. She cajoled the fish towards her spear, using a tone of voice similar to that with which she induced me to start the engine each morning, or hunt for firewood for her stove. Her head ducked through the foam, and long legs kicked the air. Her childhood and adult life were merging into each other, as they had done for a few dangerous moments when she first tried to shoot me.

Rifle raised, I stepped between the trees. Groves of small tamarinds had sprung from the damp soil, but I could see the open savanna a hundred yards away, a wilderness of scrub and dust. The bank shelved steeply below my feet, leading me down into a narrow valley that seemed to emerge from the shoulder of the channel.

I looked down at the rounded stones and striated boulders, and realised that I was standing on the floor of a broad wadi, the dried skeleton of a river that had flowed towards the south-east from the Chad border. The Mallory had overrun this ancient water-course, crossing it at right angles, and the shoulder of silt along its banks had filled in the gully through which the current might have escaped.

I heard the ring of the anchor chain, and Noon's triumphant cry as she speared a fish. Usually I made a point of being present when she caught our lunch, so that I could give her that praise she had never received, but now I ignored her call. I drove my feet into the soft bank. If I dug through the damp wall I would literally pull the plug on the Mallory, breach its western banks and disperse its great watery mass into the waiting desert.

I listened to the current, hesitating before I searched for a spade in the ferry's tool locker. For the first time the future of this great waterway and its abundant life lay within my hands. I felt nervous of harming them, and yet uncertain about the whole purpose of this strange adventure. I remembered my first appointment after graduating, when I had hesitated in the same way, before deliberately turning down a much sought-after fellowship in the United States. My friends and family had seen this as a self-destructive act, a wilful refusal to accept the possibilities that my own talents had earned. But my refusal, like so many others in my childhood and adult life, had been designed almost consciously to resist the over-warm embrace of the world. Even the smallest nod of approval, like those my father gave me when I passed my first school examinations, filled me with a special kind of irritation. Surprisingly, these refusals opened the door to other possibilities, and at least I stood on my own ground.

The water rushed past, sliding confidently along the bank. I picked up the rifle, slinging it over my shoulder. Already I had begun to resent the river, and realised that in the Mallory I had created a dangerous rival.

19

The Lanterns at Dusk

Death, so eagerly invited, for once failed to keep its appointment. Three hours later, under Noon's disapproving eye, I had cut a narrow ditch through the bank, and watched the first water tumbling towards the white floor of the wadi. As I lifted my spade and removed the last section of dripping sand, the thin stream raced between my legs, eager to escape from the confines of the Mallory and find a new life in the desert.

I stood back, exhilarated by the work. My fever had returned, but I had managed to harness the waves of nausea and delirium. My arms and legs were smeared with silt that overlaid the earlier layers of oil, rust and paint. Resting on the spade, I watched the narrow stream course past and kept careful watch on the level of the river, almost expecting to see it sink like the contents of a drained swimming-pool. By evening the wadi would be filled. An immense lake would lie across the arid savanna, and there within a few days the body of the Mallory would expire. . . .

Irritated by all this, Noon gnawed the nail of her thumb, tapping her foot against the rifle stock, as if wondering how to shoot me. I left her to the problem, and walked down the sloping ground, following the stream. I stumbled, and slid among the dry stones and remnants of bone. Far from forming a pool, the bright fluid failed to reach the floor of the wadi, sucked into a porous earth as waterless as the clinkers in a firebox.

"Noon! Come and help! You can shoot me later!"

I threw the spade towards her, knelt in the sand beside the gully and scooped the water with my hands, driving it down the slope.

The bright fluid fell on to the dry soil, the drops hissing like miniature bombs, as if setting off the fusing mechanism of life itself. I watched the wadi below me, waiting for the first sheet of water to form.

"Noon . . .!"

She stood on the bank, sunk in a depressive slouch, staring at me like a disapproving bride. Already the gully had been blocked. The soft walls had collapsed in on themselves, and the sand was drying in the sun. Bored with me, Noon's eyes moved to the great green back of the Mallory.

I drove the spade into the wet sand, deliberately spattering Noon's legs and feet. Happy to explore the wadi, the water raced down the slope, tumbling cheerfully among the dust and bones.

At dusk I was forced to stop. I sat naked in the bows of the *Salammbo*, under the Toyota awning, as a soft haze of cerise light lay like a quilt over the sleeping river. The fever which had spurred me on now bathed my body in a chilling sweat. The moisture soaked the canvas chair and stained the shabby fabric with the oil and paint that engrained my arms and chest. Like a snake unable to shed the skins of its previous incarnations, I bore these layers of dirt that marked out the earlier chapters in this serial of futile efforts. All I had to show for the hours of useless work were a recurrent fever, my guilt at abusing Noon, and a wasted afternoon which might well have put another ten miles between the ferry and Captain Kagwa's helicopter.

Below me, across the thirty feet of dark water, was the narrow cut through which I had hoped to empty the contents of the Mallory. By late afternoon it was six feet wide. When Noon took the spade from my exhausted hands and broke through the last wall of dissolving sand the river had burst forwards in an unexpected cataract, and cascaded down the ravine into the wadi. The mass of exuberant water threw up a cloud of dust and insects, but within minutes the flow had ceased. Like an immense arterial system, the Mallory was able to seal any wounds in its own walls, and this small haemorrhage was quickly blocked by silt and sand swept into the cut, by dead foliage and clumps of leaves and sudd.

Confused by all this, I slapped Noon when she tried to return to the ferry. Shaking with fever, I hurled the spade into the wadi, and was forced to watch as Noon, without being asked, stoically climbed into the ravine and retrieved the tool. When I tried to thank her she levelled the ragged blade at my face.

But now, at dusk, I could hear her swimming in the dark water below the ferry's stern. The glimpses of her naked body, partly hidden from me by the vessel's after-peak, reminded me of other confusions, and of the great stream with which she had identified herself, that river in my own name which I had created and still meant to destroy. Figment of a dream, she had little or no idea of the larger dream that lay around her. I needed to destroy the Mallory, but at the same time I wanted to enlarge it, to encourage it to inundate the Sahara before it died. Digging my pathetic canal, I had pushed myself on with a feverish vision of refilling all the wadis in Africa, of seeing the ancient fossil channels of the desert run with rivers in my own name. . . .

The smell of simmering rice crossed the evening air from the stove beside the wheelhouse. Noon had swum to the starboard side of the ferry. She lay on her back in the dark water, her legs breaking the surface as she lifted her knees, admitting the river like a lover between her thighs. The platinum foam, the soft teeth of this black admirer, played across her small nipples. Was she, in her child coquette's way, trying to draw me back to the river, to ease my fever for ever in that cool draught between her legs?

I heard the water drip from her body as she stood on the car-deck. I pushed aside the awning and rose unsteadily from the canvas chair, slipping in my own sweat. Trying not to frighten Noon, I leaned against the body of the limousine. From the rear seat rose the faint odour of her skin, which had sustained me that afternoon as I laboured over my canal.

She saw me in the darkness, and moved defensively towards the wheelhouse. I wanted to apologise to her, and reassure her how much I admired her skills, and play her one of the instructional cassettes, perhaps one devoted to the harmony of the sexes.

The sweat from my arms and chest formed oval pools on the

black paintwork of the Mercedes, the glistening imprint of a suitor's body. Deciding that I had no need to hide from Noon, I stepped around the car and walked between the oil drums.

"Doc Mal . . .!"

Lights flickered across the water, blue and ruby bars reflected in the dark surface. A river craft was approaching, its hull hidden in the shadows over the water. Trying to remember where I had left the rifle, I watched them emerge from the misty air. A quarter of a mile downstream, the lights swung together like Chinese lanterns, the eyes of a pantomime dragon, perhaps a water-borne shrine with which some superstitious member of Kagwa's advance-guard was trying to placate the spirit of the Mallory.

Noon had not yet dressed, and watched this strange apparition from the door of the wheelhouse, one hand over her mouth as if stifling the few western sounds that might emerge inappropriately. With the other hand she reached inside the door and passed the rifle to me.

The lights floated on the water, rectangles of red and emerald blinking like traffic signals in the darkness. As they drifted towards us I could see the dark curve of a wooden prow, and then more clearly the bows of a motor launch, a gleam of brass around its anchor. An engine was beating slowly, a tired rhythm that rocked the vessel and tilted its small cargo of lights towards the water. Hidden behind this array of lanterns was a freight of packing-cases swathed in canvas, a dark cargo about to be tipped into the water. The launch was almost awash, and on the port side only a few inches of freeboard separated this clumsy freight from the night stream.

"Mal. . . ." Noon gripped my elbow with her sharp fingernails, making certain that I woke from my fever. The moribund vessel passed within fifty feet of the ferry, and we could see its helmsman sitting with his back to the tiller. Slumped against the wooden seat, he steered the launch with his slim shoulders, each twinge of weariness giving the vessel a tilt to port or starboard.

How long this navigation by ordeal had lasted I could only guess, but as the launch passed the stern of the *Salammbo* I recognised the decrepit figure of the young Indian botanist slumped across the tiller.

"Mr Pal . . .!"

Its gunnels awash, the launch headed towards the beach. The prow ran on to the sand, and the engine raised its voice for the last time, the propeller screwing wearily into the wake before lying dead in the water. The cargo shifted, leaning over the side, and I realised that the magic lanterns had in fact been the reflections of the setting sun and the forest wall in two dust-caked monitor screens.

Mr Pal sat back against the tiller, staring stiffly at this beach on which he had come to rest. Even in the dim air I could see his emaciated arms and the exposure sores on his forehead and cheeks. His hands rested limply on the wooden seat, legs outstretched between the empty food cans and plastic bottles.

Embedded in this collection of rubbish, as if he had been tipped from a dustbin, was the launch's passenger. Like an old rat in a safari suit, he scrummaged about in the debris, and then heaved himself against the tiller beside Mr Pal, who spoke a few words of reassurance. The passenger pressed the sunglasses over his eyes. He gazed at the stern of the ferry above his head, where Noon and I stood together, our naked bodies lit by the last bars of sunset. The light glowed in the mud-streaked television screens, as if reminding these inert tubes of the long-lost images of the forest and river bank that now played upon our bare skins in the camera obscura of dusk. Together they seemed to bring his mind to a momentary focus.

"Dr Mallory. . . ." Professor Sanger gestured reassuringly from the rubbish on the deck around him. "Mr Pal tells me that we have saved you once again. . . ."

20

The Documentary Film

All morning the warm sunlight had pressed upon the river, drawing from its surface a vivid mist that blurred the trees on the distant shore and turned the company of soldiers into a wavering phantom army. Four hundred yards upstream, I sat on the floor of the steel tank above the railway water-tower, and watched Captain Kagwa's expeditionary force preparing to make camp. As the river moved around a sand-bar that lay on its inner curve, a stream of colder water came to the surface. For a few seconds the haze dissipated in the cool air, and Kagwa's spectral soldiers turned into a force of strong-backed men busily erecting their tents and unloading their weapons from the grey-hulled landing-craft.

Soon after sunrise I had left Noon in command of the *Salammbo*, and set off with Sanger and Mr Pal in the patrol launch, retracing our journey in the hope of identifying the exact size of Kagwa's private army. In the three days since our meeting at nightfall, Sanger's estimate of the force's strength had grown geometrically by the hour, and I began to fear that the Captain had at last called in the central government and notified them of the birth of the third Nile. If so, my quest for the source of the Mallory had already run aground. At night, as I lay in the wheelhouse, listening to Mr Pal's soft sing-song commentary on the stars, I could hear the distant mutter of the landing-craft's auxiliary motor, and see the bonfires reflected in the underbellies of the cumulus clouds, another army of ghosts that haunted the night air.

The *Salammbo* was moored in a quiet inlet on the western bank of the Mallory, protected by a shingle bar that almost blocked its entrance, and by the overhanging fan-palms. At dawn Noon watched us go, standing among the sections of film equipment like the adolescent curator of a futuristic museum.

She had been annoyed by the arrival of Sanger and Mr Pal, and the prospect of more mouths to feed, but the sight of the television screens had soon pacified her. She immediately took charge of this mud-covered cargo, eagerly helping me to transfer the cabinets and aerials to the car-deck of the ferry.

Leaving her behind, we set out in the launch, sustained by Mr Pal's eternal wild-life commentary.

". . . wild magnolias and many small tamarinds, with comfortable footing for passerine birds." Exhausted by the ordeal of the past weeks, Mr Pal murmured away, shielding his tired eyes from the overlit water. "The river is some eight metres in depth, moving through an ample basin of washed granitic marl, well-stocked with aquatic life. The warm waters offer a friendly refuge to snakes and lizards. . . ."

"Mr Pal. . . ." I cut the throttle in protest. "For God's sake—you sound as if you're stocktaking on the last day of creation. . . ."

"Well put, doctor, that describes it exactly. . . ." Nodding sagely, Sanger leaned against Mr Pal as they sat propped together against the engine locker. Sanger nudged the Indian, urging him to continue. His sun-blistered face lay against Mr Pal's shoulder, eyes hidden behind the dark glasses. For the first time I suspected that this documentary film-maker was almost blind, and accepted his whole world through the reassuring clichés of his handyman-scientist.

But before Mr Pal could go on, we heard the blare of Captain Kagwa's loud-hailer across the water. We were now two miles downstream of the ferry. I steered the launch into a shallow creek that ran into a grove of palms. After mooring the launch to a pair of waterlogged trunks, I set off down the beach. Sanger stood upright, almost sitting on Mr Pal's head, mentally filming my imminent capture by Kagwa.

I moved between the trees towards a water-tower that leaned across the shallows. At its feet a spur of the railway line from Saliere ran through the sand and vanished into the river. A metal ladder ran up to the tank, and the steel pylon shielded me from the sergeant keeping a look-out on the bridge of the landing-craft.

Dropping into the drained chamber, I pulled aside one of the rusty plates and took stock of the expeditionary force now pursuing us. Despite the impressive bulk of the French landing-craft, I could see that this military unit was little more than a private posse. There were some sixty soldiers, with their families and hangers-on, and the same weapons, stores and radio equipment I had last seen at the Port-la-Nouvelle airstrip.

So the Captain still kept the River Mallory a secret, carefully wrapped inside his dream of a green Saharan kingdom, Kagwana. My confidence rose. The effort of climbing the steps to the water-tank had left me breathless. Our daily food ration had fallen to a handful of boiled rice and a few pieces of snake. Sanger and Mr Pal had brought nothing with them — after escaping from the unguarded police barracks at Port-la-Nouvelle they had exhausted their own supplies within days. Now that we had entered the upper reaches of the river, Noon found it more difficult to hunt the abundant fish in the faster-running waters, and had little bait with which to tease them on to her spear.

I looked down at my calves and arms, at the balls of muscles that hunted beneath the thinning skin. I had lost at least twenty pounds in weight, and my hip bones jutted above my shorts like the rim of our empty rice basin. I imagined my once plump mesentery as a fraying clothes line, on which was strung an ever-more hungry intestine. Nonetheless, I felt stronger than at any time since leaving Port-la-Nouvelle, and eager to cope with the exhausting task of steering the ferry and moving the oil drums to the fuel manifold.

Scanning the mildewed road-map, I estimated that we were some ten miles to the west of the rail terminal at Saliere, and perhaps half-way across the central plain of Northern Province. Beyond the margins of the river the once green savanna was already turning to desert, a terrain of abandoned farms and villages picked over by a few nomads heading for the forested river valleys of the south. We had now covered almost a hundred miles in our northward journey from Port-la-Nouvelle, and I calculated that we would need another month to find the source of the Mallory, perhaps eighty miles upstream in the foothills of the Massif du Tondou.

However difficult it became to plan ahead, to think in terms other than the next few minutes, some care would be needed to get us there. Our small reserve of rice barely covered the bottom of the hessian sack, and now had to be divided among the four of us. Already, for some reason, I discounted Sanger and Mr Pal, as if certain that they would soon be leaving us. Noon objected to my system of rationing, putting it down to some blindness on my part to the needs of the present. In her eyes the Mallory would provide all, its cool waters assuaging our hunger and soothing the overheated plates of the *Salammbo*.

I assumed that, like a child, she found it difficult to count more than three days ahead. Beyond the fourth day lay infinity. Meanwhile, a resplendent present was waiting to be seized. I appeased Noon by passing much of my own ration to her, which she treated to a snooty gaze and then gobbled down with gusto. Half-consciously, I wanted her to grow for me, to become the young woman I saw waiting in the wings of her child's slim body. . . .

Thinking of Noon, I lay on the shadowy floor of the water-tank, and massaged the blood back into my thighs. I listened to the river drumming against the rusty pylons of the tower, and began to count the soldiers unloading their equipment across the lowered ramp of the landing-craft.

There was no sign of Kagwa or the helicopter. No further reconnaissance flights had taken place, and I could well imagine the Captain's annoyance on finding just how much fuel the machine consumed. Besides, Kagwa was fully aware that the car ferry was ahead of him, that sooner or later our own fuel would run out and he would find us waiting for him on a convenient beach with our backs to the desert.

A series of sharp snaps crossed the air. Parties of soldiers were moving along the bank. Blades flashed in the sunlight, as they cut down the bamboo saplings around their camp, gathering firewood for the galley stoves on board the landing-craft. Again I felt a pang of regret, as if pieces of my own body were being cut down, my nails crudely pared to the quick. I allowed Noon to gather only dead wood and underbrush, and never to kill the birds or the small mammals who drank at the water's edge. The fish were the one order we could cycle through our appetites, returning them in due course to the passing stream.

A high squeal pierced the air, the cry of a forest pig trapped by the soldiers in a pit. I winced at this, and was about to lower my eyes, when a strange vessel emerged from the shadow of the landing-craft. A shallow steel lighter rounded the curve of the river, a police patrol boat lashed to its side and providing the motive power. Roped to the deck was Captain Kagwa's helicopter, its yellow floats anchored between four fuel drums of aviation spirit. The young French pilot lounged in a canvas chair beside the bubble canopy, reading a newspaper like a tourist. Kagwa stood in the stern of the lighter, signalling to the helmsman to moor alongside the landing-craft. He had exchanged his police uniform for army camouflage jacket and trousers, and wore a small beret in place of his peaked cap.

When the mooring had been completed to Kagwa's satisfaction, he strode to the bows of the lighter and gazed across the river. His eyes swept the wooded banks, examining every beach and inlet, and then came to rest on the sunlit water-tower. He stepped forward, staring at the steel tank in which I knelt, as if he had guessed that I was spying on him. In that chilling moment I knew, not only that he was determined to kill me, but that I felt a strong sense of guilt for all that I had done, for the death of the Japanese photographer and for this entire military operation.

Confused by the sight of the helicopter, and by Captain Kagwa's threatening stare, I closed the steel plates. I shut out the sunlight, and crouched in the metal cell thirty feet above the water, listening to the rapid beating of my heart, as it thrust itself against my rib-cage like a creature frantic to escape its pen. I was giving way to my own panic like a trapped animal, but I could scarcely control myself. The long journey up the Mallory, the hunger and exposure, and the inundation of my mind by the simple paradise I had helped to create, together left me unable to rally myself against anything but a direct physical assault. The unspoken threat in Kagwa's gaze, the promise of retribution to come, belonged to the punitive world of my childhood, and had confused me like a schoolboy faced with the abstract symbols in his first algebra class. I was now moving into a realm of unthought responses to pain and thirst, to the sun and the air.

Against my thighs, I felt the smooth rush of water between the pylons of the tower. The river was trying to reassure me. Calming myself, I stood up and watched Kagwa climb the gangway into the landing-craft. Clearly he was after bigger game than the car-ferry — any action he took against me for firing a bullet through the helicopter's pontoon would be in the margins of his concern. According to Sanger, the southern reaches of the river were filled with fishing craft of every kind that had crossed Lake Kotto, with scores of smugglers' rafts and trading skiffs.

I lowered myself down the ladder and jumped into the waist-deep water, then waded ashore to the cover of the palms. When I returned to the launch Sanger and Mr Pal were still sitting together against the engine-locker, two Alice-like figures stranded in this backwater of the wrong dream. As I stepped on to the beach Mr Pal noticed me and began to speak to Sanger. The dark glasses rose, a semaphore of light reflected from the black lenses, as if Sanger were in some kind of secret communication with the world beyond the river. His explanation of his escape from the police barracks, that Mr Pal had bartered both his release and the use of the launch in exchange for a video-camera, seemed wholly suspect, assuming a remarkably developed taste for the home movie among Kagwa's illiterate rural policemen. . . .

"Mallory — ?" As we slid from the mouth of the creek, following the foliage along the western bank, Sanger leaned forward and gripped my arm. He was forever fondling my wrists and hands, confirming those changes to my physique and character that Mr Pal had quietly confided. "You saw the soldiers? Are they troops of the central government?"

"No, he's still keeping it to himself — there's not much more than the gendarmerie unit at Lake Kotto." I listened to my matter-of-fact voice, so at variance with my real feelings, a layer of response I wanted to shuck. "About sixty soldiers, a French pilot and the helicopter."

"Good. . . ." Sanger seemed relieved, and allowed himself to sink back into his fatigue. "So, doctor, it remains your river."

"It always has been. If you remember, you registered it in my name."

"I remember. Little did I know what a genie would spring from your head." Sanger leaned over the gunnel and dipped a hand into the speeding stream, then fingered the drops as if testing their vintage. He splashed the water over his sore-infested skin. "The Mallory . . . Are you still hoping to destroy our third Nile?"

"No, Sanger. . . ." I was wary of revealing myself to this likeable but sly opportunist, particularly as I was still unsure of my own motives. He and Mr Pal clearly regarded me as some wild man of the woods. They almost welcomed my slide into eccentricity, aware that this would make useful footage for the documentary they were filming inside their heads. My ambiguous relationship with Noon, my periodic nakedness and bouts of fever, and my still infected head-wound, for them spelt out a clear physical and moral decline, since they failed to grasp the real changes that were taking place. "I've never wanted to destroy it. I'm only concerned with the irrigation project at Lake Kotto — all this water is simply surplus to requirements."

"Nobly absurd." Sanger leaned back, sighing to himself as if this alone justified all that he had suffered. Undernourished and showing the first yellow tint of infective jaundice, he had lost the porcelain crown of his left canine, and his derelict figure more and more resembled the decaying stump. "This river may well be the most important African waterway since the Suez Canal — another Nile sprung upon the people of this doomed province by scarcely less than an act of God, with a little help from an erratic country doctor. It can drive the Sahara back to the 15th parallel. Is that not so, Mr Pal?"

"Quite correct, sir." Mr Pal emerged from his fever to parrot his statistics. With its swollen eyelids and fungal skin infection, his youthful face ressembled that of a starved apprentice in a back-street tannery. "Estimated flow-rate is some 10,000 cubic feet per second, capable of irrigating 10 million hectares, and together make it the 57th greatest river in the world. . . ."

"Only the 57th — ? These figures are vital, Mr Pal, they carry authority. I hope you can revise them upwards for the commentary. However, doctor, you can see that you are conducting your private duel with a mighty opponent."

From the tiller I gazed at this derelict pair, held together only by their bogus documentary. Like Captain Kagwa, Sanger had kept all news of the river's existence to himself. His original scheme for a filmed record of the Mallory had been given several added layers of interest — the irrational quest of its self-styled creator, and Captain Kagwa's heroic attempts to arrest him before he could divert or destroy this life-giving channel.

How many feet of film had Mr Pal already shot? Whenever we moored, the botanist would wade shakily to the nearest beach and drive a calibrated stick into the sand, set up his camera and then shoot across it as soon as Noon or I filled the background, hunting for water-snakes or fuelling the diesel engine. My menage with this under-age girl (under-age in Düsseldorf or Osaka, though not within 2,000 miles of the Mallory), and my absent-minded tendency to go about naked, together convinced Sanger that he had found the perfect centre-piece for his film. Meanwhile, my clear dislike of his documentary would give his armchair viewers a gripping sense of authenticity.

Moreover, my hostility involved a strong element of rivalry — each of us was trying to impose his own image upon the Mallory. I had helped to create this unique waterway, and filled it with an Eden of birds and flowers, which Sanger was now smothering beneath his cheap commentary. His pseudo-scientific prattle assumed that television's flattering revision of nature was an act of creation as significant as the original invention of this great river and its abundant life. Both, to Sanger, were equally plausible and equally meaningful. By conjuring the Mallory into existence, I had merely imposed a fiction of my own upon the desert. The feather-palms and wild lavender, the scented groves and thrilling bird-song were simply images on my retina searching for a comment-ator. I stared at the exposure sores on Sanger's jaundiced skin, wondering how in due course he would explain his own disease away in a set of reassuring clichés . . . I only hoped that I would be able to help him.

Noon, to my annoyance, the former child-guerilla and freedom fighter, adored the transparent flattery of the lens. As we tied up alongside the ferry I could see her among the cabinets and control panels stacked beside the Mercedes, playing the film cassettes on the battery-powered monitor and miming to her own images on the screen. The audio-tapes in the dashboard of the limousine had been cast aside. Once she discovered vision, the sound-world palled. Speech bored her, and the alphabet and syntax of the film were all she needed.

The stove was cold, and a pan of half-cooked rice sat on the embers of a few sticks. Noon had done no housekeeping or fishing while we were away.

"No fish, Noon? No snake? We have to leave now." When I reprimanded her she shrugged like any teenager. "Captain Kagwa's coming — big guns, they'll catch Noon."

When Mr Pal found the cut-off switch and dimmed the screen she promptly elbowed him aside and pressed the toggle, throwing up again the pictures of herself emerging bare-breasted from the river with a fish impaled on her spear. I remembered her primitive autistic drawings on the beach at Port-la-Nouvelle. As a child Noon had possessed almost no image of herself, and these cassettes had allowed her to describe herself for the first time. I imagined her becoming a princess of the river and the forest, ruling the leopards and the giant oaks with an authority and allure modelled entirely on the poses in Sanger's tawdry films. In many ways Noon's progress charted the future of a special kind of self-consciousness, pandered to but constrained by the limitations of this small screen. In a few months she had stepped from the Stone Age and crossed from the spoken to the visual realm in a single stride, dispensing with language on the way.

But I was happy to let her play these games of hide-and-seek. As I stood behind the helm and steered the ferry into the main channel I felt the powerful shoulder of the Mallory press against the vessel's hull. The steady surge of darker water beneath the veneer of light reminded me of my real purpose. Below the wheelhouse, Noon hopped from one foot to another, as she discovered the stop-frame and the fast forward, playing games with time and space like any child in a western suburb. Around her the river preserved a more real world.

21

The Skirmish

Even Mr Pal's everlasting commentary failed to upset my good humour. An hour later, when we were five miles safely upstream of Kagwa's bivouac, I was at last able to relax and again become the captain of the *Salammbo*. Sanger and Mr Pal sat together under the awning in the bows of the ferry, too tired to chop the firewood, extemporising a child's guidebook to the surrounding terrain. Mr Pal's voice floated back over the drumming of the diesel, the sing-song patter of a salesman selling the world.

"... already we see the first ferns and bromeliads happily filling their ecological niches. The alkaline soils have encouraged a host of species to enjoy the welcoming micro-climate."

"Very good, Mr Pal . . . but what about the river?"

"Still enlarging, sir, flowing comfortably between ample banks. Rails and heron are present on the shore, and two men in military uniform are washing in the warm waters, whose dissolved minerals — "

"Men? Military . . .?" Sanger turned and waved to the wheel-house, then ordered Mr Pal to warn me.

However, I had already seen the soldiers. Dressed in the uniforms of Kagwa's expeditionary force, they stood on a narrow beach a hundred yards ahead. They had cut down the young bamboo to provide a small clearing. Parked in its centre was Kagwa's seven-ton truck, from which the soldiers were unloading the sections of a metal hut. A wooden watch-tower rose above the trees, and a soldier on duty lounged behind his light machine-gun. On the beach below the tower was a rubber inflatable with an outboard motor. A second group of soldiers were trimming the branches from the saplings and using the bamboo stakes to build a landing-stage. Waist-deep in the water, they drove the spears into the soft silt of the river-bed.

Gripping the helm, I gazed at this scene of activity. I realised that Kagwa's men were setting up a customs post, with a toll house, inspection jetty and gun emplacement. The truck and its platoon of ten men had debarked from the landing-craft several days earlier. They had then driven on ahead, picking this point where the river's banks were constricted by a granite outcrop. Across its worn shoulder the water foamed and leapt through the hoops of vivid rainbows.

"Dr Mallory! There are soldiers here! Change course, sir!"

Mr Pal had left the bows and was clambering over the television equipment stored amidships. He pushed past Noon, who sat in her electronic den surrounded by images of herself, and disconnected the battery leads. He scrambled back to the wheelhouse and pressed his exhausted face to the broken glass.

"Dr Mallory . . . do you wish to run us aground, sir?"

I was still staring at the soldiers in their customs post. The *Salammbo* drummed its way across the breaking waves, heading directly for the wooden jetty. The soldiers stood on the bank, shouting and waving their machetes. The lookout in the watch-tower adjusted the sights of his machine-gun. We were now less than fifty yards away, and I could see their wide-eyed expressions when they recognised Captain Kagwa's limousine, puzzled why he should have chosen to deliver the vehicle to this small advance-post. I felt equally confused — it had never occurred to me that Kagwa would order his men to leave the river and drive around it. In some way this broke the rules of the contest between us, and denied the unspoken agreement that we would act out our duel within the river alone.

"Dr Mallory!" Mr Pal reached through the door to seize the helm. "Sir, this is not a time for going mad!"

I swung the helm to starboard, throwing Mr Pal to the deck. The alarmed soldiers ran from the beach to the nest of rifles stacked beside the truck. The ferry slewed across the water, its rudder handicapped by the weight of the patrol launch lashed to its side. The bows struck the end of the pier and dragged the piles from the river-bed. The concertina of green saplings sprang like a bow, and then collapsed into the shallows, chopped to pieces by the propeller.

The *Salammbo* veered away from the bank, rolling in the confused current, and tossed a heavy brown wave across the beach. The soldiers raised their rifles, still uncertain whether to fire at the Mercedes and the shabby European seated under the awning with a film camera in his hands. I crouched over the helm, and steered the ferry into the centre of the channel. Below the wheelhouse Mr Pal was grappling with a 50-gallon oil drum that had broken loose from its ropes, like an exhausted instructor trying to waltz with an overweight pupil. Noon had abandoned her television studio and retreated to the safety of the limousine. We passed the rubber inflatable, where the sergeant who had once ordered Noon's execution stood thigh-deep in the water, his strong fist pulling at the outboard motor's starting cord. As Noon ducked into the Mercedes he pointed to her, like a wildfowler spotting a rare bird across his sights. Open-mouthed, he pushed away the rifle levelled at the girl by the excited soldier staggering in the foam beside him.

We were four hundred yards upstream when I heard the sound of the outboard. Already I knew that they would catch us within a few minutes. The sergeant stood amidships, legs braced against the wooden frame-boards, loudhailer raised to his chin. Mr Pal had returned to the bows, where he squatted under the awning beside Sanger, regaling him with a vivid commentary on my foolishness and our imminent capture. Noon sat in the front passenger seat of the limousine, watching me in her nerveless way. Did she imagine that the sanctuary of Kagwa's Mercedes would save her when the sergeant stepped on to the deck?

The rubber speedboat was alongside, throwing up huge plumes of spray as its flat hull struck the bow waves of the ferry. The sergeant exchanged his loud-hailer for a light carbine handed to him by the soldier in the bows. We sped along together, the inflatable leaping from crest to crest, the *Salammbo's* funnel pumping out a plume of black smoke that uncoiled across the river.

Balancing on his stocky legs, the sergeant surveyed the ferry, taking in Sanger and Mr Pal huddled beneath the protective ensign of the Japanese car company, latter-day non-belligerents under the world's most neutral flag. He shouted to the helmsman, then raised the carbine and fired a shot at my head through the open window of the wheelhouse.

I heard the bullet whine across the open water towards the far shore, a harsh whoop drowned by the crack of the cartridge in my ear. I swung the wheel, trying to drive the inflatable into the bank, but the helmsman had already cut his speed. The rubber craft rolled in the ferry's wake, but the sergeant was already bracing himself for a second shot. I reversed the wheel, deciding to run for the opposite bank, where Noon would have a chance to flee through the forest, and perhaps make her way back to the mountains.

The untethered oil drum slid along the deck and collided with the cargo of film equipment. The ferry sheered across the stream, and a huge wave rolled against the wheelhouse. The motor-launch lashed to the port side rose over the gunnel, crushing the metal rail. As the mooring lines parted, the craft fell back, shipping half the ferry's wake. Still moving, it began to capsize and almost ran down the speeding inflatable.

Across the river, in the trees above the beach, lights glowed from the undergrowth like the eyes of a dozing cheetah. A camouflaged jeep reversed on to the beach, turned sharply and sped along the water's edge. Two armed men in the combat fatigues of General Harare's guerilla force stood behind the driver. They steadied themselves against a machine-gun mounted on the roll-bar above the driver's head, and trained the weapon on the rubber inflatable.

Already Kagwa's sergeant had lost interest in us. He sat in the bows of the speedboat, and signalled to the helmsman to turn back. In his panic the young soldier stalled the engine and the craft slumped into the water. Over my shoulder I watched it wallowing in the ferry's wake, the sergeant lying between the frame-boards as the machine-gun in the racing jeep tapped out a brief burst of fire.

Although these were Harare's men, I stupidly expected them to offer us their protection. The jeep kept pace with us, its wheels sending up fans of spray as they cut the water's edge. Then the machine-gun turned towards us, and I saw the soldiers prepare to fire.

I eased back the throttle, idling the engine so that the *Salammbo* was stationary, its propeller keeping pace with the current. The jeep stopped where the beach petered out between the exposed roots of the palms growing in the water. Its wheels half submerged, it sat in the shallows, the driver waiting as the two gunners readied their weapon. Through the door of the wheelhouse I looked down at the bright water below the starboard rail, and hoped that I was strong enough to swim the hundred yards to shore.

A door of the Mercedes slammed in the quiet air. Noon stepped from the passenger seat. She had taken the combat jacket from the windowsill, and now wore this man's garment whose bulky shoulders swamped her own. She crossed the open deck, buttoning the lapels over her small breasts, and then puffed out the sleeves, so that the camouflage pattern of Harare's army stood out clearly in the sun.

The soldiers in the jeep watched her over their gunsights. From a distance her face must have seemed calm and expressionless, but as she approached the wheelhouse her mouth and cheeks were crimped like those of a child too terrified to scream. Ignoring me, she reached into the wheelhouse and picked up the rifle, then raised her left palm to the sun, knuckles touching the shoulder-flash of her jacket, in Harare's characteristic salute.

The ferry moved away under the uncertain sights of the machine-gun, gaining speed as the channel widened and the current slackened. A quarter of a mile of open water separated us, and the guerillas seemed to lose interest. The driver began to reverse along the beach.

"Noon . . .?"

I held her shoulders when she placed the rifle behind the door. She was staring at the guerillas, the expression of fear on her face slowly giving way to disgust. Watching them coldly, she spat between my hands on to the deck.

The Skirmish

I tried to embrace her, and felt her sternum throbbing with fear against my ribs, a hammer pumped by her heart, but she slipped through my arms, shrugging off the jacket. Holding the mud-caked garment, I watched her walk across the deck to the cargo of film equipment. She squatted down in this electronic bower, tapping her teeth with her nails. She switched on the small monitor screen, and stared raptly at the image of her face that swam towards her through the dusty glass, with the gaze of an old woman seeing once again the lost world of her childhood.

22

Into the Lagoons

My courtship of Noon, which had sustained me for so many weeks, now took second place to our survival. Soon after our escape from Kagwa's speedboat, we entered an unexpected sector of the Mallory. The river issued from a wide plateau of marsh and salt-desert, a terrain of mists and melancholy birds shrieking to each other across the solitary lagoons. Beyond the rim of the plateau we could see the foothills of the Massif du Tondou, whose secret valleys concealed the source of the Mallory.

The river, meanwhile, had changed its character. Although the volume of its waters remained the same, the main channel had divided into a maze of swamps and reed-covered islands, as if trying to conceal its identity from itself. On the third morning, within an hour of setting sail from the island where we had moored through the dark, I lost sight of the river's banks and entered one of the huge lagoons that lay like inland lakes between the causeways of papyrus and bamboo. Fed by all this moisture, a heavy mist lay between us and the sun, and at midday this miasma turned into an amber haze, so that we seemed to be forever drifting within the mirage of a golden sea. The air was filled with unfamiliar birds which had made their home in these marshes, hunting for the snakes and small frogs which were now the sole marine life. Their unwearying cries crossed the bronze air, as their winged bodies, the cryptic letters of a stylised alphabet, whirled over our heads like fragments of a threatening message, a warning to me from the mountains of the Massif. Through the overheated light I saw the movement of another craft. A local fisherman punted his outrigger two hundred yards away, the wavering image of his black figure like a painted stroke on a Chinese scroll.

"Noon . . . I need you here. . . ."

Deliberately I cut back the engine, and allowed the ferry to drift across an island of reeds. The serrated fronds rasped against the hull, scraping away the layers of rust and mud. Noon's head emerged from the miniature studio amidships where she spent her day under the makeshift but stylish sunshade of a photographer's silver umbrella. She glanced at the static expanse of the lagoon, and at the narrow causeway which separated us from the river. Treating me to an impatient glare, she left the studio and made her way to the bows, stepping over the reclining figures of Sanger and Mr Pal under their Toyota awning.

I watched her as she glanced matter-of-factly into the mist and heat-haze, like an experienced housewife inspecting the stalls of a strange market. As always, I marvelled at how quickly she could orient herself. Unerringly she would pick out the best course for us to take, as if her mind was equipped with some underwater sonar, avoiding a submerged shoal of rocks or the roof of a mining company silo. At times I suspected that she knew, perhaps unconsciously, the whole course of the Mallory.

This intimacy with the hidden fathoms of the river, its longest reaches and eventual source, I took to be the reason for her attachment to me. Unlike the others, Sanger and Captain Kagwa and Nora Warrender, she accepted that the river and I were one. This awareness of the real nature of the Mallory was a fore-knowledge of my own body. The fish and snakes she beguiled from the water in order to feed us were the hopes and fears that had sent me on this quest. I knew now why I liked her to bathe naked in the river, to immerse herself in that larger dream that sustained our journey. Already, as we moved upstream, my wish to destroy the river was giving way to the belief that there was some secret at the Mallory's source, and that Noon alone would guide me towards it.

She touched the hazy air with her hand, nosing it like a wine-taster inhaling a bouquet. The contours of unseen deeps moved on the light, mapping themselves on the screen of some concealed compass behind her eyes.

She ended her survey with a flourish, glancing at the digital watch on her wrist. The gesture was for my benefit. Sanger had given the watch to Noon, bribing her to bring water to Mr Pal, and she now wore this cheap chronometer as if it were the most elegant piece of jewellery, recognising that its liquid crystal display and press-button functions belonged to the same family of signals as the captions on Sanger's documentaries. Was she using the watch to calculate true north? But in these marshes and lagoons the sun was scarcely visible in any direction, and seemed to emanate from a glowing haze all around us. The *Salammbo's* crew comprised an oracular child and three men with blurred shadows.

Noon whistled to me, rousing my attention as I dozed over the helm. She pointed to the remote north-west corner of the lagoon, a waterlogged area of crumbling embankments and small islands.

"Noon . . .? Is this another game?"

I swung the wheel to starboard and eased forward the throttle. Smoke pumped from the funnel as the *Salammbo* pushed through the shallow water. Noon squatted in the bows, now and then scowling at Sanger and Mr Pal, who sat slumped together under their awning. We approached a palisade of tall reeds that grew from the submerged banks, the air around them festering with flies and mosquitoes. A host of small frogs filled the water, feeding on the algae that turned the surface of the lagoon into a translucent jelly. A nervous egret plunged through the haze, hunting the small snakes that in turn fed upon the frogs. It burst from the water and screamed across the ferry. The wriggling form in its beak covered the air with a calligraphy of pain.

Looking down at these primitive creatures, I realised that we had left behind forever the domestic realm of the small mammals in the lower reaches of the Mallory, the passerine birds and flowering plants. We had returned to the more primitive world of the amphibians and raptors hunting among the walls of reeds that stood like bronze spears in the humid light of a younger sun.

Here, the car-ferry with its limousine and television equipment seemed as exotic as a visiting spaceship.

The helm spun through my fingers, as the bows of the ferry sheered to port. We were about to run aground on a causeway of mud that formed the northern wall of the lagoon. The reeds rasped against the hull, thrusting at my face through the broken windows of the wheelhouse.

"Noon . . . get down!" I began to reverse the engine, but at the last moment a breach appeared in the palisade. The ferry slid through the gap, its propeller thrashing the yellow spears into a trail of crushed basketwork. We entered a wide and silent channel, a wandering arm of the river which Noon had identified from the centre of the lagoon, in some way reading the scents of fresh water among the screaming birds.

At the mouth of the channel, where the great back of the Mallory swept past through the haze, I saw the remains of a military bivouac. A squad of Harare's soldiers had camped on a small island, whose grass they had burned back to give them tent-space.

I uncoupled the propeller, letting the ferry drift into the reeds. While Sanger and Mr Pal watched me glassily from beneath their awning, I jumped into the water and waded ashore through the scorched grass. Around me were the remains of the soldiers' camp — the baked shards of an earth stove, beer cans lying in the ashes, a rusty ammunition box filled with spent cartridge cases, ragged rubber boots. I searched among the debris, hoping to find a single round for the Lee-Enfield.

As the smoke lifted from the ferry's funnel I kept careful watch for this passing patrol. I assumed that the river now emerged from a zone controlled by Harare's forces. Our supplies of food were almost exhausted — barely six cupfuls of rice remained in the sack, and we would run out of both food and fuel within three days, long before we reached the headwaters of the Mallory. The strain of serving as the ferry's captain, chief engineer and stoker, the effort needed to decant the diesel oil into the fuel manifold, and the unending pressure of the helm against my arms had together drained half the blood and muscle from my body. Exposure sores covered my face and forehead, flourishing in my beard like fungi in a damp meadow.

Despite these handicaps, I was determined to press on. My own fever and light-headedness, and Noon's guile, had carried us to within sight of the Mallory's source.

"Doctor! Mr Pal's eyes — !" Sanger crouched under the awning, swaying feebly against the guy ropes. Burning tinder crackled in the stove on the deck beside the wheelhouse, warming up a pail of frogs, and Sanger coughed on the green smoke. I returned to the ferry, climbed past the mud-spattered limousine and went forward.

"Mallory, I'm concerned for Mr Pal — his eyes are troubling him." Sanger snatched at my hand and squeezed the wrist-bones, again making sure that I was not some impostor. "Try to remember your other self. . . ."

The two men sat together under the awning, the remains of several meals scattered at their feet. The set of once-elegant department store mess-tins were caked with burned rice and fish scales. All day they huddled side by side in their deck chairs, shabby-genteel passengers who had taken one tramp steamer too many. Sanger's face was hidden by the brim of his straw hat, but I could see that his lips and cheekbones were pocked with insect bites that had festered for weeks, his neck inflamed by a sun-induced viral response. He placed an arm around Mr Pal's shoulder, and listened impatiently to his heart.

"The birds, doctor — I can't hear a thing. Call away your birds!"

Beside him, Mr Pal lay slumped in his chair. He had bruised his abdomen while wrestling with the fuel drum, and an ascending liver infection had given his face the pallor of tarnished copper. He sat back with closed eyes, but then began a gabbled description of the lagoons and reed-islands, the commentary on a dream.

". . . these lagoons support an extensive marine life, amphibians and gravel feeders . . . the nutrient-filled waters also provide a home for estuarine crocodiles — "

"Crocodiles? We are far from any estuary . . . but crocodiles would be useful, Mr Pal. Keep an open eye. . . ."

". . . in addition, certain species of salamander bask in the afternoon sun . . . at dusk the phoenix flies. . . ."

Already the commentary was touched with fantasy, but as I knelt in front of Mr Pal he placed his hands on my chest and forced me away, fixing me with a sudden grimace.

". . . a highwayman approaches, sir, an evil dacoit who will abduct your daughters. . . ."

"Quiet, Mr Pal." Sanger restrained him, holding his hands like a mother calming a fractious child. "You see, Mallory, you must do something for Mr Pal's eyes. Remember that you were once a doctor."

"Noon is cooking a meal. Afterwards he can lie on my bunk in the wheelhouse." I peered briefly at the blanched inner lids of Mr Pal's eyes. "In the mountains it will be cooler."

"Mountains? That is mirage-talk. We should turn back, doctor. Mr Pal is clearly very ill."

Looking down at the jaundiced Indian, I decided to give him half my ration. I knew that I had neglected the botanist. In a curious way, my moral standards and sense of responsibility had declined, although I had become a more generous and a happier man. And, for the moment, I needed him alive. Recalling Harare's vanity, it occurred to me that Sanger and his television unit might at last prove useful. The film camera was probably the one passport that would allow us through the guerillas' lines.

"Doctor? Bring your mind to some kind of focus!"

"He'll recover. It's a transient fever."

"There's an epidemic of them on this ship. We can cure the entire outbreak by altering course for Port-la-Nouvelle."

"No — we'll go on."

"You're still obsessed with this absurd dream? To reach the source of the river? Look at yourself, doctor!"

"Think of the documentary, Sanger. I know it will astound the Japanese."

"Foolishness, Mallory. We must turn back now."

"We've come too far." I looked out at the broad stream, its surface tinted gold by the hazy sun. "We'll reach the source — it's a point of honour."

"It's a point of lunacy — you're a small man, Mallory, and a small man's madness can take dangerous forms."

Sanger stood up, trying to guide me back to the wheelhouse, his head lost in the Toyota awning. Behind the mud-spattered glasses his weak eyes flinched from the sun. As he fumbled with the canvas flag I realised that Sanger would soon be wholly dependent on me.

"Noon! Bring water!" I pushed Sanger into his seat. Noon was squatting by the stove, pulling the legs off the hundreds of small frogs she had caught, and tossing them into the frying-pan. She left the stove and came forward, carrying a video-cassette in her hand. Tapping her teeth in her substitute for speech, she rattled it in front of the two men.

Mr Pal revived at the sound, and reached down to the leather bag which lay on the deck beside his chair. This held a small library of cassettes, the most valuable currency on board the ferry. He and Sanger loaned the cassettes to Noon in return for various favours. She would bathe them, carry water, clean the deck around their feet, wash their clothes, and then retreat to her electronic den with a fresh cassette.

To my surprise, glancing over Noon's shoulder as she sat before the monitor screen, I noticed that many of the cassettes consisted of extracts from old-fashioned commercial documentaries, sequences of elephants rolling logs, warriors stamping at the coronation of a paramount chief, bare-breasted women carrying water-pitchers on their heads, and other clichés of the earliest days of the wild-life film. These, Sanger had explained, supplied a useful model for his own films, and a stream of pseudo-authentic footage consonant with the images deeply implanted in the minds of their audiences. I had strongly disagreed, and pointed out that the West's image of Africa was now drawn from the harshest newsreels of the civil wars in the Congo and Uganda, of famine in Ethiopia, and from graphically explicit films of lions copulating in close-up on the Serengeti or dismembering a still breathing wildebeest. But Sanger claimed that these were merely another stylised fiction, a more sensational but just as artfully neutered violence, and that an authentic first-hand experience of anything had long ceased to be of meaning in the last years of the century. "The truth is merely the lie you most wish to believe," he liked to opine. "After all, your creation of the river has sprung from a familiar repertory of childhood clichés. I even suspect that your wish to destroy it is really an attempt to destroy television's image of the world. . . ."

While the frogs simmered in the pan, Noon bathed Mr Pal, first stripping him to the waist and then rubbing his swollen abdomen with the wash-leather from the chauffeur's glove compartment of the Mercedes. She scraped the mess-tins with a handful of sand, and then poured water over the half-conscious botanist. Mr Pal revived briefly. He lay back, swallowing the sweat that fell from his forehead, eyes fixed on the island of burned reeds beside the jetty. Then he lapsed again into his fever.

There was little I could do for him. Even if I set off down-river and managed to surrender to Captain Kagwa it was most unlikely that he would send Mr Pal on south to Port-la-Nouvelle.

When we had finished our meal I siphoned a dozen gallons of oil into the diesel's fuel tank, started the engine and cast off from the island. As we moved forward, leaving the waterway and entering the main channel of the Mallory, I listened for any sound of Kagwa's expeditionary force. Across the reed islands and lagoons the noise of the landing-craft's engines would be audible for miles, and the layer of sun-lit haze that covered the water would conceal us from the helicopter.

I needed Noon to sit in the bows beside Sanger and Mr Pal, ready to warn me if we ran into one of Harare's patrols. However, she remained in her den, ensconced in front of her television monitor. All the hours I had spent trying to teach Noon the rudiments of alphabet and speech in an attempt to widen her world had clearly been wasted. The more improbable the picture of Africa, the greater was Noon's fascination. What most held her attention were the clips that Sanger had salvaged from a Hollywood melodrama of the nineteen-forties, which described the adventures of an African warrior queen, and drew Noon's eyes to within six inches of the cathode screen. Chin on fists, she gazed at these glimpses of a female Tarzan, played by a statuesque Texan blonde, hunting on elephant-back, rallying her lions, leading the cowed villagers against a gang of white slave-traders. These hackneyed images seemed to provide Noon with the first dream of herself. I remembered her wading bare-breasted as she hunted for the frogs, and realised whose cues she was heeding.

In the early afternoon, when the heat from the sun seemed to melt the surface of the water, the fumes leaking from the diesel at last forced me to leave the wheelhouse. I shut down the engine and let the ferry coast into a shallow creek between two sand-bars on the western bank of the river.

Exhausted by the effort of holding the helm, I sat down in the shadow of the wheelhouse. We had covered some three miles, but in this vast archipelago of reed-islands there seemed no sense of progress, as if the Mallory had lost itself in its own watery vastness. Barely recognising my body beneath the oil and sores that covered my skin, I listened to the shrieking birds as they hunted the lagoons, and to the feverish murmurs of Mr Pal lying beside Sanger in the bows of the ferry.

Noon, however, seemed to come alive in the heat. I heard her hooting and grunting to herself, supplying the missing soundtrack to her favourite film. She had switched off the monitor, shrewdly conserving the battery for the late afternoon, and well aware that it would soon run down once the diesel's generator was no longer charging it. Oblivious of the heat, she skipped about the deck, riddled out the stove and cast the ashes over the side, watching with a stylised scowl for the few small snakes to rise to the speckled surface. Machete in hand, she leapt into the knee-deep water, and began to hack at the bamboo, as if the saplings were lances borne by an army of opposing pikemen. In her naive way she had modelled her behaviour on the actress she had seen in the film clips, perhaps thinking that these were newsreels of an existing tribe of warrior queens.

Already I was obsessed by Noon, by her slim fingers quick as a card-sharp's, by her scarred instep and the warts on her left knee, like the markers of some erotic encounter to come. I followed her around the deck as she gathered the kindling. Her eyes never left the satchel of cassettes that lay between Sanger's feet, a set of instructional tapes from which she would construct a newer and stronger woman.

Perhaps I could insinuate myself into her mimicry of these film roles, model myself on the behaviour of these lovers of extraordinary women? Noon was the first person whom I had completely shaped, and I was reluctant to surrender her to Sanger. In many ways I was running about at her beck and call, but she still existed only within my duel with the river. The confident and intelligent women whom I had known as a young doctor in London had been too tolerant and too affectionate to seize my imagination, however fond of them I had become. Perhaps, in the future, those unique marriages of memory and desire would only take place within some obsessive and distempered union, like that which existed between myself and this great channel. . . .

"He's dead, Mallory! Mr Pal is dead!"

"Mal! Doc Mal!"

Noon's fist rapped against the wheelhouse, rousing me from this confused reverie. Sanger was calling from the bows of the ferry, arms thrashing about as he struggled with the awning. I went forward and freed him from the guy ropes.

"Let me see him. Stop acting all the time. . . ."

"Doctor, Mr Pal is dead!"

"Dead? You can see him moving."

The botanist was slumped in his chair, head lolling as if his neck had been broken. Rotted by the moisture that poured from his body, the canvas seat had split and he lay on the deck within the wooden frame, surrounded by a pool of sweat and urine.

"Stay with us, Mr Pal." Sanger knelt beside him, shouting into his ear. "We are going back to Port-la-Nouvelle! Dr Mallory will give you medicines!"

Remembering that I had once been a physician, I examined the Indian. No longer conscious, he was expiring inside his inflamed skin, brain cooked by his fever. The enteritis and the ulcerated mucous membranes of his mouth indicated a severe attack of sprue, overlaid by exposure and countless opportunist infections.

"I've nothing — there are no medicines here. Not even a bottle of Scotch."

"You fool. He's a Moslem." Sanger pushed me away, raised the botanist's face between his hands and began to massage his cheeks. "Mallory, listen to me! We leave now. Start your engine and set course for Port-la-Nouvelle."

I tried to move away, but he seized both my wrists and twisted them in his strong hands, as if trying to knot my arms together.

"Turn the ship around! It's a bad dream, Mallory. There is no film now. Look at yourself, man, you're more desperate than Mr Pal!"

He tried to propel me towards the wheelhouse, and then stumbled into the awning. I watched him grapple with the air and sunlight. Noon stepped behind the limousine, gazing without expression at this confrontation between a blind man and his shadow.

Should we turn back? Around the ferry the mist cleared. The harsh, insect-filled light lay over the refuse and vomit on the deck, over the derelict crew of this derelict ship. In a brief moment of lucidity I looked at my reflection in the muddy paintwork of the Mercedes, at my ragged shorts, emaciated body covered with infected bites and exposure sores. Dimly I could remember a lost self, a responsible older brother who had mistakenly sanctioned this absurd journey. I tried to stand back from my own obsession, but I could no longer separate myself from my dream of the Mallory. Was my attempt to scotch the river nothing more than the last instalment of that suicide by easy payments on which I had embarked by first choosing to work at Port-la-Nouvelle? I had killed Miss Matsuoka, and Mr Pal would follow; sooner or later we would all be killed in the coming clash between Harare and Captain Kagwa. Noon would perish before any of us.

"All right, Sanger." I beckoned Noon towards me. "Put Mr Pal in the wheelhouse. Then we'll turn around and go back to Port-la-Nouvelle."

23

Journey Towards the Rain Planet

Smoke pumped from the funnel of the *Salammbo*, diffusing into the deep haze that lay over the lagoons. Somewhere through this amber glare I could see a drifting image of the sun, so close that it seemed suspended from a gantry above our heads. When I engaged the reversing gear the diesel juddered against the walls of the engine pit, shaking the wheelhouse like a rotting cage. Mr Pal's right arm flopped from the bunk onto the deck, and then began to draw the rest of his body towards the floor at my feet.

"Noon — !"

Refusing to cooperate, Noon sat in the driving seat of the Mercedes with her fist against her chin. She flicked at the controls, as if calculating an alternative itinerary.

"Trust me, child. . . ."

One hand on the helm, the other easing forward the throttle, I stepped back across the wheelhouse floor. I pressed my right foot against Mr Pal's chest, forcing the botanist back on to the narrow bunk. His eyes opened and a confused fragment of his endless commentaries came from his lips.

". . . soft waters, made plentiful by a benevolent rainfall . . . clear streams will cool all fevers. . . ."

I ignored him, steering the ferry into the main channel of the river. The eastern shore was barely visible through the haze, lost somewhere among the reed–islands and sand–bars.

Pulled by the propeller, the ferry reversed into the centre of the channel. The current turned the bows towards the south, pointing the *Salammbo* on the long voyage to its home port. The waves clicked and tutted against the hull, as if regretting that its rusting plates and weary timbers lacked the resolve to carry her through the rigours of our quest.

"Doctor! Which way . . .? Tell me our bearing!" Sanger was shouting from the bows, hands raised to catch the confused air streaming around the vessel. For a few seconds he disappeared in a cloud of smoke from the funnel, and then emerged like a magician sprung from a pantomime trap-door.

I shielded my face from the sun, listening for any sounds of Kagwa's helicopter. The wavelets chattered against the hull, dribbling their half-forgotten messages, their whispered secrets which they had carried all the miles from the spring waters of the Mallory.

"Doctor! Our bearing?"

"South . . . we're making our journey towards the rain planet."

We were drifting downstream at two or three knots, the current outrunning the slow thrust of the propeller. I eased the helm to starboard, drawing the ferry stern-first across the channel. Noon looked up from her sullen perusal of the car's instrument panel, staring at me as if she suspected that hunger had made me lose my sense of direction. I avoided her eyes and let the ferry complete its sternward arc. When we lay beam-on to the current, I disengaged the propeller, and wound the helm hard to port. The cutwater of the vessel began to point into the stream, bearing north as the stern swung round and tucked in behind the bows. Re-engaging the propeller, I gradually increased the throttle setting.

We were moving north again, towards the source of the Mallory. Unaware of this simple deception, Sanger leaned back in his deckchair and set his hat at a satisfied rake.

So Sanger's myopia, perhaps aggravated by scurvy, was as total as I had guessed. For how many years had he concealed this, relying for his picture of the external world on the reports brought back to him by his assistants, filming his scientific documentaries that were as fictional as Dürer's rhinoceros . . .?

Noon, meanwhile, had stepped from the Mercedes. Keeping the hull of the limousine between us, she stared at me across the grimy roof, clearly puzzled by this small show of duplicity. I realised that she cared nothing for Mr Pal, and found it hard to grasp why I should bother to trick Sanger into thinking that we were returning to Port-la-Nouvelle.

Yet the deception had served its purpose. I had never intended to abandon the hunt for the Mallory, but this small deceit was a last act of deference to those human and professional debts which I would once have owed to the dying botanist.

I stood against the helm, clasping it to my bare chest, feeling the teak crosspiece cut into my breastbone. The pain bonded me to the *Salammbo*. As I swung the heavy wheel, steering the ferry down the centre of the channel, I happily felt the infected wound on my head, a gaudy plume of hair and blood that I wore like a cockade. I pressed the throttle forward, listening to the smoke beating like a fist inside the funnel.

"Doctor?" Sanger shouted from the bows. "Conserve your fuel. The current will carry us."

"Don't worry, Sanger. We're in good time."

"When will we meet Captain Kagwa? His forces must be close."

"Soon, Sanger. We'll meet him soon."

"We'll transfer ownership of the Mallory."

"Of course, Sanger. We'll call it the Kagwa."

"No, no. It remains the Mallory. How is Mr Pal?"

"He's resting — his dreams are calmer."

"Good. He's dreaming of the Ganges and the Irrawaddy."

Noon had left the Mercedes and stood by the wheelhouse door. She glanced down at Mr Pal, who was lying on the floor beside the bunk, and then turned her attention to me, tapping her teeth like a cashier as she made a rapid inventory of my feverish state.

"Not too good, Noon? You may have to take over from me."

For the first time I noticed the machete in her hand. She was staring in a hard and adult way at the bows of the *Salammbo*. Sanger had left his deckchair and was separating himself from the awning. Eager to check on our progress, he felt his way past the Mercedes, and then climbed hand over hand around his film equipment. His face masked by the sunglasses, he poked among the lights and monitors, nostrils flicking at the passing air for any scent of

Captain Kagwa. As he swung between the silent screens he resembled a blind Quasimodo sniffing his bells.

"Mallory?" His hands scrabbled through the broken windows of the wheelhouse. "Are we on the right course? All these channels, I can hear the grass breathing. You've constructed a maze."

"We'll find our way back. I recognise all the landmarks."

"Good . . . there's a map inside your head. You're feverish, doctor. How is Mr Pal?"

"He's a little calmer. The infection has passed. Some water-borne fever."

"A disease called a river. A dose of Mallory. . . ." He ran a hand across the sores on his face, as if trying to recognise himself. "I blame only myself, doctor — I urged you on. This small eccentricity, how could I know that you would go so far? Now it's all lost. . . ."

"You'll make your film, Sanger."

"No — there's no film . . . everything is finished for me. You must rest yourself. We can sit here and wait for Captain Kagwa."

"We'll move on — I'm stronger now."

"You're a sick man. Even the Captain may forgive you."

Losing his footing, he slumped against the oil drums. Noon stepped out of his way. She stood beside the stove with the machete, splitting the bamboo poles into thin spears. She watched me calmly, as if calculating how many more hours or days I could be relied upon. Then, reluctant to take her eyes from me, she skinned the end of her left thumb.

"Mal . . .!"

I left the helm and pushed the machete aside. I squeezed her thumb, expressing a few drops of blood. As the wound blanched, I could see a splinter of bamboo lodged in the quick. I raised the thumb to my mouth and teased the splinter between my teeth. I sucked the blood from the small lesion, tasting the faint tang of frog and snakeskin, and a stranger, softer flavour of a woman's skin.

Wincing with pain, Noon hopped on one foot, gripping the machete in her free hand. As I sucked each of her fingers I knew that she might split my neck with a single slash of the blade. But she let me touch her, and draw the blood from her thumb as if I was lying

165

at her breast. Would she use her sex to ensure that I sailed on to the source of the river? My hand lay against her cheek. I placed my arm around her shoulders, holding the wheel with one hand as I searched the sun-filled channel for a quiet inlet. There, on the cool banks beside a drowning pool, among the lilies and the tamarinds, we would come together, deep in the drowsy silks of her body.

The soft river airs, the sweetened odours of lagoons, breathed over me as I clung to the helm. And so the fever-boat sailed on among the dreaming fish and the giddy birds. . . .

"Mal!"

The ferry heeled to starboard, its iron rudder scraping an underwater obstacle. The helm spun through my fingers, the spokes beating my hands as if punishing me for falling asleep. Thrown across the deck, Mr Pal lay under the bunk beside the rifle. In the bows Sanger had slipped from his chair, dragging the awning with him. He clung to the forward capstan, clearly fearful that the ferry was about to capsize.

We had struck the remains of a wooden bridge that had once spanned the ancient wadi that now lay in the bed of the Mallory. Crushed by the weight of the ferry, the waterlogged timbers rose briefly above the surface like a group of disturbed crocodiles, and then sank below the foam. I stopped the engine, disconnecting the propeller as the ferry remained motionless in midstream.

Aided by Noon, Sanger leaned against the radiator grille of the Mercedes, right hand fumbling at the headlamps and chromium emblems, his left hand dangling in the water to gauge the direction of the current.

"Your engine, doctor! Start your engine!"

"It's all right, Sanger. We're safe."

"Your engine!"

As the propeller began to turn, pushing the ferry upstream, Sanger plunged his hand into the current. He took off his glasses, blind eyes raised as he offered his cheek to the sun.

So Sanger now knew that we were sailing north. He had tried without success to test the true direction of the *Salammbo*, confused by the relative motion of the river. But the sun's hot light striking his face from the western bank left him in no doubt.

"Mr Pal! Take the helm!"

He stood up and swayed around the limousine with outstretched hands, ready to wrest the wheel from me. When he reached the open deck he tottered near the edge, the spray from the bows soaking his trousers. I swung the helm to port, trying to throw him into the leaping bow-wave, but he dropped to his knees and groped his way past the film equipment. As his hands moved along the metal deck Noon backed away from him, almost inviting him to seize her ankles, the machete swinging between her knees.

"Ignore him, Noon. He won't hurt you. I'll put him ashore."

"Leave the wheel, Mallory. It's over now."

"We're on course, Sanger. The ship's following its compass."

"Turn back!"

Sanger beat his palms against the deck, drumming out all his hatred of these rusting plates. He clutched the wooden pillars of the wheelhouse, trying to throw the entire structure overboard. Across the broken window I could feel his breath panting into my face through caried teeth. His strong hands seized my shoulders. He fumbled at my skin, feeling the grease and sores on my chest, the oily beard on my face, at last convinced that an impostor who could mimic my voice had taken command of the *Salammbo*.

"Who are — ? Dr Mallory?"

I pushed his hands away, and threw him against the oil drums. As I freed myself from his thrashing limbs I heard a familiar concussive noise above the beat of the diesel. An ungainly shadow crabbed across the water. The rotating arms chopped at the air, dappling Noon's frightened face. Looking upwards through the broken roof of the wheelhouse, I saw Captain Kagwa's helicopter, machine-gun in its glass canopy, yellow pontoons like two large gas cylinders. Three hundred feet away, it followed the west bank of the river, then crossed the water and began to circle the lagoons and papyrus islands beyond the eastern shore.

Concealed by the mist, and camouflaged by the dirt and leaves scattered across its decks and cargo, the *Salammbo* had escaped the pilot's notice. I throttled back the engine, and let the craft drift into a patch of deeper haze that lay near a grove of tamarinds along the shore.

The helicopter clattered across the river. Head down, nails tapping a frantic semaphore against her teeth, Noon took refuge in the rear seat of the Mercedes. Sanger had returned to his deck-chair, and sat with a canvas bag across his legs. Among the tape-recorders and aerosols of mosquito repellent he had found a small chromium pistol. He sat stiffly with the weapon raised above his head, like a starting official at a regatta.

As the noise of the helicopter enveloped him, Sanger fired into the air. The brief crack was lost in the thumping blare, but Sanger cocked the slide and raised the pistol through the bedraggled awning. Was this blind man trying to shoot the helicopter down with a hand-bag weapon? Even Noon was watching him curiously from her passenger window.

When he fired a second shot at the helicopter I realised that Sanger was hoping to catch the pilot's eye with the sharp flashes from the gun's barrel. But the helicopter was moving upstream, gaining height as the pilot took care to avoid any possible ground fire from Harare's guerillas. Lit by the afternoon sun, its exhaust trailed behind the craft like the golden brush of an aerial fox.

"Stop the engine, doctor! You're a sick man. . . ."

With the last sounds of the helicopter, Sanger moved forward, hand over hand among the empty fuel drums. Noon sat circum-spectly in the Mercedes, like a princess watching a street-corner brawl from the safety of her limousine.

"Mallory — you will place yourself in Mr Pal's custody. . . ."

I cut the engine, listening to the last shudder of the diesel. The ferry lost way and drifted on the current, rocked by the faint swell, waves clicking against the hull as if waiting their time. Behind me Mr Pal lay below the bunk, babbling a delirious botany to himself.

Sanger had reached the television screens, marooned among the silent pieces of an electronic chessboard. His free hand searched the greasy tubes. I left the wheelhouse and moved to the starboard rail, but he heard my feet on the deck. He pointed the pistol towards me and fired a single shot, sending the small bullet into the door pillar a few feet away.

I crouched by the rail, trying to calm my shaking hands. For a moment Sanger had tricked me. He had needed the silent engine in order to hunt my clumsy footsteps. I waited as he reached the wheelhouse and seized the broken window frame, cutting his hand on the triangles of jagged glass. Blood dripping from his palm, he swayed into the doorway, and fired a third shot into the rocking helm that creaked beside him.

The shadows of the tamarinds lay like bars of camouflage across the open deck. Masking the sounds of my feet, I sidestepped between the fuel drums and backed into the circle of television monitors. Kneeling among the silent screens, I waited for Sanger to lose his way in the wheelhouse and blunder over the ferry's after-peak.

But his sharp ears, their acuity honed by years of myopia, had heard my laboured breath. Before I could move, he had left the wheelhouse. He stepped quickly on his small feet to the cluster of fuel drums, and waited there among the barred shadows.

I backed against the metal cabinets, my feet crushing a dusty cassette. I picked up the plastic sleeve, hoping in a muddled way that one of these absurd films could deflect a bullet so small as to be almost cosmetic.

Hearing me, Sanger lunged forward from the fuel drums. He stood only six feet from me, and behind the cracked sunglasses I could see his emaciated face, covered with insect bites and exposure sores. The small pistol was pointed at the rattling cassette in my hand, as he tried to remember, from whatever evidence, whether I was left- or right-handed.

The deck tipped slightly under our feet, shifting the cargo around us. I steadied myself as the metal cabinets scraped against each other, looking round for some means of escape. I saw that Noon had released and reapplied the handbrake of the Mercedes, pitching the heavy car against its guy ropes.

". . . the river as ecological stereotype, saved by Kagwa's wise administration, has . . ."

Confused by his own voice emerging from the limousine's speaker, Sanger turned his shoulder to me. Before he realised that I was beside him, I raised the cassette and struck the sunglasses from his face. I seized his shoulders in both hands, ran him forward across the deck and pitched him head-first into the water below.

As he drifted across the shadow-filled waves, arms raised in a struggle to remain afloat, Noon turned up the volume of the speaker, drowning his cries in fragments of his own monologue.

Later, when I had fished Sanger from the river with a boat-hook, I went forward and ransacked his canvas bag. Sanger lay on the deck beside the Mercedes, breathing in sudden gasps, his safari suit threaded with water-weed. His pallid face was stained with oil from the propeller shaft, as if his immersion in the Mallory had transformed him into one of those black-skinned natives celebrated in his bogus documentaries.

Noon crowded my elbows while I rooted in the canvas bag. She hopped about, tapping her teeth in relief, snapping her fingers at Sanger and uttering a stream of subvocal epithets. I hoped to find another pistol or, conceivably, a few cartridges that would fit the Lee-Enfield rifle. But among the mosquito creams and vitamin capsules were a half-empty flask of whisky, and a cassette with a label in Mr Pal's handwriting: "Dr Mallory and native girl bathing naked."

I placed the cassette in her hands.

"They misjudged you, Noon. . . ."

"Mal?"

"You've got us all under your thumb. God knows where you're leading me. . . ."

I admired her for the canny and self-contained way in which, despite her fear, she had distracted Sanger, and even for the touch of cruelty she had shown in turning up the volume as he floated helplessly in the river, ducking him in the sounds of his own voice.

I threw the bag at Sanger's oily feet, and looked up into the late afternoon air, listening for Kagwa's helicopter. Too exhausted to continue our voyage, I shut down the engine and moored the ferry

against the western bank. Bands of cerise cloud crossed the sky to
the east as the dusk advanced through the papyrus swamps. The
light was softer, and the saffron air above the river was still warm
and honeyed, but in the shadows of the tamarinds the deck of the
Salammbo seemed suddenly chill. My fever had begun to shake me
again, and a frozen sweat bathed my arms and chest.

I unscrewed the flask and drank a draught of the whisky, gasping
as the spirit stung the sores on my lips and gums. I leaned against
the Mercedes, trying to stiffen my unsteady legs. At my feet I saw
Sanger's broken sunglasses, cracked mirrors reflecting my emaciated body, the crooked captain of a crooked ship. . . .

I bent down to reach the glasses, and fell across the deck, spilling
the whisky on to myself. I held the black frames, and then hurled
them over the rail into the water. I remembered slapping the glasses
from Sanger's face when I should first have knocked the pistol from
his hand — but these opaque sunglasses symbolised that imaginary
vision of the river which Sanger had tried to impose upon my own.

". . . came a crooked camera, cruised a crooked river, caught a
crocodile. . . ."

Mulling over this jingle, I wandered back to the bullet-riddled
wheelhouse. Mr Pal had moved himself across the floor, and now
lay below the helm, his hands gripping the spokes as if trying to
reverse the course of the *Salammbo*.

I bent down, seized his legs and pulled him from the helm. His
hands clutched my ankles, but I kicked them away and began the
task of starting the engine.

Dusk had fallen, twenty minutes later, when the ferry pulled
away from the tamarind grove, and a sepia light lay over the river.
Panels of dark air rose from the surface, as if sections of a dream
were being screened from a sleeping mind. I steered between them;
alcohol and fever guided my hands. The Mallory had spread
outwards, as if making its last attempt to deceive me, dividing itself
into a maze of channels between causeways of papyrus grass that
formed blood-red palisades. The water had ceased to move, and I
reduced the ferry's speed to a walking pace. The shallow bow-
waves moved across a surface of oiled silk. Their gentle motion

soothed Mr Pal as he sank into the deep peace of the hepatic coma, rousing him to a murmured description of the last truth he had glimpsed at the doors of his own death.

". . . environmentally . . . paradise . . . may be seen as an excess of solutions in search of a problem . . . Professor, Nihal, Madhur. . . ."

By evening, as the last ruby light slipped away through the mist, I found that we had entered a large lagoon. I stopped the engine, and let the *Salammbo* drift across a dark mirror that contained no reflections.

Noon was sitting in the Mercedes, too tired to tap her teeth. When I touched her shoulder she looked up at me with surprise, as if no longer remembering who I was. In the faint light reflected from the instrument panel her face was thin and drawn. She seemed to have grown younger, once again a child, and I realised that she was starving.

"Noon . . . Let me sit with you. I'll keep you warm. Tomorrow we'll trap the birds."

I was about to climb into the car, but the far-side passenger door had opened. In the darkness she slipped away from me, her feet limping across the deck as she retreated among the cases of film equipment. Faint with hunger, I swayed against the car. I finished the last of the whisky, and then walked forward, tripping over Sanger's outstretched legs.

Behind me I heard voices across the lagoon. An engine sounded beyond the wheelhouse, as if the diesel had come to life on its own. A small wave tapped the hull plates, and the ferry rocked on the stationary water. I slipped on the oily deck, and tottered backwards into the mast.

A spotlight flared across the water, its harsh glare illuminating the *Salammbo* and its cargo. The beam picked out the chromium triton of the limousine's radiator, and Noon's blanched face as she crouched behind the fuel drums. Shielding my eyes, I saw that another vessel had crept alongside us and had coasted to a halt twenty feet from the starboard rail. Two figures stood below the open bridge, pointing the spotlight into my face.

I pushed myself from the mast and stepped unsteadily across the over-bright deck with its shadows swerving like hallucinations. Were these sudden visitors the members of a film crew who had come to help me in my seduction of Noon?

Then a woman's voice called from the darkness.

"Dr Mallory — you can take Sanger and the river. But we'll take the child."

24

A Dream of Fair Women

I woke into a dream of fair women. I lay across a dusty mattress on an ornate bed whose gilded headpiece rose towards a painted ceiling. Beneath a sky of electric blue a group of nymphs swam around the fountain of a celestial swimming-pool. Their breasts played like porpoises among the waves, and the foam leapt between their welcoming thighs.

The cheap paint flaked from the ceiling, above which I could hear footsteps and a woman's voice calling across the lagoon from the deck of this water-borne brothel. The frogs honked mournfully in reply, as the mosquitoes circled the tiny cabin, dodging the fragments of plaster that each footstep released from the ceiling.

Rested after my long sleep, I lay in this fine rain of the bodies of beautiful women, each like a mature Noon, that fell upon my oil-smeared skin. The wooden shutters were latched across the small window, shielding me from the bright sunlight beyond the iron casement, but through the cracks in the rotting timbers I could see the spears of papyrus grass twenty feet away at the edge of the lagoon.

Gripping the rails behind me, I pulled myself upright. The figurine of a naked dancer topped the brass column, and shed her skin of cheap gilt into my right hand. I wiped the metal flakes on to the mildewed mattress and gazed round the small cubicle, some-where under the restaurant deck in the stern of the *Diana*.

As I opened the shutters, the hot sunlight flooded the cabin, warming my skin. My fever had subsided, and I felt strong but empty-headed, as if part of my brain had been siphoned away during the night by the women whose firm hands had seized me in the wheelhouse of the *Salammbo*.

A sluggish wave crossed the yellow surface of the lagoon, losing itself in the reeds and papyrus grass. For all the intense light, the water seemed inert, as if the Mallory had been infected with the same fever, and was waiting for me to revive before it could flow again. A few rails and coucals called to the air in a half-hearted way, but they too seemed defeated. Even the river, I reflected, was waterlogged.

Leaning through the window, my head against the metal grille, I saw a rubber dinghy approach the starboard gangway. Two of Mrs Warrender's women stood shoulder to shoulder, each pushing on an oar as they rowed across the water. Behind them, in the stern, was a packing-case loaded with film equipment and television monitors. Three hundred yards away, the *Salammbo* sat abandoned in the centre of the lagoon. A slack anchor chain hung from its bows, and the forlorn craft seemed about to sink under the weight of the dusty limousine.

I stood up, steadying myself against the door. Already I felt exhausted, but it was time to collect Noon, borrow the inflatable and make our way back to the ferry. I brushed the flaking tempera from my arms. Above a cracked bidet, stained with all the forgotten pleasures of the Lake Kotto oil-workers, was a mirror smeared with lipstick. I looked at my heavy beard, a ragged but almost messianic bush that sprang forward from the exposure sores on my cheeks. My eyes were flecked with yellow motes and my thinning gums gave my drawn mouth a wolfish smile. I knew that I was still infected with an intermittent fly fever. A posse of armed gendarmerie was after my blood, I was infatuated with a teenage girl, and almost everyone I had recruited to my bizarre cause was either dead or dying. Yet I felt more determined than at any time since leaving Port-la-Nouvelle. I thought of the lunatic events of the previous evening, of Sanger's attempt to kill me. But these had already taken their place in the continuum of strangeness which had enveloped my life since the birth of the Mallory.

I turned the rusty handle of the door, only to find that it had been latched from the companionway.

"For God's sake . . . Mrs Warrender!" I drummed my fist against the tempera breasts above my head, dislodging a plaster nipple that burst on the floor among the empty lipsticks and faded film magazines. The pair of sturdy feet which patrolled the deck now came to a halt. The woman consulted Mrs Warrender, her voice like that of a keeper discussing an uncooperative beast in her charge.

I remembered the *Diana* running alongside the car ferry. One of the African women had stepped through the glaring spotlight. She had leaned into the Mercedes and put her arms around Noon's feverish shoulders, taking the cassette from her like a headmistress putting an end to a dormitory prank. Once Noon and Sanger were safely aboard the *Diana*, the women had come for me as I knelt in the wheelhouse, my mouth pressed to Mr Pal's, trying to breathe life into his lungs. Their strong hands had seized my arms, hustled me through the chairs and tables of the restaurant deck, and then bundled me down a companionway into the airless cabin with its reek of stale scent and damp plaster.

"Mrs Warrender — !"

I was about to burst the rotting door from its hinges, but a hand turned the latch. In the corridor stood Fanny, the oldest of the African women, the broad-shouldered bouncer and bar-keep at the oil-riggers' saloon. She gazed imposingly at me, as if I were an unruly customer who had failed to pay his bill.

"You can go on the deck. Your time for fresh air."

"Thank God for that . . . now, where is Noon?"

"The child? She is resting. With Professor Sanger — you leave them now."

"Listen to me — I want to see them. They need my help."

"Your help? No thank you, doctor. No more strange medicine from Dr Mal."

Unsure what to answer, I followed her large and purposeful buttocks up the companionway. Although a handsome woman, whom I had often admired from the windows of the clinic at Port-la-Nouvelle, she now belonged to another, remote order of womanhood.

We stepped on to the open deck, and the sunlight soon shortened the focus of my eyes. The ancient timbers of the *Diana* had been scrubbed to a lime-like whiteness. The blanched planks formed a marquetry of bones, as if the skeletons of all the oil-riggers who had lain in the cubicles below the restaurant had been placed side by side, a brothel-ship built from the ribs and skulls of its patrons. The once derelict barge had been transformed by Nora Warrender and her companions. Every inch of ornamental paintwork had been scraped and scoured, the grime from its hundreds of decorative scrolls reamed out like dirt from all the ears in a boys' reformatory. The *Diana* gleamed like old ivory, emitting an eerie sepulchral light, as if the vessel were a funeral galley being prepared for a water-borne cremation. Above the dance floor the women had roped a canvas awning between the funnel housing and the wooden roof of the restaurant, and even this canopy had the look of a flayed human skin stretched out to dry, its balls and tassels forming a frieze of pizzles and scrota.

At the edge of the dance floor, shielded by the awning, stood a group of animal cages that I had last seen in the breeding station at Port-la-Nouvelle. A pair of macaques and several marmosets clambered across the bars, intrigued to see me and obviously eager to welcome a sympathetic spirit to their disciplined realm.

The two women, Louise and Poupée, who had rowed the inflatable from the *Salammbo*, now moored alongside, and began to lift the electrical units on to the deck. I stepped forward, about to offer my help, but Fanny pushed me away, huffing at the very idea of my assistance, as if more than my token presence on this ship of bones was an intrusion.

Under the awning in the stern of the *Diana* sat a fourth young woman, recruited since my departure from Port-la-Nouvelle. On the table beside her stood a collection of ornamental lanterns, whose casements of coloured glass she buffed with a leather cloth. Was this female self-support group planning to reopen the *Diana* for business? Curious about this brisk housekeeping in the old brothel-boat, I crossed the dance-floor to the semicircular bar behind the funnel. Through an open hatchway I could see into the engine-room, where the elderly gasoline engine had been restored and polished like the most proudly owned kitchen appliance.

Could I commandeer the ship? Peering into the small bridge-house I had a sudden image of myself at the trimly centred wheel, captain of an all-woman crew. I stepped forward to the bridge-house, about to test the pliant wheel, but Fanny caught my arm.

"Doctor, you stay on the dance-floor. Or you go below."

"Dance-floor? Look here . . .!" I tried to free my elbow from her strong grip, slipped and fell to the deck at her feet. She pushed my head away with her heavy thigh and then lifted me on to my shaky knees. Steadying myself against her muscular arms, I looked down at my gasping chest that pumped like a leaking ventilator at the humid air. Far from being able to commandeer their vessel, I was at these women's mercy.

"Where you belong, Dr Mal!"

"On the dance-floor? Right . . . what's happened to Mrs War-render?"

"She's here . . . out hunting. She wants to talk to you later."

"Good. But first I ought to see Sanger and Noon."

"The child? Well. . . ." Fanny turned towards Louise and Poupée, who were dusting the screens of the television sets. I saw no recognition in the young widows' eyes that I existed, but Fanny gestured me to the companionway. "You can see the child and Professor Sanger. Just for a few minutes. I don't want you making them sick, doctor."

It was only then, as I carried out my brief examination of Sanger and Noon, that I realised once again to what physical extreme we had been carried by our voyage in the *Salammbo*. Sanger lay on the semen-stained mattress in the cubicle beyond my own, a pair of woman's sunglasses clasped in both hands, eyes fixed on the naked figures who swam across the unseen electric sky above his head. Resting there in his ragged clothes, he resembled an elderly vagrant who had returned to the abandoned nightclub where he had spent the dreams of his youth. His irregular heartbeat, the rash of impetigo that covered his chest, and the wasted arms and legs jutting like poles from the torso of a scarecrow, together reminded me how much I had neglected both him and Mr Pal.

"Mallory. . . ." He pressed the diamanté frame of the sunglasses into my shoulder, a kindly gift from Nora Warrender. "It was all nonsense. Madness on that mad ship. We'll go back to Lake Kotto?"

"Yes, we'll go back."

"And Mr Pal?"

"He's already left. You'll join him soon, Sanger."

"Good . . . I miss Mr Pal. . . ."

I unpicked his fingers from my hand. His fever had abated, but I felt unable to do anything for him, because I had ceased to think and act as a physician. During the voyage of the *Salammbo* we had moved into a realm where sickness and obsession, health and sanity had ceased to be opposites.

Even when I saw Noon, lying like an undernourished child with her bony forehead hidden by a small pillow, I could only think of her as the young woman she had become during our voyage from Port-la-Nouvelle. I held her stick-like wrist, searching for the uncertain pulse, trying to will her back to the car-ferry abandoned in the centre of the lagoon. I needed to feel again the spring of the *Salammbo's* decks beneath my heels, to see Noon in the bows swaying her adolescent thighs as she steered me between the sand-bars whose submerged forms, touched by the keel of the ferry, stirred my half-conscious dream of caressing them.

However, those dreams had reduced this once beautiful child to little more than a skeleton. As I wavered, my confidence ebbing in myself and our eccentric voyage, I became aware that Noon was watching me with her sharp eyes, the patient assessing the physician. She counted the sores on my face and arms, estimated the strength that remained in my chest and shoulders. I realised that she was asking herself if I was well enough to go on.

"Doctor . . . time for your cabin. You must rest your mind."

Fanny stood at the foot of the companionway, calling me from Noon's cubicle. She returned to the deck when I closed the door behind me. I stood in the narrow corridor, with its musty planks smelling of coffin-wood, wondering how I could smuggle Noon from the vessel. Across the windows of the cubicles were the same metal grilles, placed there to prevent any paying customers from taking a short cut to their pleasures. Even if I could kick the rusty frames from the rotting timbers neither Noon nor I were strong enough to swim to the *Salammbo*.

Exhausted by the heat, and by the patient industry of the women above my head, I leaned against a padlocked door behind me. The latch jumped from its socket, pulling the hasp from the spongy wood. The chain and padlock fell to the deck, and the door opened on to another cubicle.

Under the same gaudy fresco lay another grimy mattress. I was about to lie on it, but the bed was already occupied. Barrels pointing towards the window, an armoury of weapons lay side by side — three French and American carbines, several Kalashnikov automatic rifles, and Noon's ancient Lee-Enfield. All had been carefully cleaned, their bolts and firing pins wrapped in oily rags to protect them from the humid air. Beside the rifles lay an assortment of ammunition clips and loose cartridges, and pieces of canvas webbing of a type worn by Captain Kagwa's soldiers and by Harare's guerillas. Shoulder harnesses, ammunition belts, grenade pouches hung from the brass rails like so many trophies.

I stared down at this substantial arsenal, wondering how the women had amassed these weapons. None had been exposed to the damp soil or air of the river valley. I picked up the Lee-Enfield, my arms barely strong enough to raise the heavy stock, and un-wrapped the rags around its breech. I guessed that the women had strayed into a former battleground during their journey from Lake Kotto.

As I worked the bolt, hoping to find a cartridge in the breech, the door opened behind me. Mrs Warrender stood with the padlock and chain in her hands. She was still dressed in the bath-robe she had worn at Port-la-Nouvelle, as if she had spent the intervening months idling about her dressing-table, and was waiting for me to join her in a nearby cabin. She had cut short her hair, almost to the shaven scalp of a concentration camp victim, exposing the pallor of her face and neck, that eerie whiteness of the *Diana*. It occurred to me that she too might be a prisoner.

"Nora — are they holding you here? We can leave on the *Salammbo*. . . ."

She smiled at me, the same wan flicker of her pale lips that I had last seen in my trailer, when I had failed to rouse her. I heard the chain run through her hands.

"You're tired, doctor — you've come a long way, and it's time for you to rest."

"Nora. . . ."

I held the rifle across my chest, pressing the bolt against the sores on my breastbone in order to wake myself. Mrs Warrender was watching me in her composed way, as if I were a figment of a dream of men from which she had at last woken and was able to remember only by an effort of will. I knew now that it was myself who was these women's prisoner, and that if I was to escape, let alone commandeer the vessel, this would be my only chance.

"Let me help you. . . ." Mrs Warrender reached out and held the foresight in her small but strong hand. I was about to wrestle the rifle from her when I saw her two companions through the window grille. They stood side by side in the inflatable, rowing towards the *Diana* from the car-ferry. Behind them, in the stern of the dinghy, reclined a small man with an olive face, one arm trailing in the flat water as if he were feeling the direction of the current.

"Nora — it's Mr Pal. He must have recovered. . . ."

Before she could close the door, I pushed past into the corridor. I heard her feet behind me as I climbed the companionway.

"Dr Mallory . . . it's your rest time, doctor."

I stood in the centre of the dance-floor, on the planks of hot bone that stung my feet, under the awning of flayed skin. I held the unloaded rifle to my chest, and watched the dinghy approach. Across the pus-like surface of the lagoon the trailing hand of the botanist drew a long palm line that returned to the *Salammbo*.

Already I could see that Mr Pal was dead, and that the two oarswomen were about to bury him. They rowed towards the bows of the *Diana*, as Mrs Warrender and Fanny stood beside me. The sun's reflection lay on the water behind them, and the intense light pressed against their backs and the top of Mr Pal's head, as if they were returning from the future with the body of the last man, removing the remains of an extinct species from their world and taking it back for burial in the past.

25

The Wildfowlers

Later, while the women settled Mr Pal into the papyrus grass on the western bank of the lagoon, I sat with Mrs Warrender among the salvaged lanterns.

"I'll want to leave soon," I told her as she polished the cheap glass. "An hour after sunset, if I can start the engine."

"Is that wise?"

"Yes — Kagwa's forces may be here tomorrow. I advise you to leave, Nora. Harare's men are all over the place."

"We've seen one or two of them. They haven't given us any trouble."

"That surprises me. All the rifles and webbing — where did you find them?"

"On the way from Port-la-Nouvelle." She stared at the burial party at work in the long grass. "They . . . weren't needed any more. I think you should rest here. Perhaps we can find someone to take you back to Lake Kotto."

"No — I have to head up-river. I'll take Noon with me."

"She can't possibly travel. Besides, are you safe with her?"

"She's the only person with whom I am safe. But for Noon I'd never have come so far. She knows the river like . . . the inside of a dream."

"She's tricking you, doctor. She'll stay with us. You've already killed two people — left to yourself, you'll kill several more."

I ignored this, and watched the two women who had buried Mr Pal walking through the papyrus grass to their rubber dinghy. After a few steps they ducked down, hearing something in the maze of waterways. In the cages beside the dance floor the macaques were picking at the bars in an agitated way. I stood at the rail and listened for any sounds of Kagwa's helicopter, but the source of the noise seemed nearer to hand. As one of the women parted the papyrus grass the other raised her rifle. After a pause they stepped into the dinghy and rowed themselves towards the mouth of a narrow channel between the walls of grass. Behind them they left eddies of rotting vegetation. Already the water in the lagoon was becoming stagnant.

I pointed to the milky surface, and to the dead weeds that cloaked the stern anchor.

"Has the Mallory stopped flowing?"

"The Mallory?" Mrs Warrender repeated the name, as if it described some obscure disease. "Do you mean the river?"

"My river."

"The river you've named after yourself, and which you want to destroy."

"It attacked my dry wells . . . in fact, I want to find its source. It's a private matter between myself and the Mallory. Sanger understands that."

"A private matter? This river can irrigate the Southern Sahara, and create a nature reserve ten times larger than the Serengeti. How can you claim that it belongs to you?"

"Because I created it. In a real sense, I am the Mallory."

Humouring me, she buffed her lantern. "You are the river? The dead snakes and the mud and the rotting fish?"

"All those — and its dream of life."

"And when you reach its source?"

"That depends on what I find."

"Perhaps you'll drown yourself there?"

"Drown myself? So the entire voyage is a suicide attempt? There must be more than that. I don't know. . . ."

"Perhaps Noon knows?"

Before I could reply, the sound of a rifle shot reached the *Diana*, its report muffled by the dense papyrus grass. Mrs Warrender's pale face swayed among her lanterns. She picked at her lips, watching the creek into which the two women had rowed the dinghy. Behind me Fanny stood by the rail of the dance floor, eyes searching the walls of grass. She and Nora shared the same nervous but expectant look, as if a prize turkey was about to be brought home for the pot. I resented the idea that they should shoot the birds, those creatures who drank from the body of the river, from the waterway that had once flowed from my own bloodstream. Even Noon and I, however hungry, had not eaten the birds.

"Harare's patrols will hear you," I warned Mrs Warrender. "There are stragglers all over these lagoons. I'll captain the *Diana* for you."

"Captain . . .? The *Diana* has no captain. We take turns here, doctor. The sort of cooperation that rouses all your suspicions. . . ."

"You'll rouse Harare's suspicions. What are you doing this far from Lake Kotto?"

"Like you, we're looking for the source of the . . . Mallory. A great river like this draws men to it."

She stared at the yellowing waters. Had she worn the shabby bath-robe during her rape by Harare's men? Like her cropped hair, it was meant to serve as a constant reminder, as harsh as a police photograph, of the crime committed against herself.

"Nora, I understand. . . you want to revenge yourself on Harare."

"Not only Harare." She polished her lantern. "There's talk of a barrage, of a wall of water held back by some kind of restraint."

"A barrage?" I rejected the idea, unable even to consider it. "There can't be a barrage."

"Why not?"

"It would be like applying a tourniquet — to my own arm. It would become gangrenous."

"So you really are the river?"

"Of course. I'm sure of it now."

She put away the lanterns, regarding me with a first show of sympathy.

"You're clearly quite mad."

★

For six days I remained a prisoner on board the widows' ship, locked into my cabin under the bordello ceiling. More undernourished than I had realised, I lay for hours on the mildewed mattress. Each evening my fever returned, as I listened to the roaring of the frogs in the dusk. By morning I would be too tired to do more than sit in a restaurant chair at the edge of the dance floor. In the afternoon the women would allow me to feed the animals in their cages, but I was still too weary even to think of seizing control of the *Diana*.

Noon and Sanger lay in their cubicles. They and I seemed overcome by a deepening lassitude, as if we were affected by my failure of will, a weakening of the imaginative force which had created the Mallory.

Talking to the macaques, I wondered why the five women chose to remain in this stagnant lagoon, away from the main channel of the river. For all the apparent amity of their new order, their greatest pleasure clearly came from the hunt. Every afternoon I was forced to listen to the unpleasant sounds of their wildfowling. Two of them would go off in the rubber dinghy, standing shoulder to shoulder with a rifle in the stern, and disappear through the papyrus grass into the hundreds of creeks that connected the lagoons. An hour later, I would be woken from my fever by a single shot that marked the end of another marsh bird.

However, they never brought their prey back to the *Diana*. In my fever I guessed that they hated the birds because they drank from the waters of the Mallory. To the macaques I confided: "They're shooting the birds again . . . they're still trying to clip my wings. . . ."

Nonetheless, I was determined to resume my voyage. Watched by Fanny or Louise, I was allowed to see Noon for a few minutes each day, as she gazed at her nightclub sky. I counted her stronger pulse, and noted her clearer eyes and healing gums, again aware that it was she who was assessing me. She watched me as I felt her liver and tapped her chest, clearly measuring my recovery by the degree to which she excited me.

Realising this, the women kept Noon from me during the few hours when she was allowed on deck. She was penned behind the galley door, kneading the sorghum cakes and picking the snails from their shells for our evening meal.

On the sixth afternoon, the first to leave me free of fever, I was feeding the macaques when the muffled report of a rifle shot sounded from the papyrus-islands to the west of the lagoon. Somewhere in the maze of waterways a flicker of movement crossed the palisades of grass, as if a wounded bird was skittering through the tall blades.

I climbed from the starboard rail on to the marmosets' cage and from there stepped out on to the roof of the restaurant. Around me the endless steaming creeks of this riverine world lay under the sun. Through the yellow haze I could see the distant channel of the Mallory half a mile to the east, the mist like vapour over a tepid vat. Not a single wave or swell crossed the surface, as opaque as amber wax. The immense volume of water was now stationary, the river waiting for me to act. The turning of some kind of inner tide was about to take place, reflecting a choice being made within my mind.

A quarter of a mile to the west, beyond the bank of the lagoon, a line of reeds had collapsed into the water and exposed a section of the levee. Along this narrow causeway a man came running, his head bowed as he tried to hide himself from his pursuers. He carried a fishing spear in one hand, and a rifle slung across his back. Whenever he ducked, the rifle stock rose above his head like the tail of a wounded bird.

Unaware of the *Diana*, the soldier drew nearer. His ragged uniform and webbing were tied together with string, and I recognised one of Harare's guerillas. Perhaps he had defected, hoping to return to his village, or was the last survivor of a unit attacked from the air by Captain Kagwa's helicopter. Although I had identified him, in some confused way I believed that he was bringing a message to me from the source of the Mallory, telling me what I should do to restart the silent river.

Without thinking, I lifted my arms above my shoulders and began to wave. Seeing me, and my empty hands against the sky, the soldier stopped and raised his head. He parted the grass, and was peering cautiously at the superstructure of the *Diana* when a second shot rang out.

The report echoed across the lagoon, taking with it the life of this starving soldier. When I raised my eyes I could see that nothing now moved along the causeway. The wildfowlers had secured their prey and would deal with him at their leisure.

An hour later Mrs Warrender and Poupée emerged from the creek. They had been sweating in the heat, but their faces were composed and emptied of emotion. Standing side by side, they pushed on their oars as the tall reeds opened and fell back around their shoulders.

With Louise and the younger woman, I watched from the rail as they docked the dinghy beside the gangway. In its stern were the rifle and tattered webbing, and a spade whose polished blade shone in the sunlight like a sword.

I climbed down from the cages and stood on the floor in front of Mrs Warrender, like a shy suitor about to ask her for a dance.

"Good hunting, Nora?"

"Not too good, doctor." She drew the dressing-gown around her shoulders in a brusque and rigid movement, reminding me of her eerie calm in the months after her husband's death. "We were unlucky today."

"I didn't know there was anything to shoot at around here."

"There isn't very much. But if you wait something usually comes along."

"I can see you found another rifle."

"There was a dead soldier on the embankment. Only a few hundred yards from here."

"Poor fellow. He was probably going home to his village. Perhaps I could have helped him?"

"No — he was quite dead."

"Too bad. Anyway, you'll find better use for his rifle."

"I think we will. We buried him under the bank. Your river will bathe his bones, doctor."

"Have you buried many dead soldiers here?"

"Not very many. Though we do seem to find one nearly every day."

"I'd noticed that — so many rifles, and so much ammunition."

"And so many dead soldiers to bury. Perhaps you could help us, doctor. There's another dead man who needs to be buried. . . ."

"Well. . . ." I followed her eye to the dinghy. As it drifted from the gangway on its mooring line I noticed that the spade was still lying in the stern. A crescent of damp earth lay against the bright steel like the first instalment of another grave.

Mrs Warrender had picked up her rifle, and was smiling at me in an open and full-lipped way for the first time since I had known her. Despite the shabby robe and her cropped hair, she looked as happy as she must have done on her wedding day. I hesitated in the centre of the dance floor, aware that the women had formed a circle around me. Fanny had left the galley and leaned forward with her elbows on the bar, watching me with a not unsympathetic gaze. Only Noon, who had appeared behind the galley door, stared at me with an expression of anger, eyebrows knitted together in warning.

"We'll go, doctor." Mrs Warrender placed her hand on my arm, and I noticed the metal polish under her chipped nails, like those of a tired housewife. "That body should be buried."

"Digging a grave . . . I'm not strong enough."

"You are, doctor. A shallow grave. Come now. . . ."

"Well, perhaps a shallow one . . . my hands are — "

Preparing my palms for the labour to come, I rubbed them against my hips. An open wound stung against my hand. Looking down, I realised for the first time that I was naked. After carrying me aboard the *Diana*, the women had stripped me of the pus-stained rags that I had worn on the ferry. During the previous days it had never once occurred to me that I was naked, even in the presence of these women. By refusing to see me as a man, they had effectively castrated me.

Trying to rally myself, I looked past the circle of women at the lagoon beyond, at the silent walls of grass. Death hid among the tall palisades, gateways into a labyrinth that ended at the door of a grave. The sunlight pressed upon the stagnant water, preventing it from coming to my help. From the deck of the dance floor rose an intense white light, like the glare from a lamp filled with lime. It blanched the coloured glass of the lanterns behind me, and turned the exposed engine of the *Diana* into a calcified skeleton. I massaged my diaphragm, forcing the blood into my head, but the light intensified, and seemed to dress these women in their shrouds, as if they were mourners who had arrived early at a funeral. All the anger of these women irradiated this ancient vessel, infecting the bones of its decks and timbers, which now gave off a withering light of their own.

A lantern fell to the deck among the restaurant tables. Startled by the breaking glass, the women looked down at the ruby fragments, whose cheap vitreous glimmer seemed to break a spell. The deck shifted below their feet, as if the bed of the lagoon was stirring through the surface.

"Fanny . . . Louise . . .! We've slipped the anchor!" Confused, Mrs Warrender gripped the bar counter in both hands, trying to steady the *Diana*. The chairs and tables were beginning to slide across the white planks. The lanterns rattled, and a second fell on to the deck. In their cages the macaques and marmosets chittered in alarm, scrambling frantically across their bars.

"Fanny, we're sinking! Poupée!"

The rifle propped against the bar toppled across Mrs Warrender's feet. A deep judder ran through the ship, and its ancient keel let out a reedy cry, the bones of a corpse racked in torment.

I looked out at the lagoon, waiting for its waters to wash across the deck. The grass towered above us on all sides, exposing the darker roots in the glistening mud of the embankment. Far from engulfing us, the surface of the lagoon had fallen. The *Diana* was now stranded on the floor, its antique hull no longer supported by its own buoyancy. Already the first sand-bars had broken through the surface, and I could see the submerged banks of the deeper channel down which Mrs Warrender and the women had steered the *Salammbo* into the centre of the lagoon before abandoning her.

I walked through the sliding tables, pushing them out of my way as I climbed the slight gradient to the port rail. Behind me, Mrs Warrender was leading her rescue of the *Diana*. Still under the impression that the vessel was sinking, she and her companions were trying to tether the craft to the bank.

I listened to them shouting to each other, a party of confused sea-wives no longer trusting their own feet. The surface of the lagoon had fallen by little more than eighteen inches. Somewhere in the maze of waterways a containment wall had given way, a silt embankment had dissolved and allowed the levels within the system to balance themselves.

Nonetheless, this meant that the Mallory was falling. The great flow of water which I had summoned from its mysterious source had at last begun to falter, as if anticipating my death at these women's hands.

"Doc Mal. . . ."

Noon stood behind me, the Lee-Enfield in her small hands, hidden from the women by the animal cages. I remembered her first prodding me on to the beach of the drained lake at Port-la-Nouvelle. She was looking at me in the same determined but wary way. I remembered, too, the snap of the bolt within the breech. Had she been given another bullet by Mrs Warrender?

She raised the heavy rifle and aimed the barrel towards the *Salammbo*, jerking her head as if puzzled by my slow response.

"Right, Noon. . . ." I took her arm and lifted her to the rail. Below us the water was little more than knee-deep. I could hear Mrs Warrender beyond the starboard rail, reassuring Sanger as he bleated in alarm from the window grille of his cabin.

I placed my hands around Noon's waist, smelling the strong odour of her adolescent body that I had missed for so many days. Revived by her, I remembered Mrs Warrender's idle talk of a barrage. Perhaps a dam had been built, trapping the stream, and the Mallory itself had not failed. . . .

I lifted Noon over the side and lowered her into the water, then handed the rifle down to her. I followed her into the warm yellow liquid, and pointed to the ripples already running from our bodies towards the *Salammbo*.

"Come on, Noon. We'll get there before Mrs Warrender. Someone is trying to steal my river. . . ."

26

The Gardens of the Sahara

Change had overtaken the river, bringing with it the threat of unforeseen dangers. For the first time my footprints remained in the soft sand of the river-bed, giving me away to any sentry or sniper. As I hid behind the trunk of a fallen palm tree, searching for the signs of a guerilla patrol, the imprints of my feet emerged clearly from the shallow water, following the shadow that scuttled between my heels like a thirsty bat. The Mallory had fallen by at least my own height, revealing the roots of the trees along the shore. Baked by the sun, the exposed river-bed had begun to revert to desert.

Fifty yards to my right was the main channel of the Mallory, now little more than half its original width. The sand-bars lay like dunes in the open sun, the first couch grass growing from their crests. A warren of small pools and inlets separated the river from its former banks, and in one of these the *Salammbo* was now moored, with Noon at watch from the wheelhouse roof.

The detached enamel door of an old refrigerator jutted from the sand, its manufacturer's medallion gleaming like a chromium cipher in the sunlight. The exposed bed of the Mallory was covered with debris washed downstream from the former French airbase at Bonneville — old tyres, pieces of beach furniture, ammunition boxes and radio spare parts. A few minutes earlier, as I waded ashore, past an aerosol can and a plastic hair-dryer, I had cut my right heel on the broken neck of a wine bottle lying in the shallows.

Limping across the white sand, I left the scanty cover of the palm tree and ran towards the hulk of a small saloon car embedded in the soft slope. Resting against the fender, I listened to the steady rumble of a truck moving along a desert road, and watched the smoke of driftwood fires beyond the palm-covered shoulder of the next river bend. Scores of the white plumes rose into the air, and confirmed that Noon and I had at last reached the centre of Harare's domain.

However, in the week since our escape from Mrs Warrender and her widows, we had seen only a single armed river-patrol, as if some shift in strategic priorities had moved the centre of conflict away from the Mallory to the surrounding arid scrub. The fishing rafts and trading canoes which we passed had all been abandoned, lying against the exposed stilts of disused landing stages. The small migrant population drawn to the upper reaches of the river in the four months since our departure from Port-la-Nouvelle had mysteriously lost interest in this benign channel. We sailed between the raised banks, now higher than the *Salammbo's* wheelhouse, and lined with forgotten windmills and water-hoists, as if the people who had once fished and bathed here had sensed in advance that the river was about to die.

Nonetheless, I regarded the Mallory with caution. Perhaps it was preparing the ultimate trap for me, destroying itself so that Noon and I would perish of thirst. But fortunately the river was still a substantial waterway, a hundred yards wide even in its shrunken form. The current pressing against the bows of the ferry showed no signs of flagging, and there was nothing stagnant or brackish in the clear, cold liquid that flowed from the mountains of the Massif, whose blue flanks were now only five miles to the north-east. For all my determination to reach the source of the river, I was glad to see that my great rival was still in good heart.

Noon, too, was as determined as ever. At first she had seemed distanced from me, and I regretted the absence of those television images that had so intrigued her earlier in our voyage. Their simplistic fictions would have helped to sustain both of us. But within hours of our escape from the *Diana* we were working together, the eccentric team that had propelled the ferry all the way from Lake Kotto. As we swam the last yards to the vessel, followed by a single shot from the tilting dance floor of the *Diana*, Noon again became the young woman I had courted from the helm of the *Salammbo*. Her pale body seemed to draw strength from the leprous yellow water. Ten feet ahead of me, she lifted herself easily on to the car-deck, the slim breasts and shoulders of a child transformed into a woman's. She took the rifle from my hands and hauled me on to the deck with a workmanlike grunt. As she guided me into the wheelhouse I felt the *Salammbo* sway under our weight, and knew that there were still a few feet of clear water below its keel.

Staying within the deeper channel, whose submerged banks we could see beneath the shallow water, we sailed through the inlet which had first admitted us to the lagoon. An hour later, after threading our way among the creeks and waterways, we at last reached the main channel of the Mallory. The warm air rushed to greet us, its soft breath whispering like a lover upon my naked skin.

Within a day we left behind the marshes and lagoons, and began to cross an area of desert savanna. Free of its cargo of film equipment, and with only the mud-spattered Mercedes amidships, the *Salammbo* made strong progress against the modest current. Our only fuel consisted of the few gallons which the women had failed to syphon from the tank — enough, I calculated, for another twenty miles. Yet the falling level of the river, and some scent in the wind, convinced me that this would take us to our goal.

As if aware of this, Noon squatted on the wheelhouse roof, keeping watch on the passing banks, and on the pursuing *Diana*. At times I would hear her teeth clicking as she pointed to the coils of black smoke, like the circlets of a wreath, visible beyond the dusty scrub. In the evening, when we moored for the night and Noon swam for fish in the dark pools, I would climb on to the wheelhouse and see the widows' white ship three miles behind us, a spectre of bone in the dusk.

But I was no longer afraid of them. The water-world of swamps and papyrus screens, their hunting-ground of lost soldiers, memories and murder, had given way to the clearly defined channel ahead, and the sharp sand cliffs which the Mallory had cut through the dry ochre soil. We were crossing the southern edges of the Sahara, and the desolate terrain seemed barely aware of the river. Stronger after my rest in the *Diana*, I steered the *Salammbo* towards its final berth.

The harsh beat of an outboard motor drummed against the rusty door panels of the car. I crouched in the back seat, and watched the guerilla patrol-craft push tentatively around the river bend. Two canoes lashed side by side to bamboo poles, it carried a crew of three soldiers. Armed men haunted the region. But these soldiers had lost interest in the drained river, and were watching the banks twenty feet above my head.

After a wary inspection, they turned back and moved upstream, soon lost among the sand-bars and rock spits. I left the car and crossed the sloping flank of white sand that reached to the exposed roots of the fan-palms along the bank. Hand over hand, I climbed the ladders of entwined roots. Already their brittle leaves were streaked with serrated yellow fibre that rasped against my arms. An overgrown path ran from an abandoned water-hoist and wound its way to the crest of a small rise.

I lay in the mossy saddle between two outcrops of rock that formed its summit, my face shielded by the fronds of a tamarind. In the distance, through a haze of sun-lit dust, the broad channel of the Mallory wound its way towards me from the blue mountains of the Massif. It flowed in a westerly course, skirting the great plain of the desert that extended to the horizon. This featureless landscape of scrub and creosote bushes was broken only by the fading runways of the former French airbase at Bonneville that lay a mile to the north.

At the edge of the plateau, the Mallory reached a series of shallow cascades, broad steps of basaltic rock that marked the navigable limits of the river. The eastern arm flowed into a calm pool some three hundred yards in width, and then emptied into the main channel where the *Salammbo* was now moored. However, the western arm, carrying half the abundant headwater, ended at a makeshift barrage which the local fishermen had thrown from the central island to the bank a hundred feet away.

After driving a line of bamboo piles into the sandy floor, they had stretched their nets across the stream to form a retaining curtain, and then filled this with logs, palm fronds, and metal debris taken from the ruined hangars and barrack-rooms of the air-base. This sling of timber and rotting vegetation contained a mass of trapped silt filtered from the flowing water. Embedded in the wall were sections of galvanised iron, metal doors and panels, lengths of radio antenna and telegraph poles. As it bulged forwards, the rope and earth barrage resembled a gigantic brassiere, whose enclosed breasts of caking silt were decorated with a lost treasure of western technology.

Water streamed through a hundred fissures in the garbage dam, spurting downwards to join the open pool, where scores of fishing craft, skiffs and rafts were moored to makeshift jetties along the beach. Diverted by the barrage, the stolen channel of the river had been turned northwards by the fishermen, and flowed out across the desert through a network of canals and creeks, finally forming a shallow pond that stretched towards the ruined hangars of the airfield.

I gazed down at this green coast, with its tracts of manioc and sorghum. I remembered my first sight of the lower Nile from the aircraft carrying me to Cairo, and its narrow bands of cultivated land lying between the river and the desert. Thanks to the theft of the Mallory, the Sahara had begun to bloom again. The nomadic farmers and herders who for decades had been driven southwards by the sun had at last begun to turn back the green line. Helped by the fishermen and by Harare's soldiers, several of whom were washing in the shallow waters of the pool, they had recolonised the desert. Despite the modest success of their strip farms and small allotments, they had turned their backs forever on the lower reaches of the Mallory.

But the river still flowed. I traced the winding course of the channel across the blue landscape of the plateau, its silver back striking sparks against the rocky outcrops. Somewhere in the dark hills lay its source — we would sail the ferry into the harbour below the barrage, beach it there and press on up the Mallory in one of

the many canoes moored in the pool. I looked up at the wooded
face of the mountains, whose lower slopes ran down to the eastern
bank of the river. The abandoned conveyors of a French mining
company ran up the hillside to the silent lift towers, standing
among the trees like signal pylons.

Still struck by the beauty of the greening desert, I made my way
back to the river. I lowered myself through the web of roots and
jumped on to the sandy bed. I followed my heel prints, in which
flies now sipped at my drying blood, past the aerosol can and the
hair-dryer, lying in the sand like objects displayed in a museum of
consumer archaeology. As I strode into the cool stream I could see
the bows of the *Salammbo* in its quiet inlet between the sand-bars. I
waded into the deep water and swam towards the vessel, waving to
Noon when I paused for breath by the anchor chain.

"Noon! The Mallory — it's still there!"

She leaned on the rail, and rewarded me with a brief smile, as if
tolerant of my strange doubts in the river and myself.

However, when I gripped the rear bumper of the Mercedes and
lifted myself on to the deck I noticed that Noon was wearing her
camouflage jacket. She carried the Lee-Enfield in her strong hands,
shoulders squared as she pointed the rifle at me. In her stance was a
memory of Sanger's warrior queen.

Behind her, two of Harare's soldiers were examining the
controls of the limousine. Their boots and trousers were soaked
with the wet sand of the narrow beach behind the ferry. Raising
their weapons, they stepped into the sun and beckoned me against
the mud-caked car. They stared at me with evident surprise,
confused by my naked and bearded figure, by my scarred thighs
and oil-smeared chest, and by the bloody heel marks on the deck.

"Noon . . .?" I waited for her to explain to the soldiers that this
wild man of the Mallory was once the physician who had treated
them at Port-la-Nouvelle. But Noon watched me without comment, her young woman's body hidden inside the baggy
camouflage. Had she tricked me all along, drawing me into a
dream of the river which would deliver me as her prisoner to the
custody of Harare?

27

The Stolen Channel

My hands tied behind me with the shreds of the Toyota flag, I sat
naked on the sun-baked boards of the open truck. Noon and a
soldier leaned against the back of the driving cabin, the chalky dust
of the broken road swirling around their shoulders. As we struck
the ridges of an abandoned railway line Noon squatted on the floor,
too tired to hold the heavy Lee-Enfield. Clasping the rifle between
her bare knees, she watched me with the resigned eyes of a farmer's
daughter taking to market an animal she had grown to like, and for
which she had once held hopes higher than the nearest meat-hook.

Had Noon always meant to betray me to Harare, or had she
disowned me out of expediency? Refusing to meet her eyes, I
stared over the rattling tail-gate at the waterway beside the road.
We were driving towards the former airbase along the western
bank of the diverted channel, through a strip of primitive farms and
allotments. The heroic attempt to reverse the advance of the Sahara
and make the desert bloom seemed far more modest at close
quarters. The farms were meagre patches of open ground between
the trees, separated from each other by creeks and irrigation
ditches, and dominated by the earthen-walled tanks of standing
water. Hundreds of these pits had been sunk into the ground, as the
farmers hoarded their booty, and immense care had been taken to
pound the walls to a tile-like hardness. By comparison, their small
dwellings were hovels thrown together from sheets of asbestos and
galvanised iron looted from the airbase.

This sense that a huge act of theft had taken place, that an illicit
prize was being hoarded among the rows of banana plants, was

reinforced by the listless and guilty character of the stolen waterway. Steadying the tail-gate with my elbow, I looked down at the slack surface that lay against the banks of mud. Half the Mallory was flowing through the revivified desert, but this substantial stream, some fifty yards wide, was as lifeless as an abandoned canal. The flat water had lost all trace of the zest and authority of the great river I had created at Port-la-Nouvelle, and whose course I had followed for the past months. The Mallory had cut its way boldly through the landscape, scoring its firm banks deep into the subsoil, but this diverted channel had left no imprint on the terrain, for all the green life it nourished.

Watching it dissipate itself through the creeks and ditches, I could see that the fishermen and nomadic farmers who had stolen this arm of the Mallory had little confidence in their booty. The truck slowed to avoid a gang of women digging a large pit beside the road. They packed the walls with stones and broken glass, aware that this reservoir, like all the others, would soon vanish if the water-table fell.

They paused over their hoes, peering into the truck and its dishevelled prisoner. Despite my thirst, I was too exhausted to ask them for water. By stealing part of the Mallory, these impoverished people had been bleeding me. I remembered the goats tethered behind the Chinese pharmacies in the back streets of Kowloon, whose exposed carotid veins were tapped by customers paying for a cup of hot blood. I resented the damage they had done to the Mallory, which now lay stolen and dismembered in these mosquito-infested pits. Flies covered my chest and legs, vibrating in a cloud that hovered above the truck. I guessed that my own end was near — as soon as Harare recognised me he would complete the execution interrupted at Lake Kotto by Sanger's arrival.

However, the condition of these people was little better than my own, as if they had drunk too much of the Mallory's poisoned waters. For all the crops growing in their allotments, the children were spindly and undernourished, their bony faces flicked over by flies. The anaemic women seemed affected by the slack water in the channel and slapped the walls of their tank in a monotonous way.

A distasteful smell hung between the palms, rising from the rank soil of the allotments, twitching the nostrils of the bored men playing cards in the doorways of their shacks.

As we moved along the road the stench gathered strength, and I realised that these desert nomads lacked the experience to deal safely with these huge volumes of water. The earth tanks and ponds beside their shacks were filled with a brackish fluid and were home to myriads of fever-carrying flies and mosquitoes, and contaminated with the human wastes with which they fertilised their crops. The water-table that sustained this irrigation of the desert was freighted with disease, which had begun to poison even the stolen branch of the Mallory that sustained it.

The main waterway began to divide, the black arms separating into a series of oily shallows divided by refuse-covered mudflats. Following the largest of the channels, we turned on to a strip of metalled road. A quarter of a mile ahead we reached the gatehouse of the former French airbase, where two of Harare's soldiers lounged by their weapons, surrounded by a lake of mud. The entire airfield was now a waterlogged marsh covered with waist-high grass where a hundred creeks and canals ran out into the desert. Two metal aircraft hangars stood in the grass, their curved, pock-marked roofs like the hulls of collapsed Zeppelins.

Around us lay the silent streets of the garrison town. There was a galvanised-iron cinema, its faded posters advertising a French tough-guy thriller, a launderette, married quarters and maternity unit, a ruined telephone exchange and even a travel agency. As the palms grew through the rusting roofs there was a sense that the late twentieth century had arrived in this remote desert site, stayed briefly and then left without looking back.

We crossed the town and approached a group of floating barrack huts. Joined by wooden catwalks, they sat in a harbour of shallow mud irrigated by the seeping waters of the river.

Prodded by Noon's rifle, I climbed down from the truck, and followed the two soldiers along a pathway that led through the high grass. Leaving Noon to guard me, the soldiers set off towards the largest of the floating huts. I stood in the hot sun, ignoring the mosquitoes that festered on my naked skin. I watched the brackish water shiver under the soldiers' heels as they crossed the catwalk. The ripples reached the channel of open water fifty yards away where a small arm of the Mallory still maintained its forward flow. But beyond the marshy perimeter of the airfield the river was dying in the desert wastes. I imagined my own life running out into the dusty scrub, taking with it all memory of my duel with the river.

"Mal. . . ."

Noon nudged me, brushing the flies from my chest. From a woman soldier in a nearby hut she had brought a camouflage jacket and a tattered pair of fatigue trousers. She hung the jacket over my shoulders, and then helped me to step into the trousers, fastening them around my waist with a length of cord. I leaned my bound wrists against her strong back, trying to read some sort of fellow feeling in her pursed lips. Her slim nostrils jumped as the flies crawled across her face, searching every orifice in a way my eyes had done so many times during our voyage.

Would she shoot me if I tried to run for it? I remembered that her rifle was unloaded. I searched for an escape path through the islands of marsh grass, and then looked for a last time at the remnants of the river, dying here in the desert as if aware of my own end. Pumped by the pressure of my feet on the catwalk, the black bilge-water was oozing a few yards upstream, as if this gangrene at the tip of the Mallory was advancing up its limbs to poison the main body. . . .

One of the soldiers leaned from a door, and whistled sharply to Noon. I followed her across the catwalk into the largest of the barrack huts. The tilting houseboat, mounted on its raft of kerosene drums, formed part of a floating field hospital. Injured soldiers lay on French army cots, gunshot wounds to their elbows and shoulders wrapped in blood-stained plaster, enveloped in a stench of pus and competing gangs of voracious flies. Most of the patients, like the women auxiliaries who shuffled about in a listless way, were suffering from that same swamp malaise I had seen in the people beside the road, poisoned by the foul waters of the diverted river.

Beyond the ward was a small dispensary. A trussed cockerel lay on the floor, eyes blinking ferociously at the male orderly, who stood beside a trestle table decorated tastefully with a selection of empty medicine jars. He was dressing a lanced boil on the cheek of a grey-faced guerilla officer who submitted with squeamish distaste. Behind the lint square, plaster and thinning beard I recognised the sometime student at the Lille Dental College, General Harare.

He frowned at me, too frayed to make the effort of remembering who I was, and then beckoned me forward.

"Doctor . . .? Lake Kotto, you were at Port-la-Nouvelle . . . with the French company, drilling for oil . . .?"

"Water, General. I was drilling for water."

"That's right — water. Quite hopeless. You can squeeze blood from the African stone, but never water. Doctor . . .?"

"Mallory. I looked after your teeth, General. I treated many of your men. The sergeant. . . ."

"Of course — you syringed his ears. You must treat him again, he can never catch my orders. Dr Mallory . . . we heard about you and one of my women soldiers. You shot two of Kagwa's men and stole a ship."

"The car-ferry *Salammbo* — we've sailed it here." As Harare nodded sagely I realised that he assumed I had defected to them. "I brought a Mercedes for you, General — it's on the ferry. Captain Kagwa's personal limousine."

"The village policeman's Mercedes? No wonder Kagwa wants to kill you . . . he's across the Chad border, buying gasoline for his helicopter, or perhaps selling his memoirs. They say he has his own television unit with him. . . ."

Harare looked up at me, as if envying Kagwa this instrument of power and fame, and hoping that I might be able to offer him some comparable facility.

"General, he'll be back. He's brought a landing-craft and about sixty men — they're fifteen miles south of here."

"We know — they are waiting in the papyrus swamps, killing my poor fishermen. You've had a fight to get here, doctor." He pointed to the rags of the Toyota flag, assuming that the red stripes were the bloodstains of a wrist injury. "Are your arms broken?"

"Kagwa's helicopter machine-gunned us." I held my hands as if they were tightly bandaged. "Luckily I've recovered."

"More lucky than you think — there are no medicines here. This hospital doesn't cure its patients, doctor, it kills them." His pallid face flushed with blood, he gripped the orderly's shoulders, trying to straighten his left leg. "Useless — from now on all I can do with this leg is kneel. And with Kagwa coming it's time to say a few prayers."

"He'll hold off as long as he can, General. He's a cautious man."

"Of course. He doesn't want to waste his gasoline. We're small beans to him. He's thinking about his Mercedes. That country policeman is going to be Governor of Northern Province."

"Then move into the mountains, General. Follow the river to its source."

Harare pushed the orderly from him. "These people won't leave. Every soldier has his family and a little farm. They have water now, doctor, their precious see-through gold."

"But the Sahara is blooming again. General, it's a lost dream come to life."

"At what cost? Our desert revolutionaries have become docile gardeners. This river has been a curse, doctor. I warn you, it's a poisoned paradise. Half these people are sick."

"Then use the river against Kagwa."

"How can I? The river has been Kagwa's main weapon, a highway that will deliver him right to our door."

"Then close it off! Build the barrage across both channels. Already the water-level is falling — if you extend the dam to the east bank you will sink Kagwa and his landing-craft right on to the river-bed."

Through a nearby window one of the auxiliaries tipped a pail of faecal waste into the water below. The stench drifted through the dispensary, for a moment subduing even the flies. Harare took the orderly's arm and rose on to his sound leg. Grimacing at the chicken on the floor, he moved to the open porch at the rear of the hut. As I stood beside him I could see him staring across the swamp grass and creeks of the airfield. He was gazing towards the south, to the hazy mist and green light that marked the southern course of the Mallory. Following his raised arm, I saw a faint plume of smoke, not from Kagwa's landing-craft, but from the funnel of the bordello-boat, the white ship of the widows.

Suppressing my fears, I turned and looked away, to the mountains in the north-east and the headwaters of the river. Under the weight of our feet the black mud oozed forwards, seeping into the clear water of the stream beyond the harbour. Already I could imagine the Mallory ligatured, its last artery tied down, and the poison flowing upwards into the trapped headwaters.

I hesitated, unsure whether to seize my chances with Harare. By completing the barrage, even though it served my purposes, I would virtually seal the fate of these impoverished people. For their sake, and for the river's, I should do my best to destroy the existing barrage, even if this sped the time of Kagwa's arrival. Yet this would be to yield to the Mallory. My own obsession, which had carried me so far, was all that I had.

Noon stood beside me, and began to undo the bonds around my wrists. She seemed business-like and confident, already refreshed after the rigours of our voyage. She met my eyes, in the shared glance of the conspirator, and then stared at the upper channel of the river, waiting for me to resume our journey. The pontoon tilted under her weight, pumping a further increment of black mud into the stream, reminding me of all the wastes that the people of this green Saharan garden would generate together, enough poison to infect the river and pursue it to its source.

I pointed to the distant plume of the *Diana*, remembering that Sanger's equipment was on board.

"By the way, General, I have contacts with a visiting television producer. I can easily arrange for you to be filmed — your interview would appear in every Japanese living-room. . . ."

28

Doctor Mal

As always each afternoon when I went out to examine the river, I saw Noon sitting in her metal skiff by General Harare's jetty, waiting for me to set off again on our journey. It was already late when I woke in the wheelhouse of the *Salammbo*, and I could hear Noon striking the water with her punt pole in a bored way. But I had been unsettled by a return of my fever, and by the distant sounds of mortar fire from the hills to the east.

All night the flashes of gunfire had crossed the darkness, reflected in the broken glass of the wheelhouse like flickers of lightning deep in the forest valleys. Around me, as I lay on the sweat-soaked mattress, I could see the flashes reflected in the chromium trim of the metal debris embedded in the barrage, the refrigerators, photocopiers and air-conditioners scavenged from the airbase. The huge brassiere of the dam, on whose left breast I and the *Salammbo* rested, glittered like the corsage of a carnival queen. The escaping waters of the Mallory spilled through the flesh of the barrage and poured into the pool below, jets of noise that even the gunfire failed to drown.

When I roused myself and stepped on to the deck I found that Noon had lost interest in me. She had moored her skiff by the jetty reserved for General Harare's escape on the upper waters of the Mallory, above the barrage and the rocky cascade. There she flirted with the two sentries guarding Kagwa's limousine — the grimy vehicle was now Noon's home — and tried to teach them a few words of her primitive English. For my benefit she pretended to entice these youths from their post, urging them to give up the fight against the Captain's forces and to take my place in the search for the river's source.

However, as I walked down the inner face of the barrage, following the pathway towards my raft, she immediately turned from the sentries and paddled into the centre of the stream. Her metal skiff was the lower half of an aircraft drop-tank, which she had retrieved from the debris as I supervised the construction of the barrage. In its way this was a small flourish of defiance, a reminder that she could still rescue some hope for our stalled expedition from the preposterous structure which now blocked the waters of the Mallory.

As she sailed across the tarry surface of the river in the afternoon light, this grey tank resembled a silver slipper bearing the princess of every fairy tale. She stood up and casually displayed herself to me, and I found it difficult to believe that this handsome young woman with her feverish but elegant pose, a high-temperature Venus borne by her aircraft shell, was only six months older than the lock-jawed child who had paddled in her coracle around the waters of Lake Kotto.

"Noon . . . come with me!" There was a small, four-horsepower outboard on my raft which could easily outrun Noon's skiff, though for some reason I could never catch her. "You look tired today — let me examine you. . . ."

But she made no reply, snorting with laughter when I slipped in the greasy scum along the rubble bank. A dead snake lay in the shallows, hidden among the rotting timbers and the oil leaking from the bilges of the *Salammbo*.

I watched Noon punt herself upstream, dismissing the young soldiers with a haughty wave while watching me over her shoulder. Before following Noon I needed to inspect the barrage. Buffeted by the left shoulder of the Mallory as it turned to irrigate the desert settlements, the mass of scrap metal, soil and rubbish was constantly shifting. The barrage was held together by the retaining nets secured to the hull of the *Salammbo*, and this precarious dam threatened at any moment to collapse and spill itself into the pool below.

Soon after my first meeting with Harare, six weeks earlier, I had persuaded the ailing guerilla leader of the need to complete the Mallory barrage, partly as a strategic blow against Kagwa — we would steal the river literally from under the keel of the approaching landing-craft — and partly as a means of extending the Saharan settlements, and attracting more nomadic farmers from whose ranks Harare could recruit his fighters.

Though fuddled by the side-effects of a discontinued brand of sulpha drug, Harare had assigned me a platoon of convalescent soldiers, who in turn rounded up a work-force of some thirty village women. They assembled by the cascade, and stared listlessly at the eastern arm of the Mallory, eager to seize these free-flowing waters but hopelessly daunted by the task.

Our first efforts to construct a containment wall of earth and masonry were washed aside by the swift current, the waters of the river escaping through our legs like spawning salmon. The villagers' ragged fishing-nets were too short to span the cascade. Soon discouraged, they began to walk back along the beach, returning to the stagnant, malarial waters of their allotments and reservoirs.

I had brought the *Salammbo* alongside a wharf in the pool below the barrage, where the soldiers off-loaded Captain Kagwa's limousine. As they pulled away the wooden ramp I stood in the wheelhouse, my hand on the throttle. I could feel the current tug at the ferry's bows, as if the Mallory were teasing me with the notion of shooting the cascade.

The last of the village women were climbing between the frayed nets, throwing their loads of stone into the water. Exasperated with them, I throttled up the engine and set off across the pool towards the lowest steps of the cascade. Behind me I heard Noon shout out in alarm. She ran along the beach after the mooring line, convinced that in my typically eccentric way I was trying to continue our journey.

Twenty feet from the cascade, the *Salammbo* ran aground on the gravel bed, almost midway between the eastern bank and the central island. Ignoring the soldiers' shouts, I held the throttle

forward, as the propeller churned up a fountain of spray that
brought the work-gang back to the water's edge. Wrench in hand, I
lowered myself through the engine hatch. As I fumbled in the dark
bilges, I felt the *Salammbo's* keel slipping on the gravel, borne back
by the rushing roar of the Mallory against the craft's hull. Then
water drenched me from the stern-cock, boiling off the exhaust
manifold in a cloud of steam that filled the engine compartment and
enveloped the startled faces of the soldiers peering into the hatch.

Within ten minutes the *Salammbo* had embedded itself securely in
the gravel bed. Impressed by the sight of this metal caisson, the
women returned to the task of stealing the Mallory. Less than a
month later the barrage across the river was complete, and the
Salammbo, which had carried us so untiringly from Port-la-
Nouvelle, sat in its last anchorage, surrounded by a refuse tip of
freezers and enamel stoves, water coolers, aircraft tail-planes and
radio antennae, together forming a terminal moraine of modern
technology.

Meanwhile I had stolen my own river. Interrupted in its passage
south, the Mallory now followed the westward course of the first
detour towards the greening desert, briefly cleansing the stagnant
tanks and irrigation ditches, and setting off a flurry of digging and
hoarding. Ironically, the increased supply of water had led, not to an
increase in the cultivated land, but to a fierce competition among the
ditch and reservoir builders. Networks of irrigation channels ran
between the allotments to the wells and standby tanks, but not a
single new maize or banana plant was to benefit. Elaborate rituals
sprang up among these debilitated people to celebrate the transfer
and barter of blocks of stagnant water and all their energies went
into disputes of ownership of this disease-infested fluid. The intense
rivalry led to bitter brawls, through which I moved unscathed,
regarded by these people as their rain-king. Harare was too ill and
too concerned with the threat of Captain Kagwa to care that I was
becoming the shabby sultan of these impoverished nomads. I patted
the sore-infested pates of their children, injected out-of-date
sulphonamides into the arms of the old men and in general lorded it
over my moribund domain.

However, I had more urgent concerns at hand. The level in the pool below the barrage fell by some four feet, but enough water sprang through the earth retention wall to sustain a narrow but navigable channel downstream. Following its course from the deck of the *Salammbo*, I watched the wounded river wind its way to the south between the great silt banks, now white as death, that rose into the sun from the retreating shallows.

As expected, the sudden fall in the Mallory had given pause to Captain Kagwa. In the weeks of the barrage's construction the sounds of gunfire had drawn ever nearer. The bursts of mortar shells and the flames from the burning trees trembled in the mountain valleys two miles to the south-east. Twice the helicopter flew over the pool before being driven away by rifle fire, the French pilot photographing the broad sweep of the Mallory as it turned westwards down its new channel.

Harare had offered to me the private quarters of the former French commander at the airbase, but I had decided to stay aboard the *Salammbo*. There were unstated bonds between myself and this antique vessel. The metal debris in which it was embedded set up a constant wailing and groaning, and in my fever I almost believed that I was embarked on an even stranger voyage across the garbage pits of the planet.

A week after the completion of the barrage Nora Warrender's floating brothel appeared in the pool. Silhouetted against the dark hills to the east, its white hull appeared to float on the sunset, a gliding sepulchre of polished bone. It arrived soon after dusk, under the wary guns of the sentries who guarded the barrage. I could see Mrs Warrender and her sisters on the bridge, Fanny holding the helm in her strong arms. They attempted to moor against the barrage, but were sent away by a patrol boat and forced to anchor by the southern exit from the pool two hundred yards away. As darkness settled, a line of lanterns glowed from the awning of the restaurant deck. The soft lights framed the bar and dance-floor, illuminating the waters of the pool. The ruby and turquoise beams shone on the drab uniforms of the guerillas who went out to inspect the *Diana*, and transformed them into actors in a harlequin pageant. Within an hour, Louise and Poupée were pushing the first beer bottles across the bar, and the soldiers hung their webbing across the restaurant chairs. Even Sanger fumbled about the dance-floor, setting up a television screen for the amusement of the customers. Watching his blind, scurrying figure, barely tolerated by the women, I could scarcely remember the sly entrepreneur I had met at Port-la-Nouvelle.

During the days that followed, the *Diana* remained moored on the far side of the pool, its lantern doused but the bar open for business, and parties of soldiers rowed out to the ship. As the men drank the stale beer at the restaurant tables and jigged across the dance-floor to a scratchy pop record, I wondered if they were about to have their throats cut, or if the cabins below deck had reopened for business. So contemptuous were the women of the men who had killed their husbands that they could sleep with these drunken soldiers without any care.

Whatever the women's motives for mooring in the pool, I was careful to avoid them. In their eyes, dreaming of death, I could see reflected only the leprous yellow spears of the papyrus swamps.

29

The Blue Beaches

For the time being, I had a far more important death on my mind. Turning my back on the pool, and the white ship with its sinister lanterns, I kicked aside the poisoned snake that lay at the foot of the barrage. The wake from Noon's skiff sent a sluggish eddy across the river. Backed up above the rocky cascade, the waters of the Mallory had almost ceased to flow, their dark surface covered with an opaque scum. Damped by this satin cloak, the ripples from Noon's craft reached my feet like a series of vague afterthoughts, as if the damming of the Mallory, the containment of a dream, had held back time itself.

Even Noon, dulled by the fever that had returned to us all, moved more slowly, paddling her silver shell with off-hand strokes, her handsome but gaunt shoulder exposed to the light in a pose imitated from Sanger's travel films. I watched her lose her footing as she passed the jetty where the young sentries leaned against the radiator grille of the Mercedes. She raised her punt pole and drew a cryptic message on the musky air, and then stumbled deliberately, sending a silken tremble through the brackish water. Was she mimicking the death of the Mallory, and the failure of my own will? As the soldiers laughed good-humouredly, Noon sat in the skiff and worked the bolt of the Lee-Enfield with a dramatic flourish. She frowned magisterially, though Harare, suspicious of her long absence, had refused to supply any ammunition for the elderly rifle.

With an effort I lowered my eyes from Noon. At my feet, beside the pontoon raft, was a dead coucal, its blackened plumage barely visible among the oil-covered reeds and rotting vegetation. I hated to see these creatures killed by the Mallory, but as I gazed along the shore line, through the blur of dung flies and mosquitoes, the success of my devious scheme was more apparent every hour.

Groups of women sat by the water's edge, guarding the entrances to their irrigation ditches but too tired to operate the water-wheels with which they topped up their precious reservoirs. Around them their crops grew strongly, a blaze of green foliage and yellow blossom. Their Eden, however, was poisoned. As I had guessed, the completion of the barrage, and a doubling of their water supply, had only added to the insecurity of these im-poverished people. Hundreds of nomads had flocked to the desert strip, staking out their allotments and hacking their irrigation ditches through the dusty soil. Every spare plot of ground had been excavated and filled with water. Whey-faced children and older men armed with sticks sat beside the stagnant tanks, a feast for the malarial mosquitoes and fever-fly as they guarded these parcels of water from their neighbours. At their feet the Mallory flowed between its greasy banks. Doubting its will to survive, they stared at the black mudflats, at the bodies of snakes, birds and fish.

I was their physician and I did everything I could to care for them but, despite myself, I needed these sick people, their fever and their wastes. This foetid paradise was an engine generating the poisons that would at last kill the river. Already there were signs that the Mallory was faltering, as the poison seeped up this flagging artery to its head. When I pushed the raft away from the barrage, and started the outboard motor, the whirling propeller spattered the rubble wall with globs of oily waste.

I set off across the stream, moving between rocky banks on which grew a few withered palms. Narrow beaches of blue pebbles paved the shore, as if cyanosed by the lack of oxygen in the polluted water. Few fish swam below the surface, and the birds kept their distance.

Noon had slipped ahead of me, hiding behind the sharp bends in which the Mallory uncoiled itself through the foothills of the Massif. I cut the engine, and let the raft drift on the faint current.

I was now half a mile from the barrage, and had entered the silent reaches of the river. Here the Mallory had erased all sound in its passage. As if dismantling itself sense by sense, it had unpacked the fish from its depths, and stripped the birds from the trees, cancelling itself as its dream died in my head.

For all the silence, this was a zone of some danger. Bandits and deserters from the rebel forces haunted the mountain valleys, and I could imagine Noon being seized by a wounded guerilla wading out to her skiff.

Over my shoulder I heard the ripple of a punt pole, the grating of a keel on shingle. Noon stood naked in her metal shell, the pole held horizontally across her breasts. While she watched me, with the same curious but calm gaze that I had first seen at Port-la-Nouvelle, the water dripped from the pole, ticking off the seconds.

"Noon . . . you're still waiting for me to go on. First we'll return to the ferry. You can rest there."

I started the outboard, reversing the raft across the current. The guerilla uniform at her feet, Noon punted the skiff through the entrance of a shallow inlet. Trying to cool her fever in the shadowy pool, she knelt in the blue water, the reflection of her arms and shoulders leaking across the surface, as if she was about to dissolve into its hidden mirrors.

"Noon . . . we'll leave tomorrow. I know I've said that before. . . ."

I let the raft run aground on the shingle. Noon fell sideways in the water, and only with an effort forced herself on to her knees. Fearing that she might drown herself in her fever, I tried to catch the stern of the skiff, but she pushed away from me. Blood fell from her mouth and formed thin streamers in the water, like the ribbons of a decoy.

From the mist-veiled hills to the east came the rumble of mortar fire. Sections of the forest canopy were burning, and the jade-green smoke drifted through the valleys, the threat of an approaching storm. Captain Kagwa's reconnaissance patrol had pushed forward to the next ridge-line, capturing the conveyor system of the mining company. Somewhere among the rock slopes Harare

213

would be trying to rally his men, one eye closed by the boil on his cheek.

Out of these sounds of discontent came a steadier noise, the deepening drone of an aircraft engine. Hidden behind its orange floats, the fuselage of Kagwa's helicopter rode across the cliffs above the eastern bank of the Mallory. It hovered over the centre of the channel and then settled towards the surface, its fans throwing up a violent spray. Captain Kagwa leaned from the observer's seat beside the French pilot, a heavy flak jacket around his thick neck. Both he and the pilot watched Noon punting her craft away from them, this half-naked guerilla in a camouflage jacket, a rifle between her feet.

The helicopter crept behind her, soon blinded by its own spray. The pilot sheered sideways, and the spray fell in a wet cloud that drenched me as I ran through the shallow water. Kagwa racked back his seat, sitting diagonally behind the pilot and giving himself ample room to aim his carbine at the young woman. Driven frantic by this threatening machine, Noon dropped her punt pole and raised the unloaded Lee-Enfield, hopelessly pointing it at the confused air.

A signal shell rose into the afternoon sky, fired from an observer's post in the lift house of the mining conveyor. A cerise star lit the sombre hills, a medallion of light that dripped slowly from its mushy wake into the forest canopy below.

Without waiting for Kagwa, the pilot broke off his pursuit of Noon. He inclined his machine and accelerated along the line of cliffs. The spray fell like lost rain on to the silver surface of the river. Noon stowed her rifle and punted with one arm, eager to return to the safety of the barrage. Unable to start the outboard, I pushed the raft into the shallows and paddled across the water, following the ribbons of her blood that trailed below the surface of that mortuary stream.

30

The Arcade Peep-Show

At dusk I found myself leaning against the helm in the wheelhouse of the *Salammbo*, the feverish captain of this landlocked ferry foundering in the garbage heap of the barrage. The last of the gunfire had subsided, but the echoes sounded in my throbbing head. Captain Kagwa's patrol had captured the mining conveyor, and the final ridge above the river valley. There they would dig in for the night, waiting for the arrival of the main force in the landing-craft. The evening mist seeped along the slopes of the surrounding hills, hunting out the narrow defiles in the forest where Harare's demoralised men waited for reinforcement. The smoke from their kitchen fires rose through the dripping trees and seemed to exchange secret signals of the coming attack, as if the unseen powers of the Massif which concealed the Mallory were about to come down on to the plain and avenge the river's death.

Through the tilting windows of the wheelhouse I watched the curling fog that followed the river on its southward course, and the steam-cloud from Kagwa's landing-craft, moored barely a mile downstream.

The tracer of a rifle bullet crossed the ridge-lines, fired by one of Harare's snipers on the defensive perimeter which the guerilla leader had drawn around both banks of the river. As the sound faded into the forest, I listened to the water seeping through the barrage, and to the rattle of my cheekbone against the bullet-marked helm.

An hour earlier, at the floating field hospital, I had injected Harare with the last dose of sulphonamide. All of us were now infected by the same fever, carried by the flies and mosquitoes from the noxious waters of the river. I knew that I should rescue Noon, and move her up-river from the final battle which would soon overwhelm Harare and his desert settlement. But the higher reaches of the Mallory frightened me with their blue beaches and dead snakes, and the palpable presence of the poison which its waters had leached from my head.

Downstream lay Captain Kagwa, with a long inventory of scores to settle. Even if we evaded his advancing force, there lay the papyrus swamps where Mrs Warrender and her women had hunted, and might hunt again.

The widows' ship was now berthed only fifty yards away, among the village of small craft which had taken refuge against the barrage. Earlier, as the sounds of gunfire drew nearer, the fishing rafts and waterborne shacks had abandoned their anchorages in the centre of the pool. The soldiers guarding the barrage had ordered them away, cutting their mooring lines when they tried to tie up beside the leaking rampart of earth and scrap metal.

Then the *Diana* had upped anchor and moved slowly across the pool, its white timbers more than ever resembling a marquetry of bones. The ghostly vapour of its slowly beating engine rose into the air like the smoke from a floating crematorium. Mrs Warrender stood on the bridge, her small face, like a sinister child's, lit by the lanterns of the dance-floor.

Remembering the papyrus swamps, I distrusted Mrs Warrender and her women, and protested to the sergeant in charge. But the guerillas had spent too many hours on the old brothel-ship, beguiled by these passive and welcoming women, by the endless supplies of cheap beer and, above all, by the primitive closed-circuit television system. Lounging around the dance-floor, their rifles leaning against the restaurant tables, they watched themselves on the screen above the bar, filmed by the camera which Sanger, fumbling about like a blind Merlin, had set up on a tripod between the animal cages.

Unable to resist the promise of stardom, the soldiers allowed Mrs Warrender to moor the *Diana* against the barrage. Followed by a flotilla of small craft, the white liner of the night lay securely against the creaking dam, a veiled assassin pressing herself to her victim's breast.

Light-headed with hunger, I listened to the water rush through the secret veins of the barrage. The noise was magnified by the metal debris and sounded like the sighing of a frozen sea. Through the ceaseless din I could hear the soft strains of old dance-band records coming from the deck of the *Diana*. Unable to sleep on the sloping bunk — feet pressed against the wall, I felt like a corpse in a bullet-riddled coffin — I left the wheelhouse and stepped from the creaking deck on to the earth embankment.

A hundred jets of water spurted between the restraining nets of the barrage and fell into the pool. Below my feet a small cave-mouth had opened within the compacted metal rubbish, a cloacal vent from which leaked a stream of phosphorescent bile. I walked along the barrage towards the *Diana*. A wooden gangway led down to the starboard rail, reached by a path from the western bank of the pool.

The lanterns glowed over the dance-floor, their eerie light reflected in the empty bottles that lay on the deck among the broken glasses and cigarette packets. Floating on the pools of beer were the loose pages of a pornographic magazine with which the soldiers had tried to light a fire in one of the amber lanterns. The bar was deserted, the untended television set recording a last party of soldiers who sat at the tables. They were trying to strike a bargain with the hostesses, two local young women whom Louise and Poupée had recruited from the widows and abandoned wives in the nearby allotments.

Mrs Warrender stood on the bridge of the *Diana*, whose rails in the darkness were like bars separating her from the shabby revels below. She had at last discarded the bath-robe, and now wore the brocaded evening gown I had seen her lifting from the suitcase on the beach at Port-la-Nouvelle. This lavish but formal garment made her seem a young woman again, as if she were deliberately returning to the naive world before her marriage. Hands folded, she watched the drunken scene like a Victorian spinster gazing down at the unlicensed behaviour of animals on the floor of a cage.

I disliked the way in which Mrs Warrender had recruited these illiterate village girls as her whores, using them as bait in whatever trap she was setting, and knew that she might well have tried to enrol Noon had I not escaped with her. For reasons I chose not to examine, the calm but threatening presence of this unrevenged woman always set off an immediate surge in my fever. Unslaked by the papyrus marshes, Nora Warrender had pursued me along the upper reaches of the Mallory, but had seemed to lose interest in me as soon as she reached the pool. Watching her from the *Salammbo*, I found it difficult to read any clear motive into her eccentric behaviour. Harare and his men had forgotten their earlier encounter with the women at the breeding station, and passed to and fro within easy rifle shot of the *Diana*. But the women had made no move.

I walked down the springing gangplank towards the dance-floor, so giddy that I almost lost my footing. Nora Warrender treated me to a tolerant smile, and then withdrew into the bridgehouse. For all my derelict condition, my power over the river still worked its authority.

In the darkness by the port rail of the restaurant deck Sanger sat with his camera and tripod, the diamanté sunglasses hiding his eyes. He had perched himself out of the soldiers' way on a small stool, his back in a niche between the animal cages. The distant gunfire of the afternoon had unsettled the nervous creatures, and Sanger leaned his left ear to a chittering marmoset, as if this frightened monkey now provided him with his entire view of the world, a faint echo of Mr Pal's commentaries. He cocked his other ear as I stumbled from the gangplank, and his sore-covered hands moved protectively around his camera. For a few seconds his face emerged from the niche, and the lantern light played over his white hair and eroded features. Sitting there in the shadows, he resembled a blind beggar on the steps of a waterfront hotel, displaying his television screen like a wound.

A lantern fell to the deck beside the soldiers' table, and the flaming paraffin floated towards me through a swill of beer. The soldiers shouted and pointed, not to the flames leaping at their feet, but to the image on the television screen above the bar.

I stood in the harsh light among the empty bottles. Sensing the patterns of my feet, Sanger fidgeted in his dark hole, waiting for the marmoset to give him a description of this late visitor to the *Diana.*

"Mallory. . . ." He clutched at my wrist. "You've come for me . . . I've been sick, doctor. We can still make the film, Mallory."

I pushed his hand away. "There's no time left for films. Sanger, I wish I could help you . . . look at yourself."

"You look, too, doctor . . . it's a good picture." He gesticulated in the direction of the screen above the bar, still hawking his shabby illusions to every passing patron of this floating brothel. "See yourself in the film, doctor. Then we'll go back to Port-la-Nouvelle . . . can you find Mr Pal . . .?"

"Mr Pal? He's waiting for you in the papyrus swamps. Ask Mrs Warrender."

"Good . . . our new film . . . I want to tell Mr Pal."

I left him muttering to himself, and swayed away through the tables. I pressed the white planks under my heels, trying to shake off the fever. The soldiers ignored me, but one of the hostesses sitting on the corporal's knee slipped through his hands and approached me.

"Come for beer? Good time . . .?"

"Is Noon here?"

"Noon . . .?"

"Have you seen her?"

"Noon busy . . . busy time. . . ."

"Where is she?"

"Oh . . . where . . .?"

Expertly she looked me up and down. Barely more than fourteen, she already had the style of a seasoned beer-hall trouper. She sidled around me in a haze of perfume and cheap spirit, searching for a gold watch or bracelet. When I pushed her away she gave a grimace of disgust, exposing her broken teeth, assuming that the wound on my scalp was an infectious eczema.

"Ugh. . . ." She turned back to her corporal. "Dirty man . . . see Noon. . . ."

Avoiding her, I stepped back unsteadily, almost burning my feet in the last of the paraffin flames. A roar of music came from the soldiers' cassette player, setting off my fever again. The pain drummed at my head, a fierce frontal migraine. In the television screen I saw myself clutching at the rail, swinging on the bars like a deranged orang in a zoo. My chin bobbed at the air, the mechanical gesture of a desperate mammal trying to reopen the sores on its scalp.

Watching this apparition, I felt curiously detached from my own body with its pains and fevers, and closer to the abstract and stylised image on the small screen. The pearly rectangle, scarcely larger than a light-bulb, shrank me down to size, like everything else on which the camera turned its eye, and stripped away the irrelevancies of emotion, pain, and motive. Only my obsession endured, a great dream made small by failures of nerve, but a great dream nevertheless.

I shuffled towards the bar, looking up at the screen as over the years I had peered dispassionately at so many X-ray plates. I reached to the control panel, trying to turn up the brightness, to bathe us all in that white dispassionate glow.

Beyond the swaying image of my wounded head and the soldiers arguing at their table, I saw that another figure had appeared among the ghostly lanterns. One of Mrs Warrender's youngest girls, some consumptive child-widow wearing a cheap dance-hall gown several sizes too large for her, leaned against the stern rail and breathed in the night air as if trying to free herself of the taste of her last client. She gripped the flagstaff, about to retch over the rail, when she caught sight of me standing by the bar. She raised her chin, recognising another customer, but then paused to stare at me. Through the garish rouge and lipstick that masked her childlike face was an expression of sudden concern.

"Noon . . .? Is that — ?"

Blinded by the white light, I switched off the screen. There was a shout from the corporal but when I turned I saw that the young woman had gone. Had Noon dressed up in this garish costume, unable to resist the lure of the closed-circuit television system? Perhaps she knew that she would only survive Captain Kagwa's arrival as a hostess in Mrs Warrender's menage.

Beside the bar was the open hatchway to the cabins below. I crossed the dance-floor and stepped on to the wooden rung of the ladder. A beer bottle rolled across the deck, kicked at my head by one of the soldiers, and shattered against the brass step guard.

I fumbled in the darkness for the corridor rail. Slivers of light slipped through the planking, and swayed like funeral torches seen through the lid of a coffin. In the darkness I was alone with my fever, engulfed by the scents of perfume, semen and mucus that hung in the corridor, forever fused in my mind with the nymphs that decorated the cabin ceilings. I thought of the young whore I had seen by the stern rail, dressed like a mock-child in an oversized gown, pretending to be some prepubertal bride. . . .

The ship swayed slightly, crowded by the small craft huddled against it. From the cracks in the barrage a hundred jets of foetid water played on the *Diana's* hull, as if all its clients were urinating on to this floating brothel in an attempt to cool its overheated decks.

Stumbling over my own feet, I fell against the door of the cubicle which had served as Mrs Warrender's armoury. The store of weapons had gone, hidden away from Harare's men. The light flickered across the bed, as the jets of water cascaded against the window shutters, transforming the interior of this sweaty boudoir into a scene from an ancient silent film glimpsed in a pierside booth.

I stepped into the small cell, inhaling the stale air filled with the tang of rifle oil and flaking plaster. In the trembling darkness I leaned over the wash-basin, and let the sweat drip from my face and chest. Too exhausted to search the remaining cabins, I lay across the mattress, my forehead against the brass bars of the headpiece, watching the light reflected in the peeling gilt. Above me, the nymphs leapt from their foamy deep, ready to carry me away to a more serene sky.

Soon after, I woke from a troubled sleep to find my legs slipping from the mattress on to the floor. I reached to the bars behind me, about to pull myself on to the bed, and felt an arm force me away. A slim-shouldered young woman sat in the darkness at the head of the bed, her narrow thighs pointing away from me towards the shuttered window. The sequins stitched to her cheap gown and the glass jewellery across her small breasts seemed to conceal her within the metal bars behind my head, an erotic child penned inside a cage of peeling gilt. In her hand she held a gauze cloth, with which she had been wiping my chest.

The light stuttered, the silver flicker of old arcade peep-shows. I could feel the feverish heat of the girl's skin. The bony thighs that kept my hands away streamed with a malarial sweat. In the trembling glimmer of the water jetting against the hull I saw the young whore's alarmed eyes as she struggled to free herself from this diseased man. I tried to reassure her, and pressed my hands between her legs, hoping to calm this disturbed patient nursing me on my own sickness bed.

My teeth tore a strip of sequins from the bodice of her gown, and the glass jewels beaded the nipples of her miniature breasts. For a moment, through the haze of perfume and the stench of the poisoned river I could smell a familiar skin, the sharp, sweet odour of the twelve-year-old who had sailed the *Salammbo* with me, down the far reaches of the Mallory. But then this adolescent I embraced became some other child of the night. I felt the loose sequins against my lips, the flat of a small hand against my forehead releasing its pressure. The stuttering light transformed us into players in a clandestine film. The silver streamers of jetting water seemed to caress the young woman's naked body. I clasped my hands behind her head and held her small face within my forearms. Her hands were trapped against my chest, but I felt her palms embrace me as our shared fevers came together in the trembling night.

31

The Death of the Diana

A heavy blow rocked the *Diana*, as if the bows had been butted by a bull elephant who had strayed into the pool. The painted nymphs on the cabin ceiling wept a cloud of white plaster on to the bed where I slept. The concussion wave of an ordnance round drummed through the hull, rattling its aged bones. A spray of water lashed the wooden shutters of the window. Roused from a cold sleep, I lay alone on the mildewed mattress, listening to the intermittent tapping of a machine-gun, the clatter of a circling helicopter and the distant throb of a large marine diesel. Soldiers were running on the path beyond the gangway, their bare feet slapping the worn mud, part of the din of battle that drowned the murmur of the river leaking through the barrage wall.

So Captain Kagwa's attack, threatened for so many weeks, was at last taking place. I pushed my legs on to the floor, and tried to steady myself, brushing the white dust from my shoulders. The fever had passed, but my body felt calm and curiously passive. For all my fear of Kagwa, I was detached from my likely fate at his hands.

A signal flare shone through the doorways of the empty cabins on the port side. I stepped into the corridor, tripping over a sequined gown discarded by one of the girls, as a tower of hissing light descended into the pool. Its vivid glare illuminated the pale dawn mist, filling the upturned faces of the fishermen in the boats and rafts beside the *Diana* with a melancholy sheen.

A stray mortar shell had struck a landing-stage twenty feet from the *Diana*, drenching the vessel and waking me from my sleep. The

broken bamboo smouldered in the shallows, its green smoke join-
ing the plumes that rose from the burning tamarinds on the ridge
above the pool. An iron warehouse of weaponry, the landing-
craft edged through the disturbed surface, almost too large for
the shrinking mirror that reflected its massive plates. Nervous of
stranding himself, the helmsman hesitated over his tiller, and the
helicopter came down through the smoke and small-arms fire and
hovered above its ramp. Captain Kagwa sat in the observer's seat,
battle-jacket open around his bare chest, urging the French pilot to
drive the landing-craft forward with the helicopter's propeller.

Hidden behind the shutters, I watched this sharp skirmish turn
itself into a battle. Harare's men were digging themselves into the
beaches that overlooked the pool. As the landing-craft advanced
towards them, it seemed appropriate that the final struggle
between Kagwa and Harare should take place on the draining bed
of the river which I had created for them, beneath the huge breasts
of the retention dam with their cargo of rusty refrigerators and beer
coolers. Already I took for granted that Captain Kagwa would win
this battle, reopen the Mallory and seize his kingdom. . . .

A mallet-like blow chopped into the deck above my head, a stray
round from the machine-gun firing from the stern of the landing-
craft. A marmoset let out a scream of terror that rang the bars of its
cage.

"Noon . . .!" Alarmed for the girl, I began to search the empty
cabins, waving aside the mist of plaster that fell from the ceilings.
In the cracked mirrors I could see disjointed sections of myself, a
naked man coated with talc in some brothel prank, playing blind
man's buff as he searched for the hiding women. The mirrors
shook to the noise of the helicopter, preparing to withdraw into
their illusory world, and the mist trembled around me in the
gunfire.

I sat on the bed in my cabin, feeling the imprint of a young
woman's body among the stains of fever that soaked the mattress. I
could smell her skin on my hands, the odours of a dream
remembered. Had Noon slept with me, or had I confused her with
one of the young widows I had seen entertaining the soldiers? I had

held Noon or her double in the darkness, tasted the lips and eyes that I had watched each day as we sailed the Mallory towards its source. I had embraced the same thighs that had clasped the pail of headless frogs, tasted the same saliva that Noon had left on the tips of her fishing spears. In the trembling dark of this dusty cabin I had felt the same care, impatience and regret to which Noon had treated me since our first meeting at Port-la-Nouvelle.

I pressed the mattress with my hands, half-hoping to find the contours of an older woman in the rotting fabric. My fingers touched a darker stain beneath the talc, a patch of bloodstained saliva, and I remembered the infected wound in Noon's mouth.

Then a second signal flare exploded above the *Diana*. Its cyanide glow illuminated the breech and barrel of the Lee-Enfield rifle propped against the wash-basin.

Arcs of blue phosphorus were falling from the sky, dripping into the disturbed waters of the pool. Terrified by the landing-craft, the fishermen and raft-dwellers moored beside the *Diana* were cutting their lines. They pushed off towards the scanty cover of the beach, where Harare's guerillas were making their last stand.

Stray bullets were striking the superstructure of the *Diana*, ringing against the iron rails and scattering the furniture on the restaurant deck. I held the Lee-Enfield, nervous of Noon's scent on the wooden stock, and stepped into the corridor. The hatch had been pulled across the stairway, and I heard Mrs Warrender and her women dragging the animal cages to the starboard rail.

"Nora . . .!"

Kneeling on the upper rungs of the ladder, I drove the rifle stock at the hatch. My shouts were lost in the blare of the helicopter. The down-draught from its propeller blades drove through the deck planks and turned the corridor into a whirlwind of dust. The white mist of the disintegrating murals seethed around me, the ghosts of these tempera nymphs lost in the corridors of this abandoned brothel.

Above the noise of gunfire came the snarl and cry of a macaque. Claws raced across the deck in a deranged skittering. There were shouts from the women, and a broom thudded against the planks. I realised that Nora Warrender was freeing her animals and driving them ashore. I tried to raise the hatch, scarcely able to move the heavy cage that lay across it. Through the dust and spray thrown up by the helicopter I saw that the women were leaving the *Diana*. Rifles slung over their shoulders, they carried suitcases and bedding rolls like members of an armed theatrical troupe leaving a besieged city at the end of the season. Between them they steered Professor Sanger, who clutched his camera like a mendicant clasping his begging-bowl.

An acrid smoke hung in the corridor, seeping through the wooden bulkhead that separated the cabins from the engine compartment. The bows of the *Diana* were smouldering, and the oil-soaked timbers gave off a foul vapour that choked my throat. Within minutes the engine and its fuel tanks would be overrun, and the bridge would collapse into a pit of burning charcoal.

Abandoning my attempts to move the hatch, I drove the rifle stock into the soft decking above my head. On the third blow I struck an ancient knot from the soft pine, forced the barrel into the aperture and wrenched the plank from its joists. Like a talcumed corpse springing through the lid of a coffin, I burst between the bone-white planks and clambered on to the deck.

Smoke swirled across the dance-floor, uncoiling among the restaurant tables. Swaying there, I braced myself with the rifle like a tight-rope walker, and ran forward on to the face of the barrage. I clung to the sisal nets that held the retention wall and climbed across the earth and metal debris.

Below me, the *Diana* was ablaze. Hidden by the clouds of black smoke that shrouded the bridge, the first flames rose from the engine-room, and transformed the floating brothel into a gaudy lantern. The mooring lines had parted, and the blackened cords smoked against the white cutwater, fuses lit beneath the skirts of the gilded princess of the bowsprit. The stern swung against the barrage, crushing the abandoned rafts and pontoons of the fisherfolk. The gangway collapsed below me, its planks tumbling into the pool.

Smoke enveloped the west wall of the barrage. The splitting timbers of the *Diana*, a ripple of fire-crackers, sounded above the drone of the helicopter and the noise of gunfire from the sand-bars beyond the pool. Rifle in hand, I searched through the smoke for Noon or Mrs Warrender, and then ran along the path to the east wall where the *Salammbo* was entombed.

After its long journey from Port-la-Nouvelle, Captain Kagwa's landing-craft now presided over the pool. The ramp fell into the shallow water beside the smouldering jetties, and a reserve platoon of teenage soldiers hesitated in the spray. Berated by their sergeant, they plunged into the water and ran along the beach towards the sand-bars, ready to flush out the last of Harare's men.

The fire had reached the cabins of the *Diana*. Jets of flame, like a score of gas mantles, lifted through the decking. Tinted by the metal salts in the mural pigments, the flames darted among the tables, gaudy geysers of zinc and copper light, as the ghosts of these nymphs put on their last performance. The entire ship was now alight and leaning against the barrage, its bows burned down to the water-line, and exposing the antique engine in the glowing debris of the bridge.

Through the clouds of illuminated smoke the helicopter appeared, the grand finale of this firework spectacular. An ugly genie, it descended to within fifty feet of the *Diana*. The pilot directed the draught of his propellers against the burning ship, trying to drive it away from the landing-craft. Bows submerged, the *Diana* drifted back against the barrage, as the lanterns and television tubes on the restaurant deck began to explode in a last display.

In the wheelhouse of the *Salammbo* I felt the barrage shift. The earth wall slackened, as if a tendon had snapped. The restraining nets of the west wall were now alight, and revealed the huge, rounded breasts of the dam in a fiery striptease. Like the straining brassiere of an overweight madame, it peeled back through the smoke to expose the unsupported bulk of overflowing earth, liquid jetting from a hundred nipples, ready to spill its wealth of metallic rubbish.

The *Diana* sank in the shallows, its fuel oil burning among hundreds of floating beer bottles. Above it the right breast of the barrage slewed round. This vast organ strained forward, as if offering its riches to the men fighting among themselves in the pit below.

Then the barrage exploded. It toppled in a rush of poisoned water, an avalanche of earth and debris that swept past in a rumbling cloud of spray, the last stricken roar of the Mallory.

32

The Poisoned Valley

At last I was alone with the dying river. I stood in the bows of the *Salammbo*, looking down at the empty valley. A veil of smoke and steam lay over the silent pool. Through the breach in the western wall of the barrage flowed a thin stream of black water, making its way past an overturned truck and the cabinet of a cold-store that lay face-up like a metal coffin dislodged from a tomb.

Draining from the creeks and canals of the desert strip, the stream ran across the floor of the pool, a garbage pit littered with the debris that had once helped to consolidate the barrage. At the centre of the pool, like the fossil remains of an ancient saurian, rested the wreck of the *Diana*, only its ribs and engine showing through the mud. Around it lay the rafts and pontoons, sections of landing-stage carried down from the farms, and the crushed barrack huts of the field hospital.

The clouds of dispersing steam seeped along the empty channel of the river between the exposed sand-bars, covered with aerosol cans and beer bottles, fuel drums and tyres. Six hundred yards away was the grey hull of the landing-craft. It rested on its starboard side, landing ramp open to the sky.

I steadied myself against the foremast of the *Salammbo*, and searched the river-bed for any sight of the rival armies. All trace of these warring men had vanished, swept aside by the flood of poisoned water as the Mallory discharged its last task. Yet for all the weapons that littered the banks, the rifles, mortars and ammunition boxes, not a single corpse remained.

So Mrs Warrender and her women had taken their revenge on

229

Captain Kagwa, Harare and their soldiers, bringing to an end the uncertain mission that had set them on their course up the Mallory. I hoped that Noon was with them, and had survived the collapse of the barrage. Her steel skiff lay moored on the upper waters of the river above the cascade, beside the soot-stained hulk of the old Mercedes.

The ferry stirred in its earth embankment, still trapped within the eastern span of the barrage. Under my feet I could hear the garbage wall moving, the dim scraping of some buried air-conditioner against the keel plates, urging the *Salammbo* to resume its voyage.

Reluctant to leave my command, the one safe haven I had known in the past months, I stepped from the bows on to the soft earth at the edge of the barrage. Carrying the Lee-Enfield, I clambered down the broken wall of the dam, a dangerous slide of charred earth, knife-sharp debris and the still smouldering skeins of the retention nets. Rifle raised, despite the empty breech, I waded through the knee-deep water towards the opposite bank. As I reached the open cold-store a dying rat trembled in the current and struck my knee, then swirled away, followed by a trio of dead fish.

I climbed to the west wall of the barrage and rested in the doorway of the deserted sentry post.

"Noon . . .! Doc Mal . . .!"

Below me the last water was running from the stolen channel of the Mallory. The oily bed was now a glistening gutter, fed by the water draining from the creeks and reservoirs. Hundreds of dead fish lay on the banks, their silver carcases giving out a speckled light. Already a few crows picked at the bodies, moving among them like members of a burial party.

The small farms and allotments had lost their bloom. Blanched by the heat, the leaves of the banana trees hung above the crusting soil. The air was filled with a dark, vibrating cloud, a weatherfront of mosquitoes thirty feet high, leaving behind their last larval pools.

There was a stir of movement in the shabby trees along the road. I picked my way along the blackened shore-line, stepping between the streams of waste. I heard a faint murmuring, passive but insistent. The branches trembled, as if the farmers' tethered beasts had been left to die in the shade.

I crossed the road, concerned only to find Noon. Then I saw the dark forms of these creatures following me behind the foliage. A dozen ailing women, sick children tied to their backs, were resting in the shade. They stepped into the insect-filled air and raised their hands to me, a walking misery of fever and disease.

"Noon? Where is Noon?"

Appalled by what I had done to these people, I waved them away with the rifle, pushing aside the outstretched hands. The women clutched at my arms, pointing to their stricken infants, hoping that I might find some medicine for them.

I broke away from the women and ran towards the pool, losing myself in the smoke that rose from the smouldering nets. Without protest, the women shrank back into the trees, hiding themselves beneath the branches like the stunted people of a fungal forest.

I stood on the western wall of the barrage. A narrow waterway still ran from the mountains towards the once wide river valley, but the Mallory was dying, the flow barely strong enough to push through the breaches in the dam. My long struggle against the river had at last come to an end, but I felt no sense of pride or triumph. I had poisoned the Mallory, but I had also poisoned Noon and these destitute nomads. Solely by accident, I had created a great river that had brought life to the waiting desert. But I had become so obsessed by myself that I had seen the Mallory as a rival, and measured its currents against my own ambition. Like a child, I had wanted to destroy the river, afraid that I could not keep all of it to myself.

I looked down at the skin of my arms and legs, covered with sores and scars. From the very start, from the earliest days at Port-la-Nouvelle, I had been wounding myself, and my attempt to kill the river was no more than a surrogate suicide.

I slid down the crumbling face of the barrage and stepped into the shallow water. In a fuddled way I was determined to save the river. Using the stock of the rifle, I began to clear away the heavy stones and pieces of metal debris. I dragged a section of steel fencing through the water, pulling with it a knot of blackened ropes wrapped around the trunk of a small palm.

Already the water flowed more freely. I slung the rifle across my shoulders and waded to the cold-store which lay open to the smoke-stained sky. As I gripped its handles, rocking the cabinet from side to side, a startled monkey leapt through my arms. One of Nora Warrender's macaques, it landed in the shallow water behind me, from which it sprang as if it had scalded its paws. It jumped to the central island of the barrage, scrambled up the rocky face and sat on the rim of an old truck tyre. Chittering into its paws, it consoled itself by licking the end of its tail, large eyes gazing dolefully at the desolate valley that was its new home.

I remembered Nora Warrender's dream of clearing the river plain of the Mallory and repopulating the empty meadows with new species of animals. I felt committed to this small mammal, which would soon perish when the land turned to desert again. Above all, I wanted to fill the draining channel with clear water. If I could reach the river's source I could rekindle its springs, send it coursing once again between its broad banks.

As the last of the smoke drifted across the pool, I carried the rifle back to the *Salammbo*, ready to lay the weapon aside. The barrage was shifting, and the bows of the ferry pointed towards the west. The partly crushed shell of a portable telephone booth had emerged from the debris, and lay beside the stern rail. Squatting inside the inverted kiosk, like a tramp taking refuge from an upended world, was Professor Sanger. He sat with his knees against his chin, eyes hidden behind his sunglasses, still clutching his cine-camera to his chest. He was wiping the dial of a white watch on his left wrist, as if he expected a telephone call from his Japanese sponsors at any moment. Then I saw that he had burned the back of his hand while crawling across the smouldering guy ropes. He had wrapped the blister in a strip of cotton torn from his jacket, but the pain of the wound made him consult the dial every other second.

For all his exhaustion, he listened keenly to the sounds around him, the faint gurgle of the Mallory through the gap in the barrage, the soft smoulder of the ropes, and the low wail of the *Salammbo's* keel. As I climbed through the rubble he could hear my panting breath, and the clicking of the rifle sling against the empty magazine.

"Mallory? Dr Mallory? You're crawling around me. Like a disease. . . ."

"Sanger — how did you get here?"

"Do you need help? I can't cure you." Sanger pointed the camera at me, as if its magic lens might ease my ills. A bullet or piece of shrapnel had penetrated the case, carrying away a section of the lens. "You escaped from the *Diana*. . . ."

I leaned the rifle against the stern of the ferry and took Sanger's wrist, my first conscious act as a physician since leaving Port-la-Nouvelle. "I'll dress that for you. Where are Mrs Warrender and the women?"

"They've gone — their task is over. Or almost over. I wanted them to kill you, Mallory."

"They didn't try to keep me alive. What about Noon? Is she with them?"

"Perhaps . . . not. I've heard her here but. . . ." Sanger lowered his ravaged face behind his broken camera, losing interest in me. "It's over for the child. And for you, Mallory. As you wished, your river is dying."

"We can still save it. Where did you hear Noon? Did Kagwa's soldiers take her?"

"Kagwa's soldiers? Dear doctor, their bodies are sailing back to Lake Kotto on the last tide. My film is done: the country doctor is mad, and his river is dead. . . ."

"No — " I stared at the sombre mountains, waiting for some encouragement from the hard blue slopes. "There's a landslip up in the gorges — some kind of obstruction that I can try to clear."

"You'll save the river? After all your efforts?" Sanger retched over his camera. "That's an improbable postscript, doctor, a touching epilogue. You should go into the film world."

"I have. Now, I'll move you to the ferry. You can wait for me there — when the Mallory flows you'll be safe."

"When the Mallory flows — ? Are such powers in your gift . . .?"

I lifted him from the booth and held his skeletal body against my chest. Together we tottered in the shifting earth, trying to find our footing in the sliding mud, two tramps dancing on a garbage hill.

"You're starving, Sanger—before I go I'll catch that macaque for you. . . ."

"The monkey — I could never eat the little beast. It would be a crime. Roast on a spit, or boiled?"

"Think of your film, Sanger. You're too weak to hold that camera. First I'll find Noon. You said that you'd heard her . . .?"

"She was here. Or part of her. The confused children . . . you poisoned her, Mallory, with your sick river, like all these desert people. They're sick with your dream. . . ."

"I'll bring them fresh water again. I've done it before, Sanger."

I propped Sanger against the rail of the ferry. The effort of supporting him had exhausted me. Bent double over the rifle, I scanned the silent beaches of the pool, and then turned to the shallow waterway of the Mallory above the barrage. Captain Kagwa's limousine waited in the sunlight, its shabby, bullet-pocked body covered with white ash, as if it had been decorated for a funeral cortege. Above the highest shelf of the cascade Noon's steel skiff was beached between the exposed legs of the landing-stage.

Through the ash and oil flecks the left headlamp of the limousine pulsed faintly, the last blurred glow of a fading battery.

"A trick of the sun . . .?" I asked aloud.

"Yes, the whole expedition. The sun tricked us from the start. . . ."

"Noon . . .!"

"Leave her. We'll eat the macaque."

Sanger's hands clutched my shoulders, feeling the hard flesh. Already I guessed that he saw me taking the macaque's place in due course. I seized his wrists and pulled his nails from my skin, then pressed the rifle to his chest and threw him across the deck. While he fumbled for his camera I ran down the inner face of the barrage, swinging myself between the pipes and girders. I clambered across the stranded raft with its outboard motor, and ran along the exposed river-bed between the bodies of the dead fish.

Noon lay in the front seat of the Mercedes, her head against the driver's door, one arm resting weakly on the steering wheel. In an effort to warm herself, she had wrapped her shoulders in the camouflage jacket.

"Mal. . . ." She smiled at me with a brave grimace. The blood from her mouth ulcer stained her teeth. Between her blanched lips they tapped out a faint morse, a deep signal to herself. The recurrent fever of the past weeks had leached all pigment from her pale skin, which seemed as ashen as the grey flakes that covered the limousine, as if she were a plague-ridden princess who had somehow survived her own funeral pyre.

"Noon . . . let me carry you." I reached into the car, which was filled with the acid odour of her sweat and the scent of the cheap perfume I had last smelled on the limbs of the young woman who had slept beside me in the *Diana*. Had I embraced Noon, or had she shared the perfume jar of the hostess into whose cabin I had blundered?

"Give me your hands. We'll get you to the ferry."

I held her arms but she slipped from me and fell against the instrument panel. Embarrassed by her weakness, she smiled at me, disguising the wound in her mouth, and concerned that I might abandon her in this derelict Mercedes. At the same time I was aware of another motive. She lay back, thighs sprawled and open, using her last fever to draw me to her. For all her distress, she was still trying to enlist me in whatever cause had sent her from Port-la-Nouvelle to the source of the Mallory.

I sat her upright, my hands under her armpits, and shook her lightly, settling her bones like the contents of a shopping-bag. Her mouth fell forward against my shoulder, leaving a bloody stain on my skin.

I held her to me, concerned for this disoriented child, but she pulled away from me, stiffening in alarm.

"Noon — it's all right. . . ."

She was pointing at the barrage. Beyond the tilting wheelhouse of the *Salammbo* came a familiar drone, the wearying sound of a helicopter.

"So Kagwa's come back . . . that's too bad for us. . . ."

Still holding Noon's head to my chest, I gripped the barrel of the Lee-Enfield. The distant ache of the helicopter's engine resolved itself into a concussive clacking. I watched its exhaust plume winding towards us like a hairless boa among the sand-bars and gravel cliffs of the drained river. The craft emerged from the empty valley of the Mallory, drawing its black trail behind it, an aerial sign advertising a death to come.

It crossed the pool and made a slow circuit of the deserted beaches and the collapsed west wall of the barrage. As it hovered above the ferry, little more than fifty yards away, Captain Kagwa sat by the open passenger door. He had abandoned his flak jacket, now that his war against Harare was over and, with it, his dream of being the Governor-General of this northern province. But his expression was as set and determined as I had ever known. He stared hard at the ferry, and then pointed to where Noon and I stood beside his Mercedes.

He signalled to the French pilot to descend, and the machine revolved twice and approached the barrage beside the *Salammbo*.

Captain Kagwa dismounted beneath the rotating blades. Head lowered, he strode through the down-draught towards the ferry. When he saw Sanger crouching against the wheelhouse he loosened the flap of his holster, but I knew from his tight mouth that he was not concerned with the film-maker. He nodded to him, and then set off down the slope of the barrage. Twice he slipped in the broken earth, stumbling to his knees, but he picked himself up and reached the narrow beach beside my raft.

I sat Noon against the passenger door and raised the rifle, drawing back the bolt on the empty breech. This time, however, Kagwa would not be impressed by the bluff. I felt calm, but empty-headed, as if a large part of my mind had already left. In a confused way I imagined that I might start the engine of the Mercedes and drive into the safety of the foothills to the east of the river. But I was too exhausted even to walk around the car.

Kagwa had left the beach and was striding up the slope to the landing-stage. His eyes noted the old truck tyres and the dead rats, the moss-covered shell of Noon's skiff between the wooden piers. His hand was on the revolver in his holster, freeing the heavy weapon.

"Noon . . . stay here as long as you can. He won't shoot you in the car. . . ."

I pushed her away from me, but she had seized my wrist and drummed with her hand at my breastbone, her teeth clicking some primitive curse. For all her fear, her eyes were fixed on Kagwa with the same hate she had first displayed at the airstrip. I looked down and realised that her fist was clenched around a silver peg, some toggle from the limousine's dashboard. She pressed it into my hand, urging me on with a rictus of her wounded mouth, as if she wanted me to attack Kagwa with this miniature weapon.

Then, as she passed it into my fingers, I saw the copper cartridge with its steel bullet. She had hidden this third round throughout our months together, saving it for a last emergency. When I hesitated, she took my hand and held it fiercely against her chest, so that I could feel the bullet and her breast between my fingers. She forced my nails into her nipple, trying to give me courage.

I raised the open breech and slid the cartridge into the barrel. I drove the bolt forward, cocking the firing-pin, and snapped down the bolt. As Noon sat beside me, pressing her hands against my diaphragm, I levelled the rifle at Kagwa.

Ignoring me, the Captain climbed the beach to within twenty feet of the Mercedes. He was breathing heavily through his strong mouth as he took the revolver from his holster, his eyes examining the damage to the limousine's fenders and bodywork, the bullet holes in the windshield, the dents and dirt that now covered its black paintwork.

When he raised his revolver towards me, I steadied the rifle and shot him through the head.

Soon lost in the noise of the helicopter's engine, the report of the rifle shot rolled among the hills, hunting the valleys among the abandoned mine shafts.

Kagwa lay dying among the dead rats and truck tyres on the oily beach, his legs stirring as the blood ran from his head to join the Mallory. The helicopter pilot sat forward over his controls, one hand on the carbine between the seats. When I raised the rifle he eased forward his throttles and took off into the morning sun.

From the wheelhouse of the *Salammbo* I watched the machine following the stream of dark water that ran southwards along the grave of the river. The engine at last faded into the dusty haze, and I could hear only Sanger fidgeting with the lens of his broken camera.

"Mallory — was Kagwa here?"

"He's gone now."

"I felt his feet on the ground. Those were the feet of an angry man."

"I know. But I explained our problems to him."

"And you changed his mind?"

"In a sense."

"You're not usually very persuasive, Mallory. And the helicopter?"

"It won't be back. Don't worry."

"That's good. Now we can go on."

I looked down at Sanger, huddled like a beggar with his broken camera. He must have known that Kagwa lay dead on the beach beside the Mercedes.

"You're ready to go back to Port-la-Nouvelle?"

"No! We've come too far now. You must find the source, Mallory. Then my film will be complete."

"Sanger, you'll never make this film. . . ."

"It's already made — all we are doing is performing it for anyone who cares to watch."

"All right. We'll go when I'm ready. I want to care for Noon. You stay here while I bring her to the ship."

"Of course. I can help her. There's a cassette in the wheelhouse. You can describe it to her. . . ."

But when I returned to the Mercedes I found that Noon had gone.

33

The River Search

"Noon . . .! There's a film for you. . . ."

Standing beside Sanger in the stern of the raft, I shouted towards the beach of blue shingle that lay behind a breakwater of fallen boulders. As I searched the empty shore I noticed once again that no echo of my voice returned from the steep granite cliffs, as if the dying river had so shrunk into itself that it had withdrawn from even the smallest response to the living.

"Noon . . .! Professor Sanger has a film. . . ."

"Doctor . . .?" Huddled in the bows, Sanger pointed his camera to left and right, trying to sense the direction of my eyes. "Is she here? Three o'clock?"

"We've lost her — she can hide behind the air."

"Our bearing? Three o'clock or nine o'clock?"

"Midnight . . . for God's sake, Sanger, there's no time here."

For two days we had sailed up the draining channel. Although we were only ten miles from the barrage beside the former Bonneville airbase, we had entered a remote mountain world, a landscape of sheer volcanic walls that faced each other across the gorges like fossilised giants. Their fluted surfaces were stained and streaked with red ores, so that the Mallory seemed to be flowing along the gutter of a vast natural abattoir. The damp air was without taste or texture, no longer touched by the spoor of birds and fish, or the scent of the flowering plants that had crowded the lower course of the river. The last heathers and old man's beard had given way to ferns, and these in turn to sedges and groundsel.

In this realm after death, we were making our passage up the leaking cadaver of the Mallory. The low sky, the ceiling of mist a few hundred feet above our heads, and the sombre beaches together formed a zone outside time or memory.

The stream tugged at the raft, urging it to change its course and join this last expedition to the desert below. Shipping the oar, I throttled up the engine and steered towards the centre of the channel. Within minutes of sighting Noon that morning, our first glimpse of the girl since leaving the barrage, a submerged boulder had punctured the starboard pontoon, splitting the cheap weld that formed its keel. Dead in the water, the craft began to founder. As Sanger clung to his camera, I jumped down into the cold stream and dragged the raft on to a nearby sand-bar. There I laboriously unwound the wire securing the pontoon to the wooden frame, and rotated the cumbersome cylinder so that the open weld was uppermost.

We had lost at least an hour, but I was sure that Noon was only a quarter of a mile ahead. Although we were handicapped by the raft and its overheating engine, she never eluded us. At times, when I struggled with the motor, she seemed even to hold back, her silver shell moored in midstream against the punt pole. She stood in the stern, chin resting against her small fists as they clasped the top of the handle. When we came into view she would lean wearily against the pole and slide away, losing herself behind the rock falls that filled the floor of the gorge. Either she wished to stay in my sight, luring me to whatever mystery lay at the source of the Mallory, or she was even more ill than I guessed and needed to spur herself on with the spectacle of Sanger fumbling like a demented photographer with his broken camera.

From the ashen pallor of her face and arms, I knew that Noon was still gripped by the fly fever. When she rinsed her mouth she would leave threads of blood in the water that clung to the bows of the raft like fading pennants. In my confused way I wanted to save both Noon and the river, and was sure that I could do so once I reached the Mallory's source.

"Doctor! The river divides . . .!"

Sanger gesticulated with his camera, pointing to the western bank. In some uncanny way his ears had sensed that a long arm of still water lay between the shingle beach and a giant's causeway of boulders that ran along the centre of the gorge.

After scanning the main channel for any trace of Noon, I steered the raft into the arm of quieter water. I cruised quietly along the inner face of the causeway, peering into the small caverns and caves where Noon might be hiding. Eighty yards ahead, the causeway sank into the shallows, leaving a narrow exit between the submerged boulders.

The rush of water disguised the soft putter of the outboard as I steered the raft among the rocks. When we swung outwards into the faster water, Noon was squatting in her steel shell only twenty feet from us. She had berthed her craft behind a shoulder of the causeway, where she waited for us to appear, watching the main channel with her back to us.

I cut the engine, leaving the silent propeller to unravel in the water, and let the raft drift on to her. Careful not to alert Sanger, who was staring myopically at the stained cliffs, I leaned over the engine, ready to catch Noon's arm. She was gazing at her pale fingers, marked like badly painted nail varnish with the blood from her mouth. Her shoulders trembled in the cool air, and her ribs pumped in a feverish shudder. From the pallor of her skin, so leached of pigment as to be a chalky white, I could almost believe that she had been rubbing herself with the cinders of a small fire.

The raft rode the last few feet of water between us. I was about to embrace Noon, but Sanger was trailing one hand in the current. Always suspicious that I would trick him again, he began to slap the water as if the river were a miscreant child.

"Mallory . . . you've changed course! Don't give up now!"

Noon turned towards me, startled by the silent rush of the raft and its bulbous pontoons. There was a flurry of the punt pole and the steel shell leapt across our bows, revolved like a surf board and sped into the open channel.

"Doctor — ! You're moving south!"

"Sanger, I had the child in my hands. . . ."

The exhaust puttered flatly as I tried to restart the engine. The

241

raft struck an anvil of submerged rock, and pitched Sanger between the pontoons. Drenched to the armpits, he gripped their plump flanks like a stunt rider suspended between two galloping horses, then slipped and was carried below the wooden frame. He screamed at me in rage, hands reaching through the bamboo grille to seize my ankles.

An hour later I at last beached the raft on a quiet beach, and persuaded Sanger to release the propeller shaft of the outboard motor to which he clung in the shallows. As I dragged him ashore Noon was again waiting calmly for us in midstream, her skiff moored against the punt pole.

Resting beside the raft, I stared dispassionately at Sanger. I had managed to light a small fire with pieces of decking and a few drops of fuel from the outboard's tank, pulling on the engine until a spark from the magneto ignited the vapour. The effort had exhausted me, and I could barely stand on the rolling shingle. Sanger lay against the starboard pontoon, wisely reluctant to part himself from the craft. His hands clasped the broken camera to his chest, this Cyclopean third eye from which he regarded me warily.

Should I abandon him here? He too was infected by the fever and malaise that had poisoned everyone at the barrage. My own condition was little better, and I now needed him to help me row the raft once the fuel was exhausted. I tried to think only of Sanger's needs, and reminded myself that he was my patient and that I was once again his physician. Nonetheless, I was reluctant to leave him, aware for the first time that I depended upon his presence, almost as if I at last accepted that I was appearing in a drama directed and overseen by him.

However, this logic would lead inevitably to his death, like those of Miss Matsuoka and Mr Pal. For his own sake, I would persuade Sanger to remain on this beach. Once I had found Noon, and revived the Mallory, I would return and collect him. Meanwhile I would leave him the last of my small stock of millet bread and strip the raft's decking to its minimum in order to provide him with a fire.

At the barrage, planning this last leg of the journey in the wheelhouse of the *Salammbo*, I had not wanted to take Sanger with me. As I prepared the raft, he had come down from the ferry, tottering among the debris of the crumbling barrage, shouting and arguing with me. The last of the villagers had left, and he could smell disease as the allotments faded, transforming themselves once again into desert. He gazed sightlessly at the silence, well aware that this was a place where a crime had been committed. But even then Sanger had been prepared to place himself in my hands.

I remembered him sitting on the raft as I dragged it into the water above the barrage. The last ebb of Captain Kagwa's life leaked down to the beach, flowing into the grooves left by the pontoons, a slipway of blood. Without speaking, I held Sanger's shoulders from behind. He had taken this as a touching gesture of solidarity, but I was about to pull him on to the beach and leave him among the truck tyres and dead rats.

Then I saw Mrs Warrender and her women on the hillside above the pool. Bundles in hand, they stood beside the ore-conveyor, ready to make their way into the remote mountain valleys. On a rusting scoop beside them, two marmosets preened their tails, grimacing at the stench from the river below, only too eager to join the women in their modest paradise. Nora Warrender watched me while I stood behind Sanger, clearly assuming that I would leave him.

Under the women's disapproving gaze, I had rallied myself, but now, only two days later, I was ready to abandon Sanger again, a blind man marooned on these cold beaches.

"Sanger — you're tired."

"No, Mallory. It's possible that I'm stronger than you."

"I'll build a fire. You'll be safer here."

"No."

"Remember to move to higher ground. You'll hear the water rushing towards you."

"Rushing water?"

"Sanger, I'm going to make the river run again."

"I must be there, Mallory. It's the climax of our film. . . ."

"Perhaps . . . but I have to find Noon."

"I should be with you, Mallory."

He was holding tightly to the outboard with both hands, revealing the unexpected strength that had sustained him since our journey from Port-la-Nouvelle.

"Mallory, I must go with you. For your sake."

I tried to prise his fingers from the propeller, but left only a smear of blood on the blades. I reached down and lifted the camera lanyard from his neck. Sanger scrabbled at the air, kicking me with his small feet.

"The camera, Mallory! We need that!"

"Let's get rid of it now! The damned thing's been a snare."

"No — the film, it's all that's left. . . ."

I was about to throw the broken black box into the river, but it seemed to cling to my hands. The pistol grip, contoured to my palm and fingers, sat as easily within my mind, offering a different perspective on our trivial quarrel. Before hurling it from my reach, I put it to my eye, curious to see the fictional space that had haunted my entire journey since Sanger's arrival.

A hundred yards upstream there was a glimmer from the water. Through the viewfinder I saw Noon's silver shell float past a rocky shoulder. Noon stood in the stern, supporting herself on the punt pole.

"Noon — she's here, Sanger! She needs us to follow her. . . ."

I stared through the viewfinder. Was she playing up to the camera, even acting out some solitary death modelled on Sanger's fictions, or was I imposing this climax upon her? I had hoped that I could draw her towards me with the promise of these dreams of herself, but it was I who had been ensnared, just as the Mallory had trapped me within its dream of a great river.

"Doctor . . . we're both too tired to argue with you." Sanger seized my foot, throwing me on to the shingle. He scrambled across the blue stones, lunging to left and right, seized the camera from my hands and struck me across the face.

Stunned by the blow, and too weak to defend myself, I lay back

244

on the shingle, feeling the old wound to my scalp. The sutures of my skull were opening, letting the cool wind into the chambers of my brain. I stared up at the cloudless, cyanide sky, like the domed roof of some deep psychosis. It occurred to me that perhaps I could remain here, resting beside a small fire while Sanger sailed on. . . .

"Doctor?" I felt his hands on my chest and forehead. "You're in a poor state. I must have caught your head. . . ."

"It's all right. . . ." I sat up and climbed to my knees. "I'll take you with me."

"You need my help, doctor."

"I know — I can't start the motor again."

"We'll have to row. You're strong enough."

He guided me down to the water and leaned me against the raft. We pushed out into the stream, and then clambered aboard and sat beside the motor. Sanger settled himself, camera slung around his neck, massaging my thighs with his hands.

"Come on, Mallory. You can paddle — the river is almost still. Don't lose faith in your dream."

"Paddle?" I began to push the water with one hand while Sanger worked away with the oar. Framed by the granite cliffs, Noon and her skiff slipped away into the mist. I watched her cross the partly submerged pillars of rock, her interrupted image reminding me of the stuttering light in the cabin of the *Diana*. I had been able to embrace Noon only through the flickering image of an antique seduction. To sustain me now I needed Sanger to tell me of some heroic voyage, against self-doubt and the fall of night, in search of a private myth, like those of Pizarro or Cortés.

"Tell me, Sanger. About your film . . .?"

"Which film, doctor? Paddle now. I've made many films."

"Your film about the Mallory. The one you started at Port-la-Nouvelle."

Sanger turned to face me, the oar motionless in the water. He had lost his sunglasses, and his myopic eyes, like closed glass, seemed to see me for the first time. "You want to hear about the film? You wish me to describe it to you?"

"Yes. . . ." The thought of this bogus documentary was strangely comforting. Already I could feel the commentary reassuring and encouraging me, in the soft sing-song of Mr Pal. "Tell me about the film, Sanger. Be my eyes. . . ."

34

The Source

Six days later, sustained by these desperate stratagems, we at last reached the source of the Mallory.

During our final passage through the misty gorges of the river, I lay beside the silent outboard at the stern of the raft, paddling with one hand as I listened to Sanger describe landscapes of imaginary splendour. In its ambiguous way, the broken camera of this blind film-maker had kept us going. Its cracked lens supported us both in the illusion that we were making a lasting record of our hunt for the Mallory. I was happy to collude in this, aware that I could distance myself from that other person I had known, a physician at Port-la-Nouvelle who had allowed a grand obsession to capture him.

The day after my brawl with Sanger, on whom I soon became almost wholly dependent, we entered an area of chilling rain cloud. The fluted cliffs which had lined the gorges of the Mallory now fell back, leaving the river to meander through a wide valley. Here we rested, and I was at last able to start the engine. On all sides there were traces of recent volcanic activity. Igneous rocks and pumice were mixed with coarse-grained gneisses marked with bands of granular material like the symbols of some stratified alphabet. On the cold shore-line there grew only a few ferns, and the empty slopes were covered with a green glaze of lichens and stunted grasses. The river, little more than fifty feet in width, flowed between small islands of red mud, and the water was opaque with a thick russet silt. The sluggish wavelets that swilled across the raft left a copper scum across the wooden frame. As a bleary sunlight shone through the mist we seemed to dissolve in this primordial soup, at one with the trilobites and ammonites washed on to the deck.

On the fifth afternoon the outboard engine failed for the last time, and I then discovered that I was too weak to help Sanger with his rowing. However, the endless archipelagos of waterlogged islands allowed us to keep up with Noon. She squatted with the punt pole in the stern of the steel shell, like a fatigued acrobat, wearily testing the maze of channels. At times she seemed to lose interest in us altogether, for hours moving away into the mist in search of that secret treasure which I now knew lay at the source of the Mallory.

On the next morning the mist was suddenly dispelled by a strong and unbroken sun, whose beams probed around us like the gaze of a friendly sentry. We had spent the dawn in a frozen sleep, adrift among the islands of mud. As the air cleared we woke to find that the mountains had receded almost to the horizon. We had entered a vast plateau, covered with red laval mud and shallow pools, the floor of a huge lake some twenty miles in width.

"Sanger . . . we're home."

He was already awake, lying across the raft with his blistered face to the sky. Without thinking, he reached one hand into the water and paddled feebly.

The raft had grounded on the bank of a shallow pool. I eased myself into the warm sulphurated water, and looked out at the damp vistas of this marine world, the bed of an immense lake that had once covered the plateau. I assumed that at some time in the recent past a tectonic shift along a deep plate-line had fractured its floor and walls. The displaced waters of this lake had formed the Mallory, first flowing through the subterranean conduit which surfaced at the Port-la-Nouvelle airstrip, and later in the channel of the Mallory itself. Nonetheless, I still believed that I had created the river. By dislodging the stump of the ancient oak I had allowed a current to flow which in turn had encouraged the waters of the lake to burst their banks.

"Sanger . . . it's still flowing." I waded around the raft, feeling the faint southward tug of the current, moving across the plateau from the secret headwaters of the river. Somewhere beyond these shallow pools, in the northern slopes of this drained lake, lay the source of the Mallory.

I released the raft and let it drift on to the muddy bank. Sanger was fretting at the water with one hand, still testing the current. He had now become more determined than I was to hunt down the Mallory to its end. He had slept fitfully through the night, constantly waking to see that I was still alive, and trying to revive me with his commentary on the shifting darkness, part delirium and part imaginary travelogue.

With his free hand he shielded his face from the vivid sun, and then launched again into his rambling exposition.

"A primaeval lake, Mallory, the original mud world, covered by a strange light . . . our lens won't care for it, so we picture you in close-up, an aggressive mammal answering a deep migratory call . . . can you see the source?"

"Ahead of us — perhaps half a mile."

"Prepare yourself, Mallory . . . now we reach our climax, returning to that primitive fount from which all the rivers of the earth have sprung, the moment when consciousness moved into the daylight, from the reptile to the mammalian brain . . . now God exists, Mallory, perhaps you have returned to Eden to destroy Him . . . a messiah for the age of cable television. . . ."

But I no longer needed his commentary. A shadow wavered across the surface of the lake; the mist had lifted, taking with it the watery, confused light. Through the clear air Noon's silver craft slid through a narrow neck of water into the larger lake to the north. She sat upright in the stern, hips pivoting as her frail arms swung the punt pole. She had recovered her strength now that the river's source was in sight.

Leaving the raft, I waded through the water, following a bank of viscous mud. I strode through the shallows, my hands warding off the hot spray that leapt into my face.

When I reached the inlet Noon had already crossed the adjacent lake. Exhausted, I sank into the warm water. My feet had dislodged part of the isthmus of laval mud that separated the two pools. As I rinsed the water across my legs, the warm mud dissolved and flowed across me, a soothing quilt that tempted me to rest forever beneath its balmy covers.

Released now, the water slid past, a brief tidal rush that raced across the surface. The quickening current carried Sanger and the raft for fifty feet, and then beached them on a shelf of copper silt.

Upstream, the next lake was emptying itself. Stranded by the falling water-level, Noon stepped from her craft. She threw the pole aside and strode through the water towards a narrow cleft in the bank. Here the last remnants of the Mallory flowed from the lava flats that formed the northern rim of the plateau.

The tepid water slid past my ankles as I followed her across the lake. Silhouetted against the lava dunes, her strong shoulders emerged through the steaming air. Watching her confident stride, I could see that Noon was now a young woman. Somewhere in this maze of pools, we would lie together and conceive a second Mallory.

I waded past her steel skiff, and approached the narrow stream that vented itself from the bank. Only three feet wide, this was all that remained of the river. Noon, however, was undismayed. Following the stream, she strode with the jaunty step of a returning traveller at last in sight of her home village.

The prints of her feet, the scarred right instep like a diagonal arrow, moved in front of me along the edge of the stream. Marooned by the falling river, islands of water lay in the sand-pits. The Mallory moved among the dunes, a faint thread only a few inches deep.

Clumsily, I scattered the drying sand into the water. I knelt down and scooped away the wet grains, trying not to disturb the stream, and hoping that in some way Noon's arrival might revive it.

In the silence of the valley floor I heard Noon's footsteps fade among the caking hills. Losing my bearings, I climbed to the crest of a dune beside the stream, and saw her fifty paces ahead. She stared at a dark scar in the sand. When she looked back at me for the last time, her eyes were those of a woman of my own age.

"Noon . . .!" As I ran towards her, the Mallory shrank into a spur of water no wider than my hand. Head down, I traced it around the base of a large shoe-shaped rock. The thin groove ran back to a basin drying under the sun.

I knelt down, trying to separate the sand grains from the winking vein. A last trickle ran between my hands as I fell to my knees and clasped it.

The Mallory died in my arms.

When I roused myself and began to search for Noon, I found no trace of her. The shallow hills of crusting lava ran for a further mile towards the northern edge of the plateau. I wandered into the hollows between them, but the scum of algae and water-weed was unmarked. A few paces from the grave of the Mallory her footprints vanished into the sand.

For an hour I blundered among the hills, calling out her name as the lake-bed dried around me. A few islands of water surrounded the draining pool in which Noon's skiff lay stranded. Kicking away their walls, I released the water in a last attempt to revive the Mallory. As I reached the skiff and collapsed into its metal shell there was a brief race of water. The wave turned the bows of the craft towards the south, then swept me into the next pool where Sanger's raft was coasting towards the gates of the valley below.

Steered by his demented monologue, we sailed into the gorge together, carried between the warning rocks and the mourning beaches, as the Mallory set out on its last journey to the sea.

35

Memory and Desire

The desert is closer today. Standing beside the abandoned airstrip at Port-la-Nouvelle, on the eroded shoulder of the dam which I once hoped would halt the waters of the Mallory, I can see the dust advancing from the northern horizon. The sharp grains slip between the stumps of the dead trees that stand along the banks of the river. An immense white dream flows silently across the land, spreading over the drained surface of the lake.

Blanched by the sun, the landscape has become a fossil of itself. Although abandoned only two years ago, Port-la-Nouvelle seems as remote as Pompeii. The police barracks, the tobacco factory and the Toyota agency are all covered with the same dust. Out on the lake the towers of the drilling project loom through the strange light like memories dressed in their shrouds. The roof of the clinic has collapsed, but the trailer is still serviceable, and on my visits to Port-la-Nouvelle I sleep on that same mattress from which I first heard the waters of the Mallory stealing across the lake.

For the past two years, since my recovery, I have worked at the WHO unit thirty miles to the south-west, but every weekend I drive here and camp beside the trailer in the car park of the clinic. Ostensibly I am still exploring the possibilities of an irrigation project, but this is no more than an excuse. As I search the sandy bed of the river I am really thinking of Noon, and waiting for her to appear again.

Below the shoulder of the dam I can see the footprints of nomads who have camped on the river-bed beside the earth rampart. I am always careful to examine the prints, and on several occasions have seen Noon's scarred instep and curious toes. I remember my final glimpse of her, and the crazed journey down the Mallory, as it flushed me away with its last waters.

Sharing Noon's skiff with Sanger, it took us three weeks to reach Lake Kotto. As we lay in the metal shell we saw the whole process of creation winding down to its starting point like a reversed playback of Sanger's imaginary documentary about my quest for the Mallory's source. The green desert had faded again when we reached the cascade at Bonneville, and below the pool the groves of tamarinds resembled pineapples run to seed. The papyrus swamps where Mrs Warrender had hunted for men were now a grass wilderness of white basins and dried-out lagoons, covered with the skeletons of millions of frogs. I almost believed that the *Diana* had reassembled its timbers and sailed southwards, casting its white death on the land.

Later, during our convalescence in the provincial capital, I knew that Sanger suspected that the entire expedition to the source of the river had been an invention. Distancing himself from me, he regaled the governor's press officer with a graphic account of the comeuppance of the renegade country policeman, the would-be secessionist Captain Kagwa. When I protested, he informed me that he was concerned with a more interesting project, and at the first opportunity flew to Nairobi. I had served my purpose for him, and he could never forgive me for having learned to take his dubious profession with complete seriousness. I last heard that he had arranged for the Mallory to be deleted from the National Geographic Society's gazetteer.

However, Sanger's insistence that I was no more than a bystander in the attempted coup saved me from suspicion. At times, as I rested in my hospital bed, I too felt that I had invented the entire adventure. The irony is that, in many ways, I remember our journey to the Mallory's source in terms of Sanger's imaginary travelogue. That alone seems to give meaning to all that took place.

Nonetheless, there is no doubt that the journey was real, as I have confirmed on two modest safaris twenty miles up the drained bed of the river. I have been shown aerial photographs of the

Salammbo still embedded in its rubbish tip by the cascade at Bonneville. Yet I have never seen any corpses of Kagwa, Harare or their men, though their abandoned military equipment is strewn along the 200-mile course of the river, and the rusting hulk of the landing-craft still lies on its side half a mile south of the barrage.

Kagwa and Harare have vanished into the nothingness of their ambitions, just as Mrs Warrender and her women have disappeared into their mountain dream of a new nature reserve, somewhere in the rain valleys of the Massif. Each of us had abused the Mallory, trying to use it for our own ends, and only Noon remained true to our first dream.

I had not invented the river and our journey, but had I invented Noon? She has a distinct physical presence that is ever more real, the smell of her hands and breasts, the endless clicking of her teeth. But was she a figment born from a river itself sprung from my imagination? Had I invented her to draw myself to the river's source, and in their references to Noon were the others merely humouring my obsession?

Fifty feet from the rampart there are fresh footprints in the river-bed, but I will explore them later. Above the dusty roofs of Port-la-Nouvelle I can hear the government helicopter. It moves over the town, its propeller sending up whirlwinds of dust that hunt the empty streets. The new district officer is keeping his eye on me. He is suspicious of my hanging about this drained river-bed, and guesses that I may be waiting for a secret plane to land here at this remote airstrip, carrying the emissaries of another secessionist movement.

I am waiting, but not for a plane. I am waiting for a strong-shouldered young woman, with a caustic eye, walking along the drained bed of the Mallory with a familiar jaunty stride. Sooner or later she will reappear, and I am certain that when she comes the Mallory will also return, and once again run the waters of its dream across the dust of a waiting heart.